ARCHIE & FRIENDS ALL-STARS

The CARTOON LIFE of CHUCK CLAYTON®

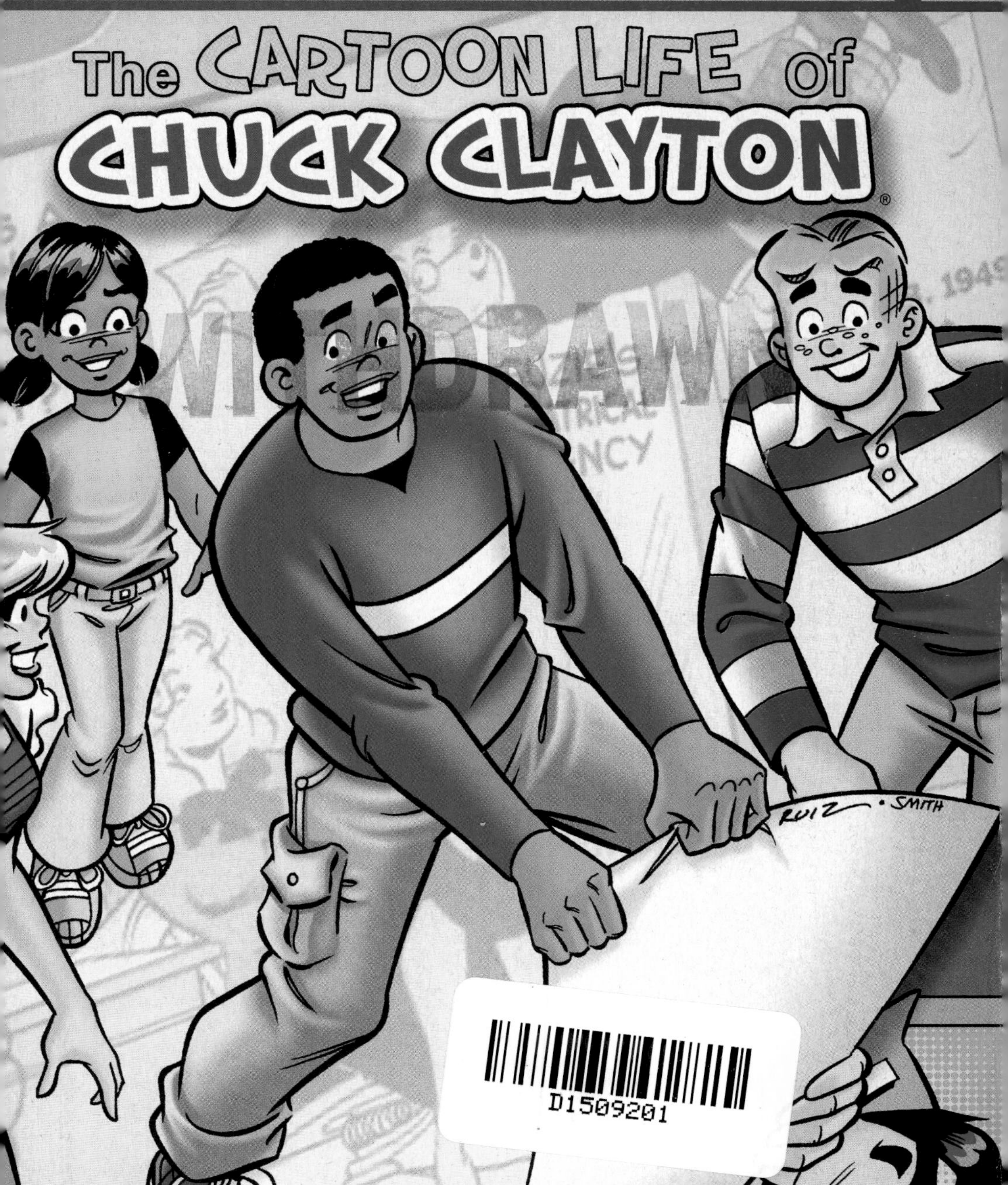
RUIZ • SMITH

ARCHIE & FRIENDS ALL STARS, Volume 3, 2010 The Cartoon Life of Chuck Clayton. Printed in Canada. Published by Archie Comic Publications, Inc., 325 Fayette Avenue, Mamaroneck, New York 10543-2318. Archie characters created by John L. Goldwater; the likenesses of the Archie characters were drawn by Bob Montana. The individual characters' names and likenesses are the exclusive trademarks of Archie Comic Publications, Inc. All stories previously published and copyrighted by Archie Comic Publications, Inc. (or its predecessors) in magazine form in 2009.

ISBN: 978-1-879794-48-1

Credits

CO-CEO:
JONATHAN GOLDWATER
CO-CEO:
NANCY SILBERKLEIT
CO-PRESIDENT/EDITOR-IN-CHIEF:
VICTOR GORELICK
CO-PRESIDENT/DIRECTOR OF CIRCULATION:
FRED MAUSSER
VICE-PRESIDENT/MANAGING EDITOR:
MIKE PELLERITO

SCRIPT: **ALEX SIMMONS**
PENCILS: **FERNANDO RUIZ**
INKS: **AL NICKERSON**
LETTERS: **PATRICK OWSLEY, PHIL FELIX & ELLEN LEONFORTE**
COLORS: **GLENN WHITMORE**

COVER ART: **FERNANDO RUIZ & BOB SMITH**
COVER COLORIST: **ROSARIO "TITO" PEÑA**
ART DIRECTOR: **JOE PEPITONE**
PRODUCTION: **STEPHEN OSWALD, CARLOS ANTUNES, PAUL KAMINSKI, JOE MORCIGLIO, SUZANNAH ROWNTREE**

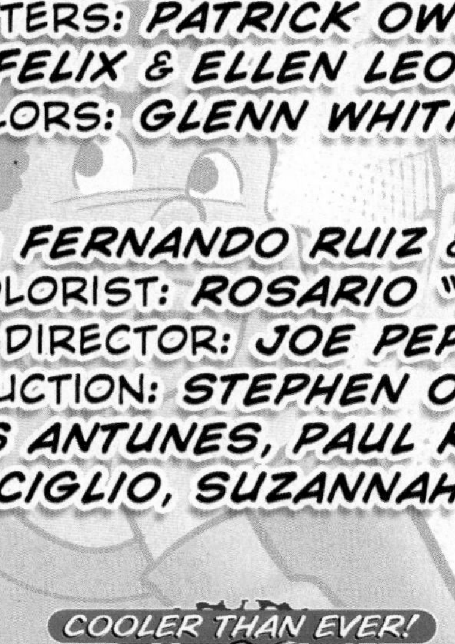

COOLER THAN EVER!
R
ARCHIECOMICS.COM

Table of Contents

4 CHAPTER ONE:
STICK FIGURES & GRUMPY ELVES
CHUCK IS ASKED TO TEACH AN
AFTER-SCHOOL PROGRAM IN CARTOONING
TO ELEMENTARY SCHOOL KIDS.

26 CHAPTER TWO:
MEET THE NEW SCHOOL
FEELING OVERWHELMED BY ALL THE COMMITMENTS
IN HIS LIFE, CHUCK COULD SURE USE SOME HELP
TEACHING HIS CARTOONING CLASS.

48 CHAPTER THREE:
A TIME TO DRAW
A HISTORY TEACHER AT RIVERDALE MIDDLE SCHOOL
WANTS TO DO SOMETHING NEW AND EXCITING
FOR HER NEXT LESSON; GOOD THING
CHUCK'S AROUND.

70 CHAPTER FOUR:
DELINQUENT DOODLES
CHUCK HELPS OUT A SCHOOL DELINQUENT
WHO IS SPREADING GRAFFITI AROUND
THE NEIGHBORHOOD.

92 BONUS:
CHUCK CLAYTON'S
CREATING COOL COMICS!

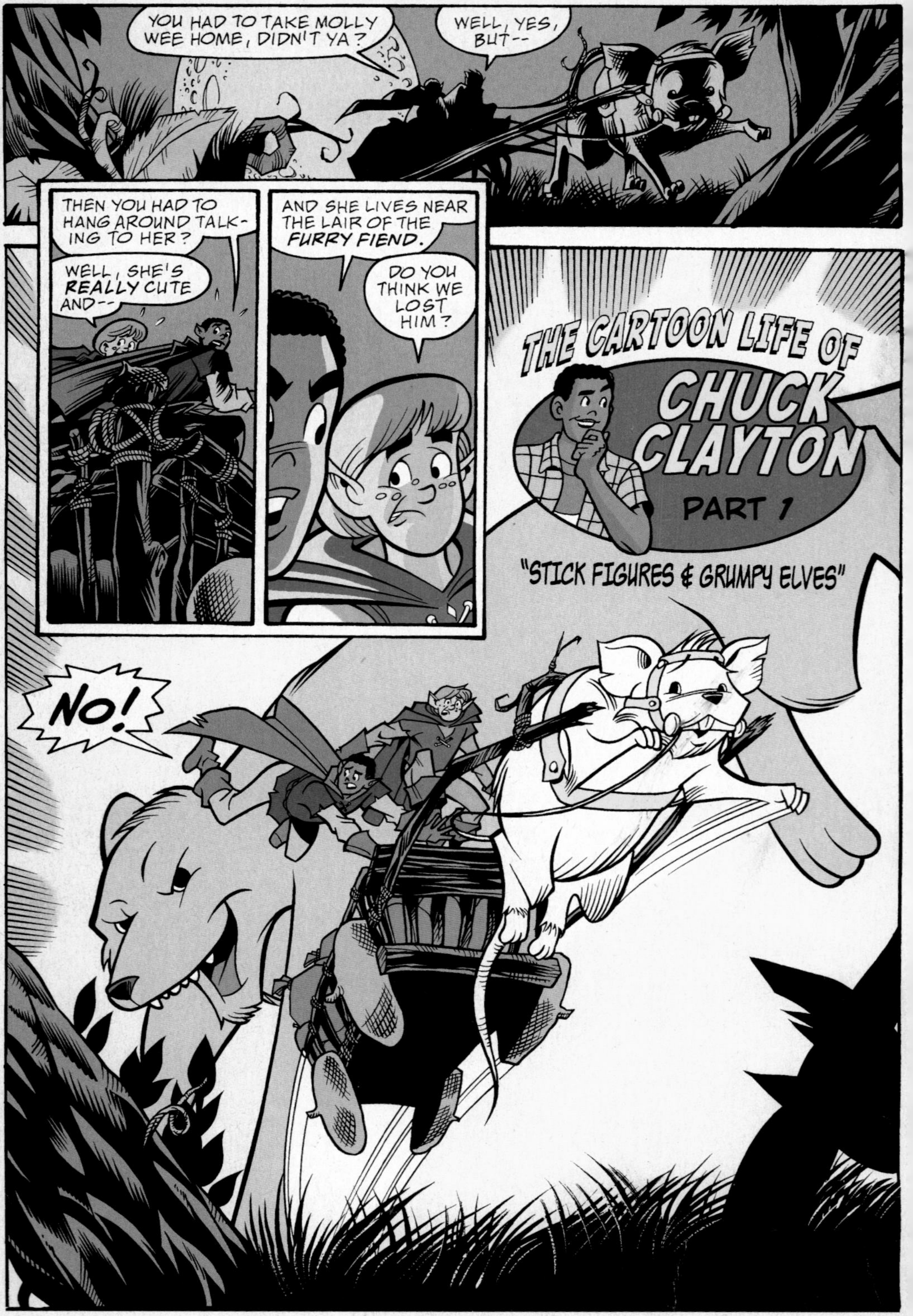
YOU HAD TO TAKE MOLLY WEE HOME, DIDN'T YA?
WELL, YES, BUT--
THEN YOU HAD TO HANG AROUND TALKING TO HER?
WELL, SHE'S REALLY CUTE AND--
AND SHE LIVES NEAR THE LAIR OF THE FURRY FIEND.
DO YOU THINK WE LOST HIM?
THE CARTOON LIFE OF
CHUCK CLAYTON
PART 1
"STICK FIGURES & GRUMPY ELVES"
NO!

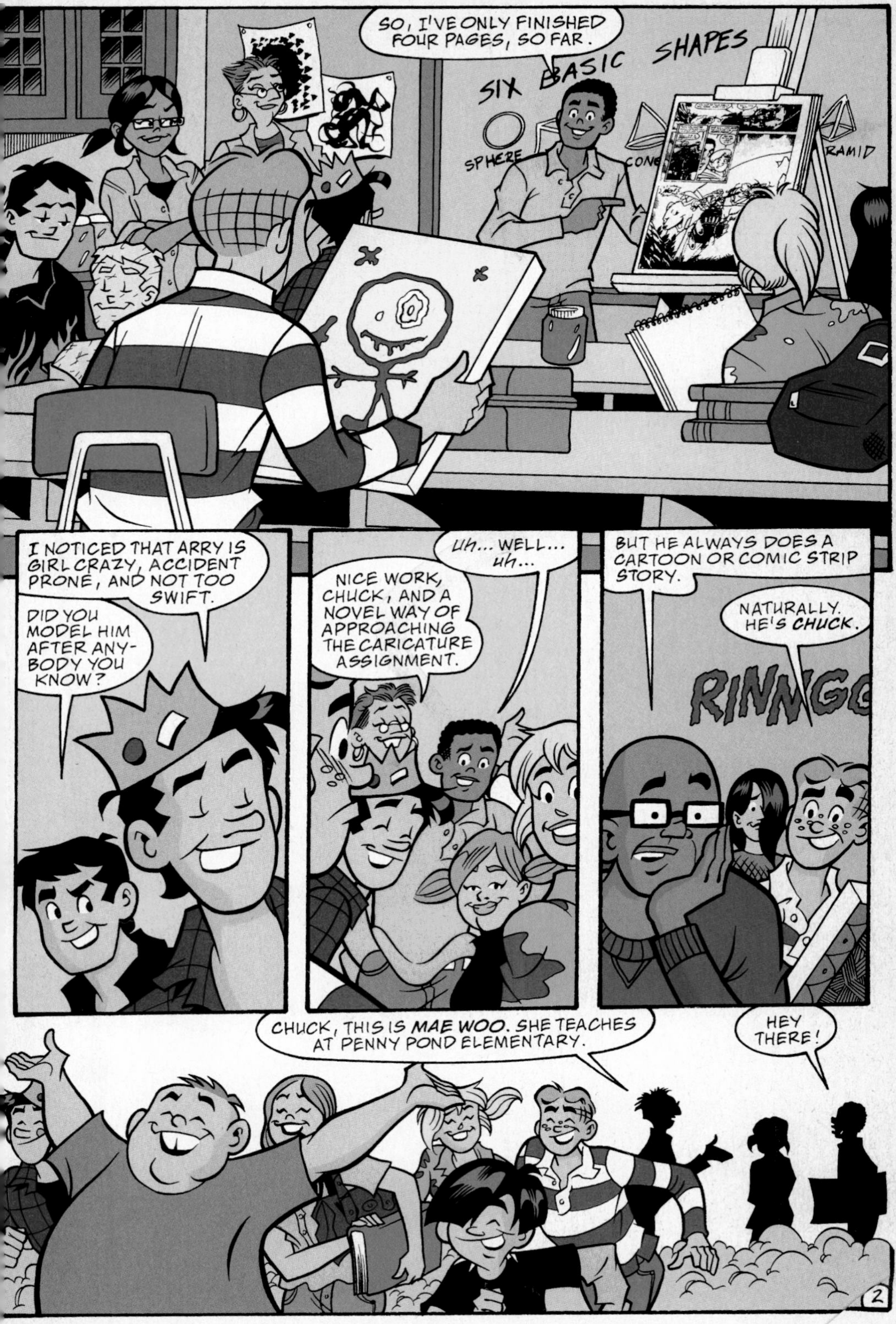
SO, I'VE ONLY FINISHED FOUR PAGES, SO FAR.
SIX BASIC SHAPES
SPHERE
CONE
RAMID
I NOTICED THAT ARRY IS GIRL CRAZY, ACCIDENT PRONE, AND NOT TOO SWIFT.
DID YOU MODEL HIM AFTER ANYBODY YOU KNOW?
UH... WELL... UH...
NICE WORK, CHUCK, AND A NOVEL WAY OF APPROACHING THE CARICATURE ASSIGNMENT.
BUT HE ALWAYS DOES A CARTOON OR COMIC STRIP STORY.
NATURALLY. HE'S CHUCK.
RINNGG
CHUCK, THIS IS MAE WOO. SHE TEACHES AT PENNY POND ELEMENTARY.
HEY THERE!
2

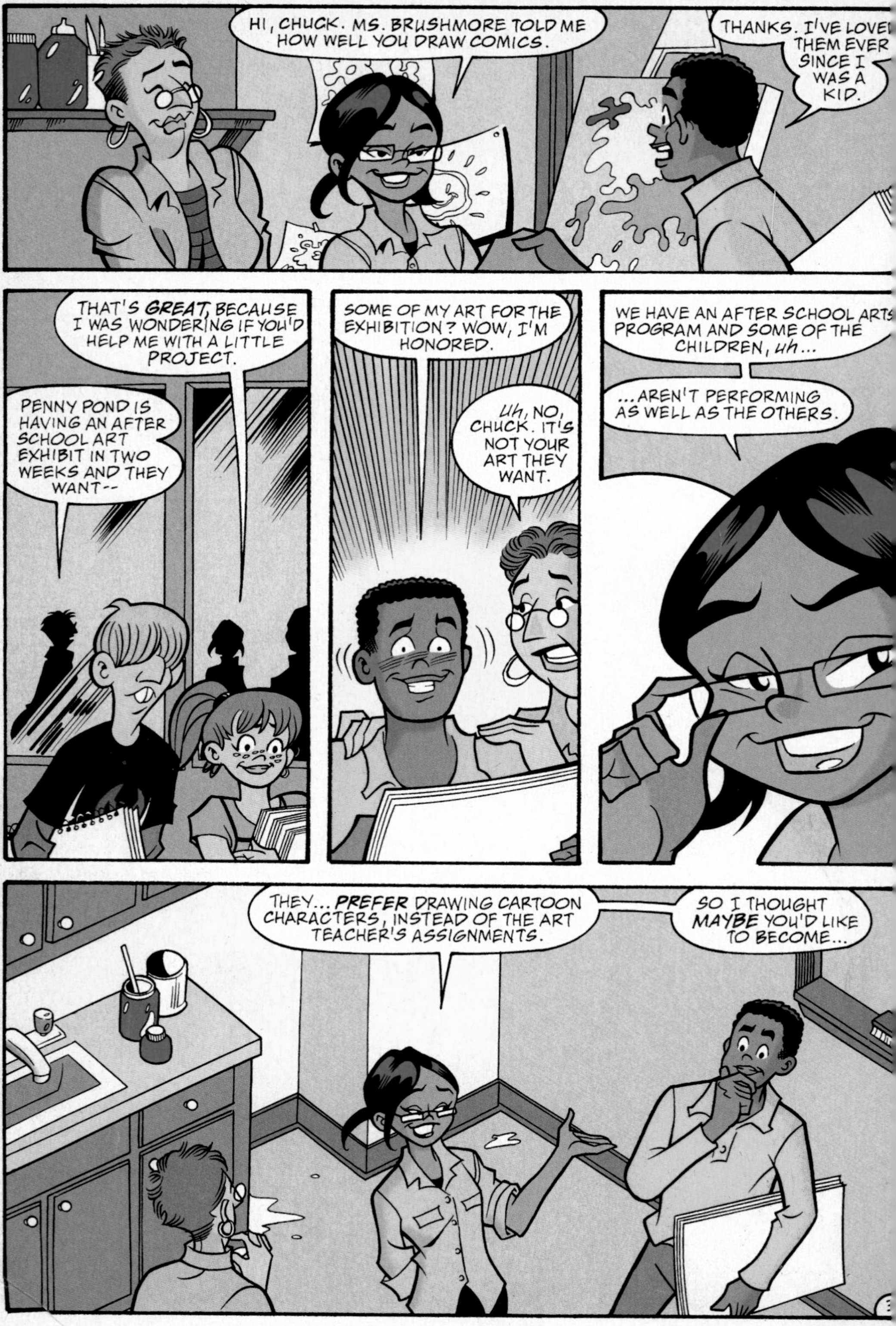
HI, CHUCK. MS. BRUSHMORE TOLD ME HOW WELL YOU DRAW COMICS.
THANKS. I'VE LOVED THEM EVER SINCE I WAS A KID.
THAT'S **GREAT,** BECAUSE I WAS WONDERING IF YOU'D HELP ME WITH A LITTLE PROJECT.
PENNY POND IS HAVING AN AFTER SCHOOL ART EXHIBIT IN TWO WEEKS AND THEY WANT--
SOME OF MY ART FOR THE EXHIBITION? WOW, I'M HONORED.
UH, NO, CHUCK. IT'S NOT YOUR ART THEY WANT.
WE HAVE AN AFTER SCHOOL ARTS PROGRAM AND SOME OF THE CHILDREN, *UH*...
...AREN'T PERFORMING AS WELL AS THE OTHERS.
THEY... **PREFER** DRAWING CARTOON CHARACTERS, INSTEAD OF THE ART TEACHER'S ASSIGNMENTS.
SO I THOUGHT **MAYBE** YOU'D LIKE TO BECOME...

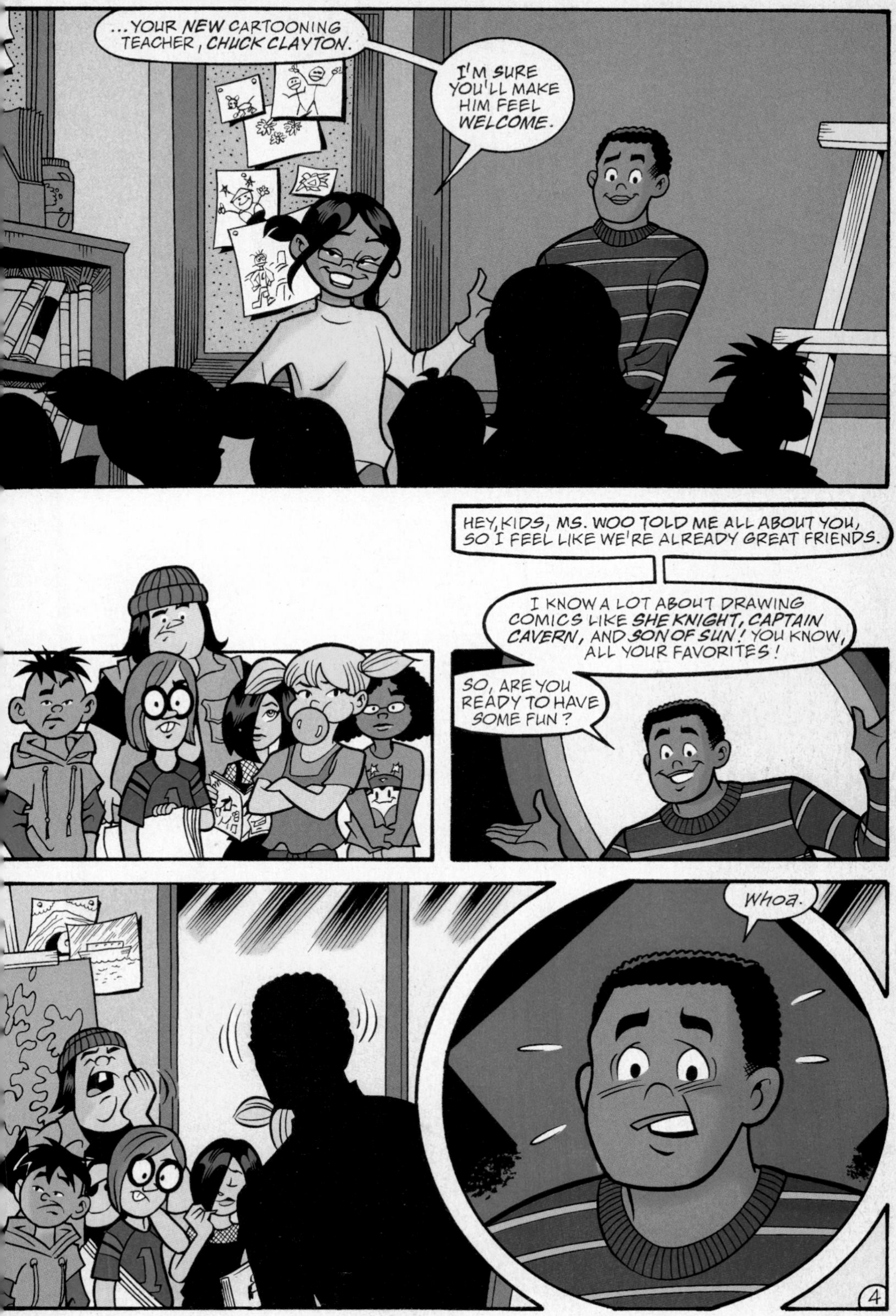
...YOUR NEW CARTOONING TEACHER, CHUCK CLAYTON.
I'M SURE YOU'LL MAKE HIM FEEL WELCOME.
HEY, KIDS, MS. WOO TOLD ME ALL ABOUT YOU, SO I FEEL LIKE WE'RE ALREADY GREAT FRIENDS.
I KNOW A LOT ABOUT DRAWING COMICS LIKE SHE KNIGHT, CAPTAIN CAVERN, AND SON OF SUN! YOU KNOW, ALL YOUR FAVORITES!
SO, ARE YOU READY TO HAVE SOME FUN?
Whoa.

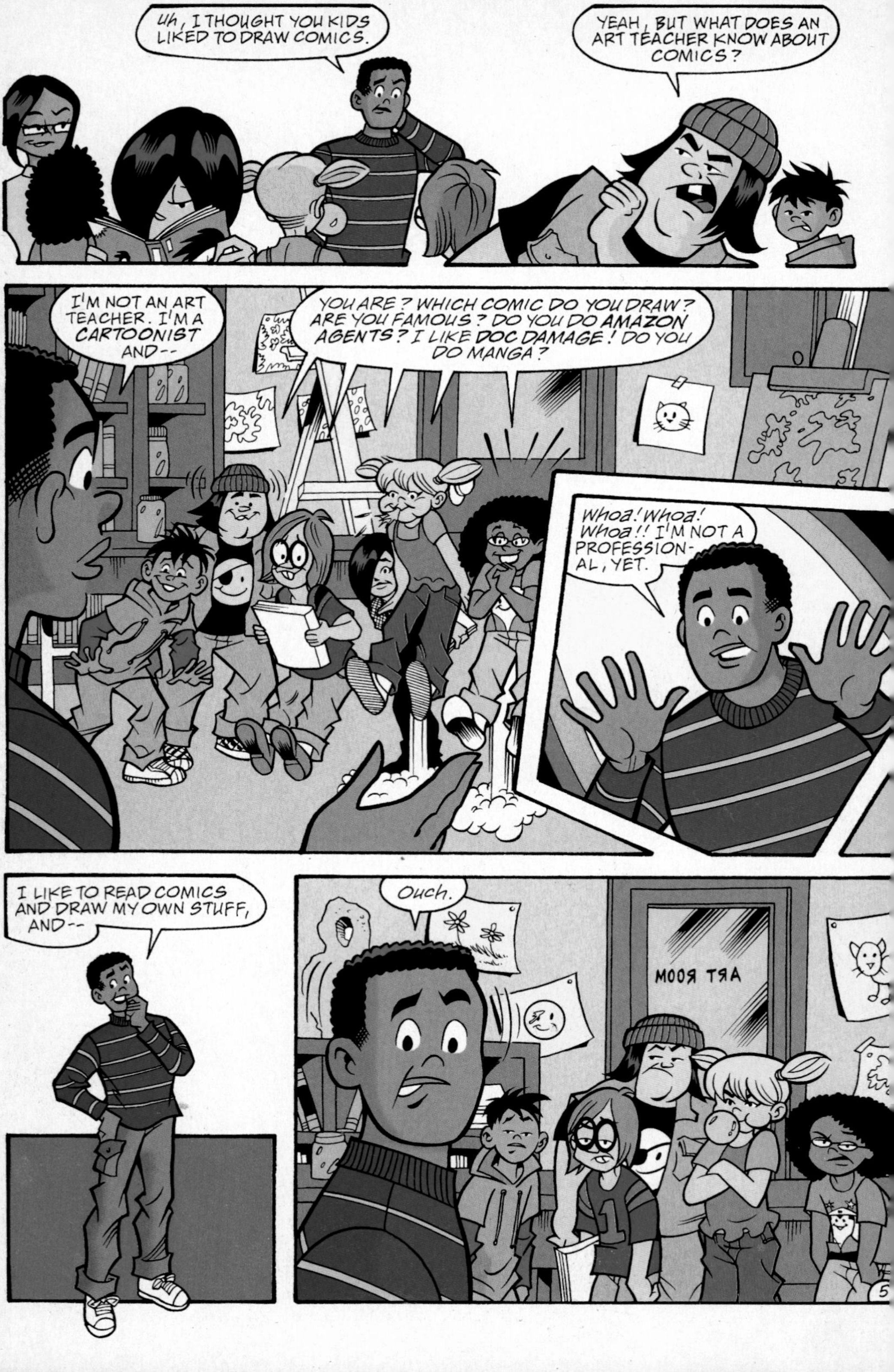
UH, I THOUGHT YOU KIDS LIKED TO DRAW COMICS.
YEAH, BUT WHAT DOES AN ART TEACHER KNOW ABOUT COMICS?
I'M NOT AN ART TEACHER. I'M A CARTOONIST AND--
YOU ARE? WHICH COMIC DO YOU DRAW? ARE YOU FAMOUS? DO YOU DO AMAZON AGENTS? I LIKE DOC DAMAGE! DO YOU DO MANGA?
WHOA! WHOA! WHOA!! I'M NOT A PROFESSIONAL, YET.
I LIKE TO READ COMICS AND DRAW MY OWN STUFF, AND--
OUCH.
ART ROOM
5

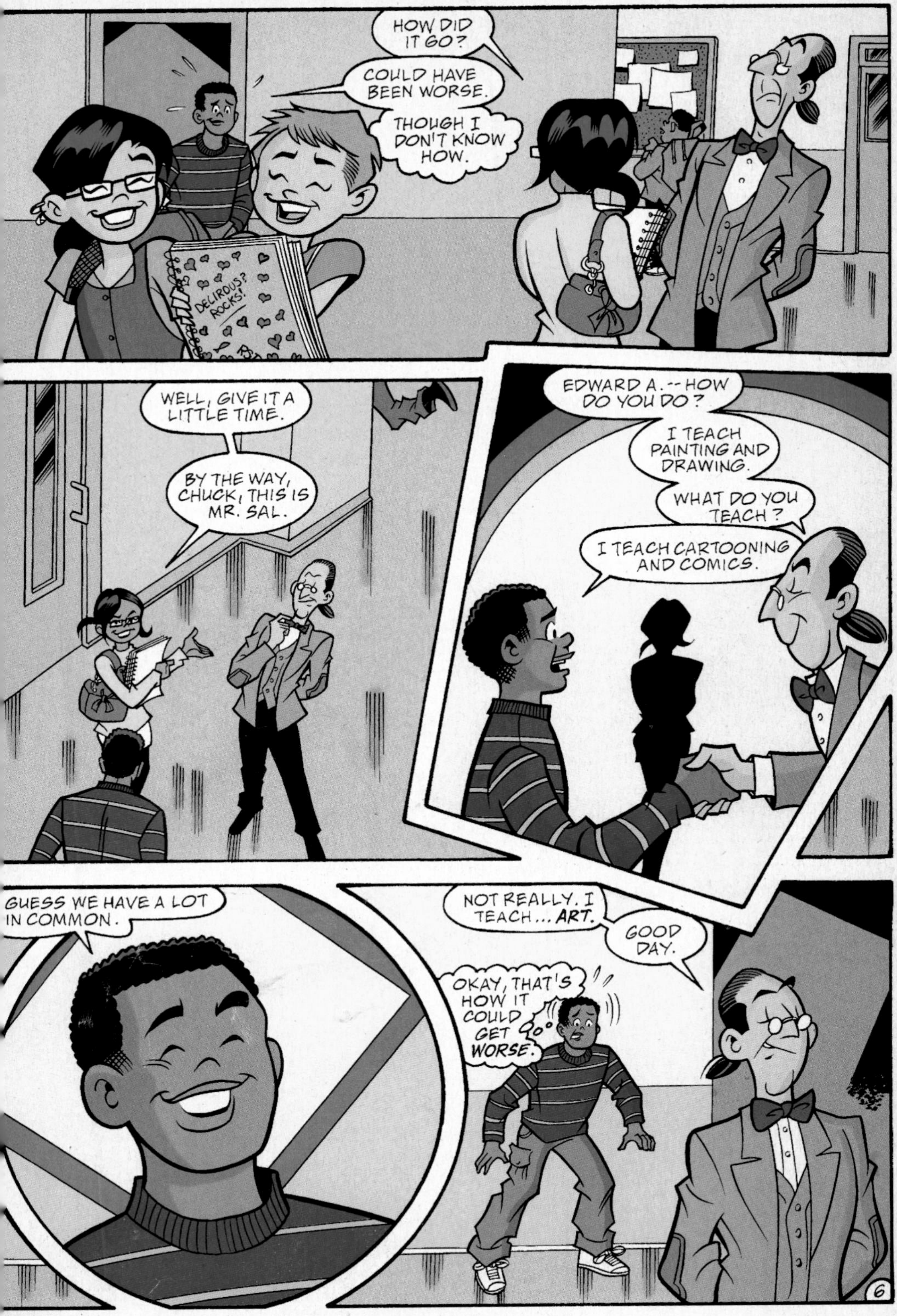
HOW DID IT GO?
COULD HAVE BEEN WORSE.
THOUGH I DON'T KNOW HOW.
DELIRIOUS? ROCKS!
WELL, GIVE IT A LITTLE TIME.
BY THE WAY, CHUCK, THIS IS MR. SAL.
EDWARD A.--HOW DO YOU DO?
I TEACH PAINTING AND DRAWING.
WHAT DO YOU TEACH?
I TEACH CARTOONING AND COMICS.
GUESS WE HAVE A LOT IN COMMON.
NOT REALLY. I TEACH... ART.
GOOD DAY.
OKAY, THAT'S HOW IT COULD GET WORSE.
6

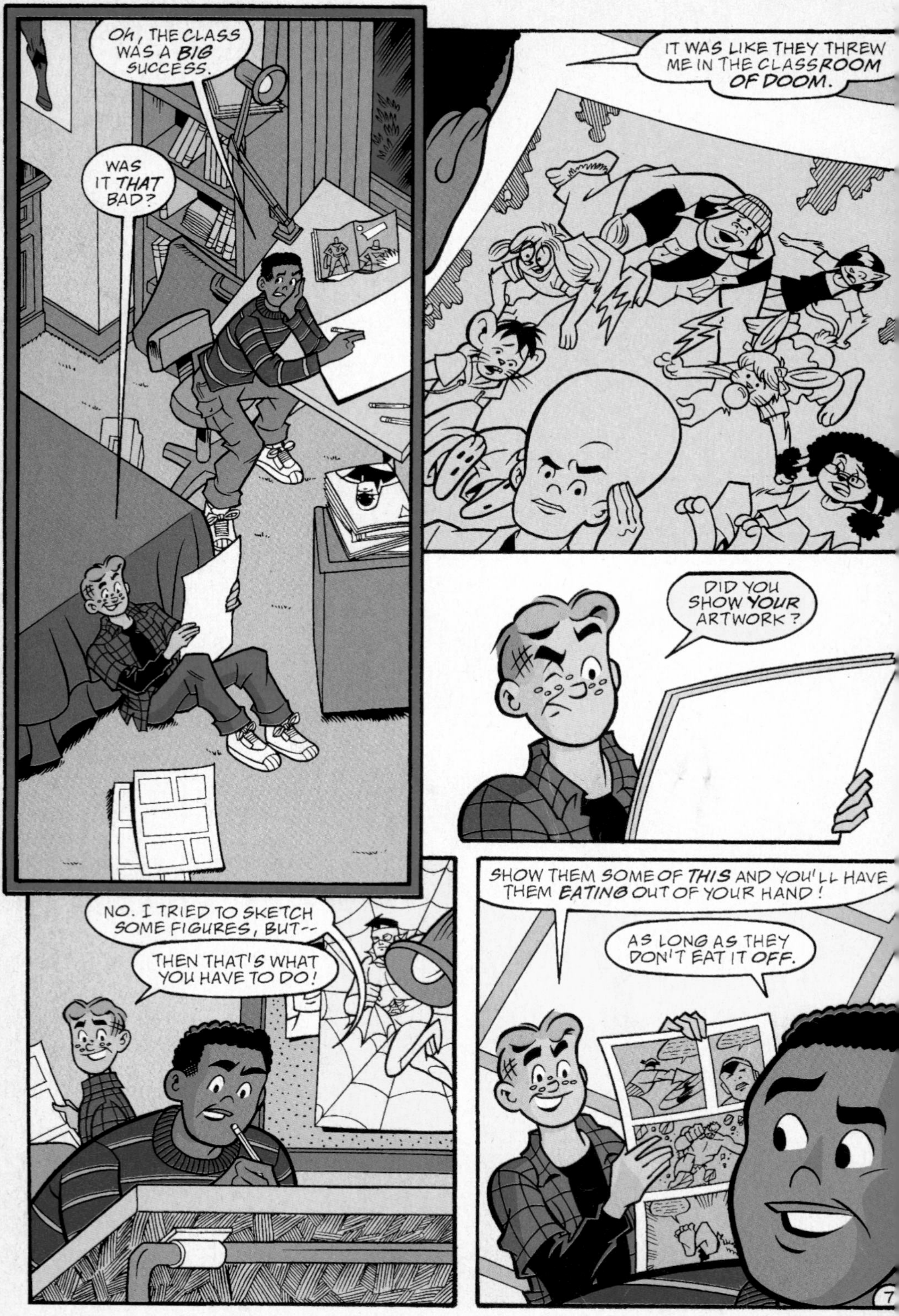
OH, THE CLASS WAS A BIG SUCCESS.
WAS IT THAT BAD?
IT WAS LIKE THEY THREW ME IN THE CLASSROOM OF DOOM.
DID YOU SHOW YOUR ARTWORK?
NO. I TRIED TO SKETCH SOME FIGURES, BUT--
THEN THAT'S WHAT YOU HAVE TO DO!
SHOW THEM SOME OF THIS AND YOU'LL HAVE THEM EATING OUT OF YOUR HAND!
AS LONG AS THEY DON'T EAT IT OFF.
7

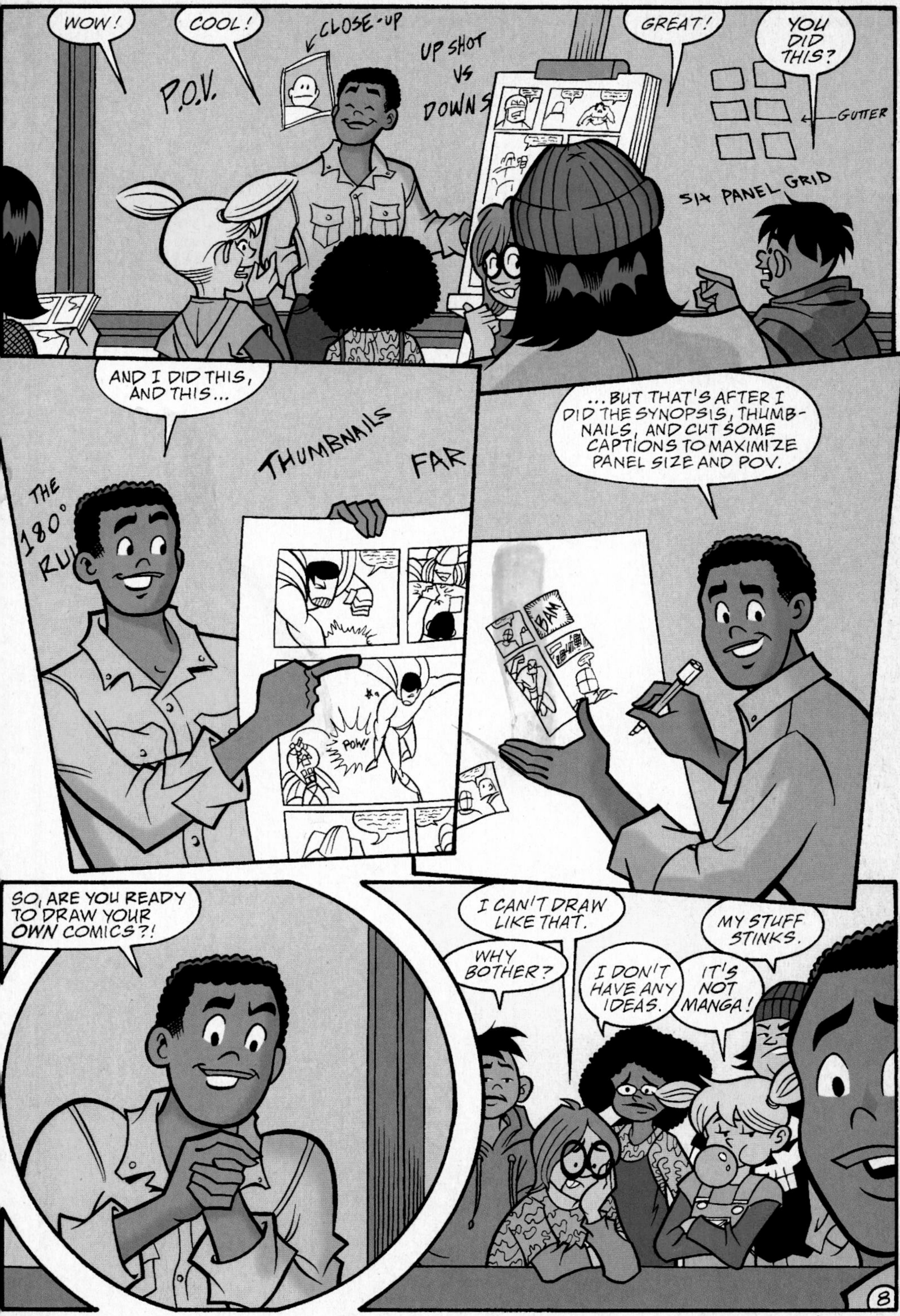
WOW!
COOL!
CLOSE-UP
P.O.V.
UP SHOT VS DOWNS
GREAT!
YOU DID THIS?
GUTTER
SIX PANEL GRID
AND I DID THIS, AND THIS...
THUMBNAILS
FAR
THE 180° RU
POW!
...BUT THAT'S AFTER I DID THE SYNOPSIS, THUMB-NAILS, AND CUT SOME CAPTIONS TO MAXIMIZE PANEL SIZE AND POV.
BAM
SO, ARE YOU READY TO DRAW YOUR *OWN* COMICS?!
I CAN'T DRAW LIKE THAT.
MY STUFF STINKS.
WHY BOTHER?
I DON'T HAVE ANY IDEAS.
IT'S NOT MANGA!
8

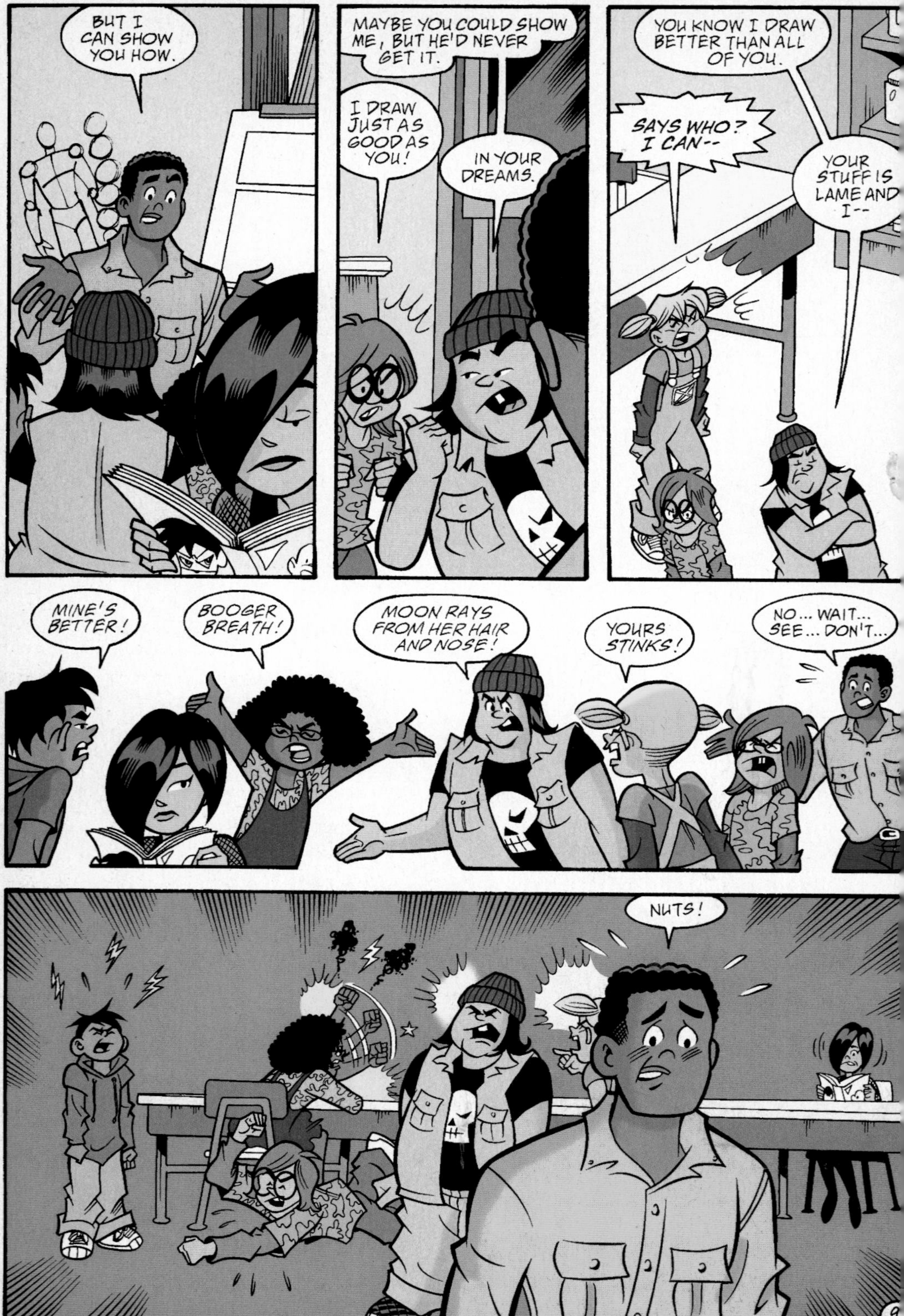
BUT I CAN SHOW YOU HOW.
MAYBE YOU COULD SHOW ME, BUT HE'D NEVER GET IT.
I DRAW JUST AS GOOD AS YOU!
IN YOUR DREAMS.
YOU KNOW I DRAW BETTER THAN ALL OF YOU.
SAYS WHO? I CAN--
YOUR STUFF IS LAME AND I--
MINE'S BETTER!
BOOGER BREATH!
MOON RAYS FROM HER HAIR AND NOSE!
YOURS STINKS!
NO... WAIT... SEE... DON'T...
NUTS!

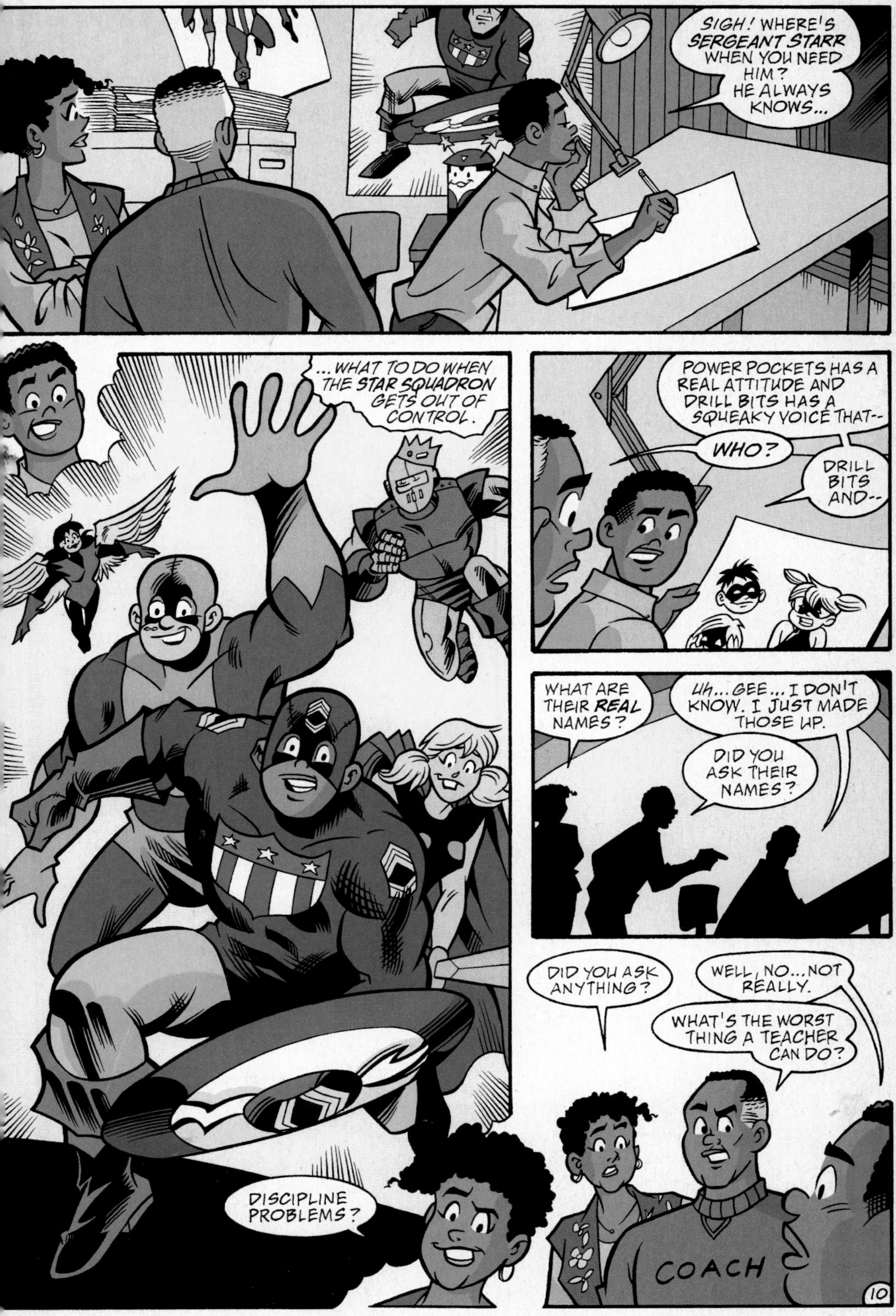
SIGH! WHERE'S SERGEANT STARR WHEN YOU NEED HIM? HE ALWAYS KNOWS...
...WHAT TO DO WHEN THE STAR SQUADRON GETS OUT OF CONTROL.
POWER POCKETS HAS A REAL ATTITUDE AND DRILL BITS HAS A SQUEAKY VOICE THAT--
WHO?
DRILL BITS AND--
WHAT ARE THEIR REAL NAMES?
UH... GEE... I DON'T KNOW. I JUST MADE THOSE UP.
DID YOU ASK THEIR NAMES?
DID YOU ASK ANYTHING?
WELL, NO... NOT REALLY.
WHAT'S THE WORST THING A TEACHER CAN DO?
DISCIPLINE PROBLEMS?
COACH
10

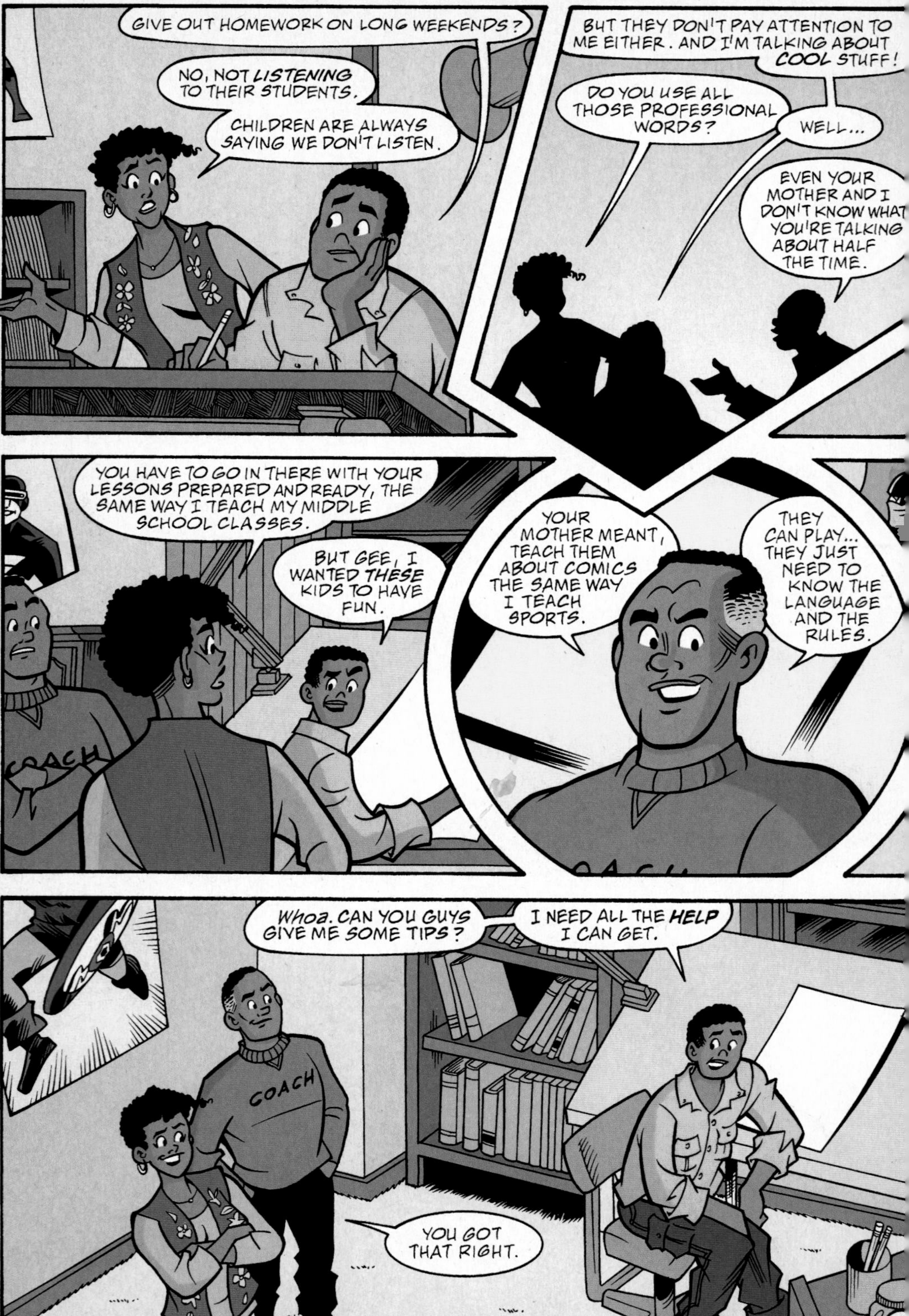
GIVE OUT HOMEWORK ON LONG WEEKENDS?
NO, NOT *LISTENING* TO THEIR STUDENTS.
CHILDREN ARE ALWAYS SAYING WE DON'T LISTEN.
BUT THEY DON'T PAY ATTENTION TO ME EITHER. AND I'M TALKING ABOUT *COOL* STUFF!
DO YOU USE ALL THOSE PROFESSIONAL WORDS?
WELL...
EVEN YOUR MOTHER AND I DON'T KNOW WHAT YOU'RE TALKING ABOUT HALF THE TIME.
YOU HAVE TO GO IN THERE WITH YOUR LESSONS PREPARED AND READY, THE SAME WAY I TEACH MY MIDDLE SCHOOL CLASSES.
BUT GEE, I WANTED *THESE* KIDS TO HAVE FUN.
COACH
YOUR MOTHER MEANT, TEACH THEM ABOUT COMICS THE SAME WAY I TEACH SPORTS.
THEY CAN PLAY... THEY JUST NEED TO KNOW THE LANGUAGE AND THE RULES.
Whoa. CAN YOU GUYS GIVE ME SOME TIPS?
I NEED ALL THE *HELP* I CAN GET.
COACH
YOU GOT THAT RIGHT.
11

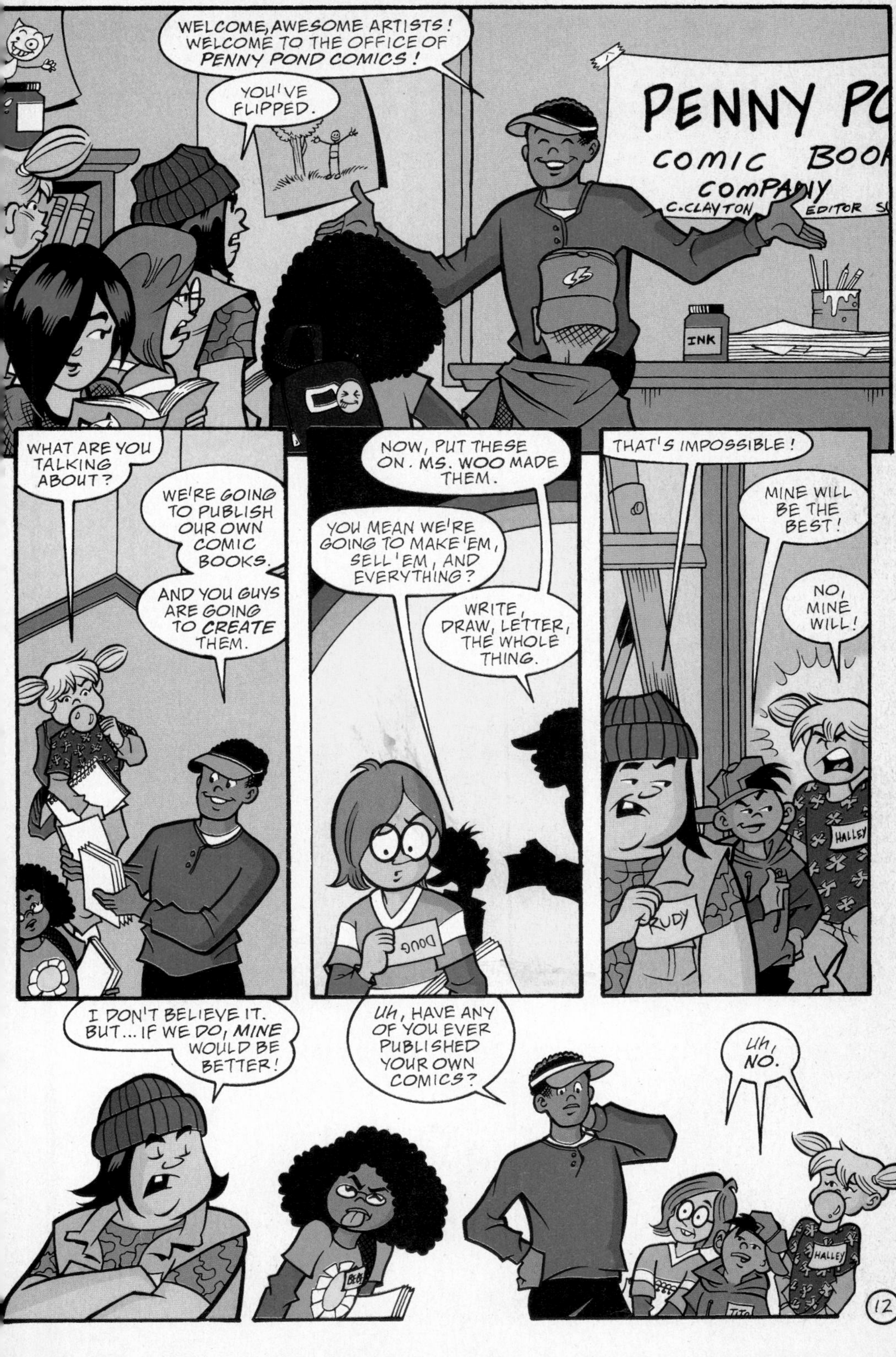
WELCOME, AWESOME ARTISTS! WELCOME TO THE OFFICE OF PENNY POND COMICS!
YOU'VE FLIPPED.
PENNY PO
COMIC BOO
COMPANY
C. CLAYTON EDITOR S
INK
WHAT ARE YOU TALKING ABOUT?
WE'RE GOING TO PUBLISH OUR OWN COMIC BOOKS.
AND YOU GUYS ARE GOING TO CREATE THEM.
NOW, PUT THESE ON. MS. WOO MADE THEM.
YOU MEAN WE'RE GOING TO MAKE 'EM, SELL 'EM, AND EVERYTHING?
WRITE, DRAW, LETTER, THE WHOLE THING.
DOUG
THAT'S IMPOSSIBLE!
MINE WILL BE THE BEST!
NO, MINE WILL!
RUDY
HALLEY
I DON'T BELIEVE IT. BUT... IF WE DO, MINE WOULD BE BETTER!
UH, HAVE ANY OF YOU EVER PUBLISHED YOUR OWN COMICS?
UH, NO.
HALLEY
TITO

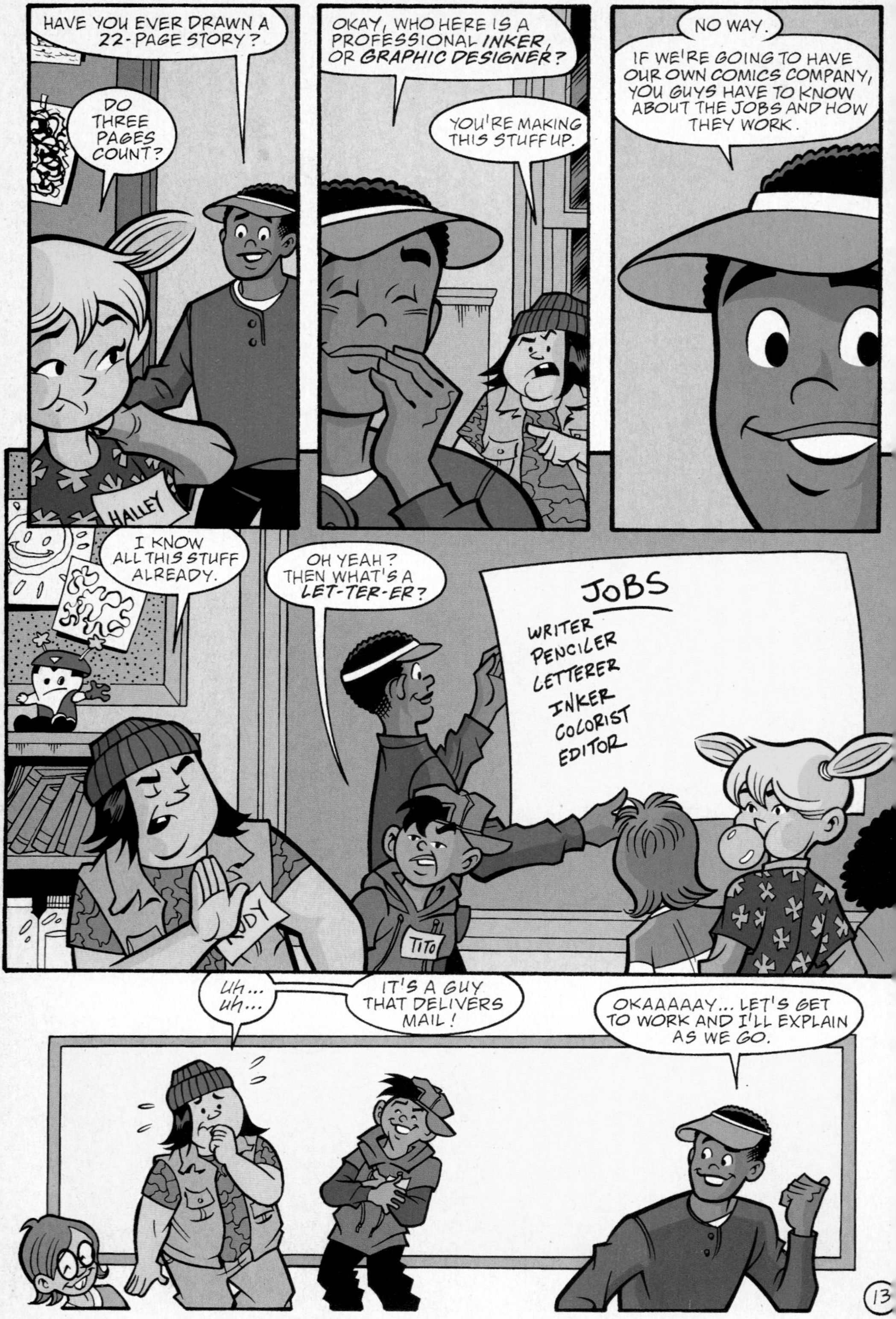
HAVE YOU EVER DRAWN A 22-PAGE STORY?
DO THREE PAGES COUNT?
HALLEY
OKAY, WHO HERE IS A PROFESSIONAL INKER, OR GRAPHIC DESIGNER?
YOU'RE MAKING THIS STUFF UP.
NO WAY.
IF WE'RE GOING TO HAVE OUR OWN COMICS COMPANY, YOU GUYS HAVE TO KNOW ABOUT THE JOBS AND HOW THEY WORK.
I KNOW ALL THIS STUFF ALREADY.
OH YEAH? THEN WHAT'S A LET-TER-ER?
JOBS
WRITER
PENCILER
LETTERER
INKER
COLORIST
EDITOR
RUDY
TITO
UH... UH...
IT'S A GUY THAT DELIVERS MAIL!
OKAAAAAY... LET'S GET TO WORK AND I'LL EXPLAIN AS WE GO.
13

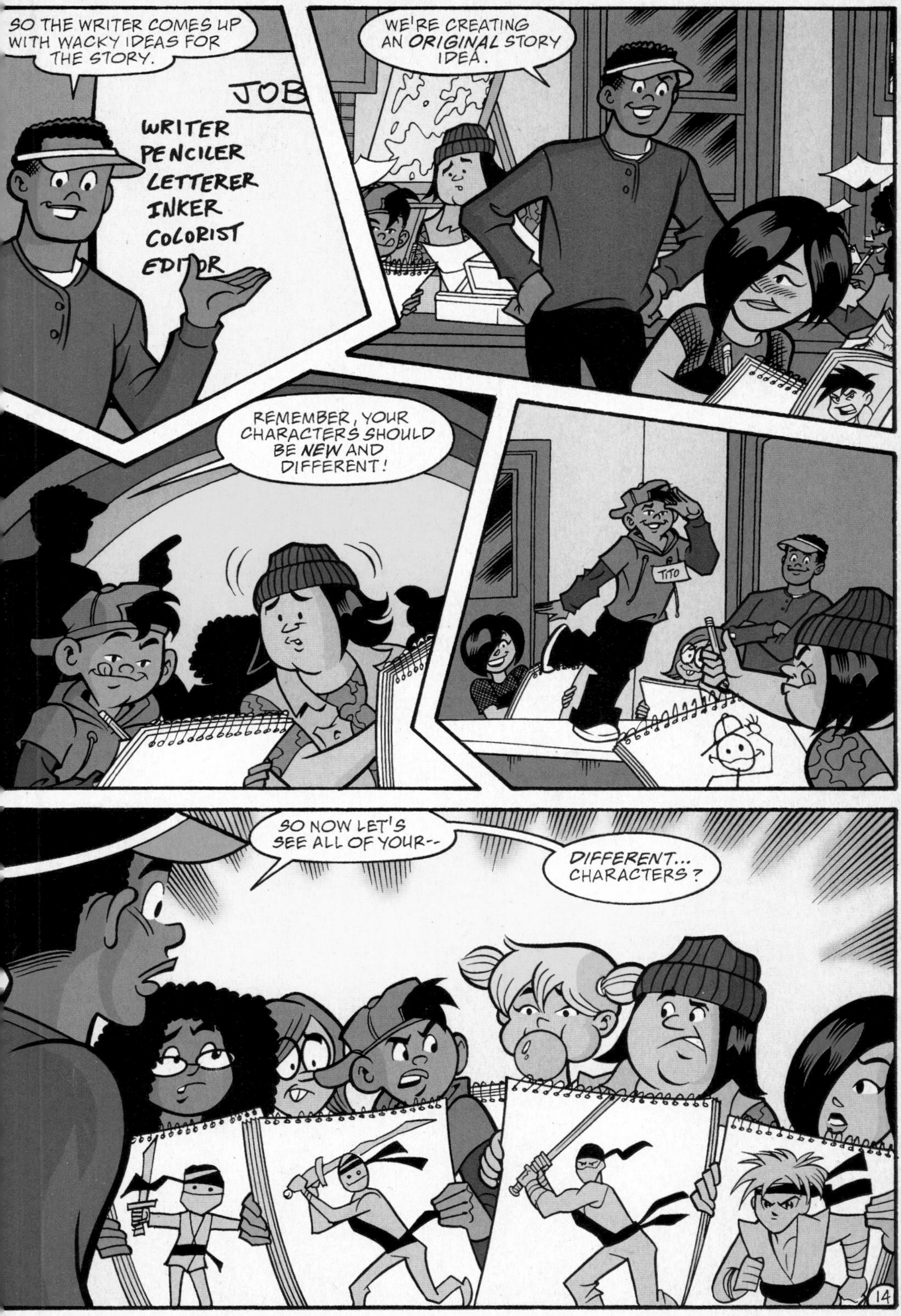
SO THE WRITER COMES UP WITH WACKY IDEAS FOR THE STORY.
JOB
WRITER
PENCILER
LETTERER
INKER
COLORIST
EDITOR
WE'RE CREATING AN *ORIGINAL* STORY IDEA.
REMEMBER, YOUR CHARACTERS SHOULD BE *NEW* AND DIFFERENT!
TITO
SO NOW LET'S SEE ALL OF YOUR--
DIFFERENT... CHARACTERS?
14

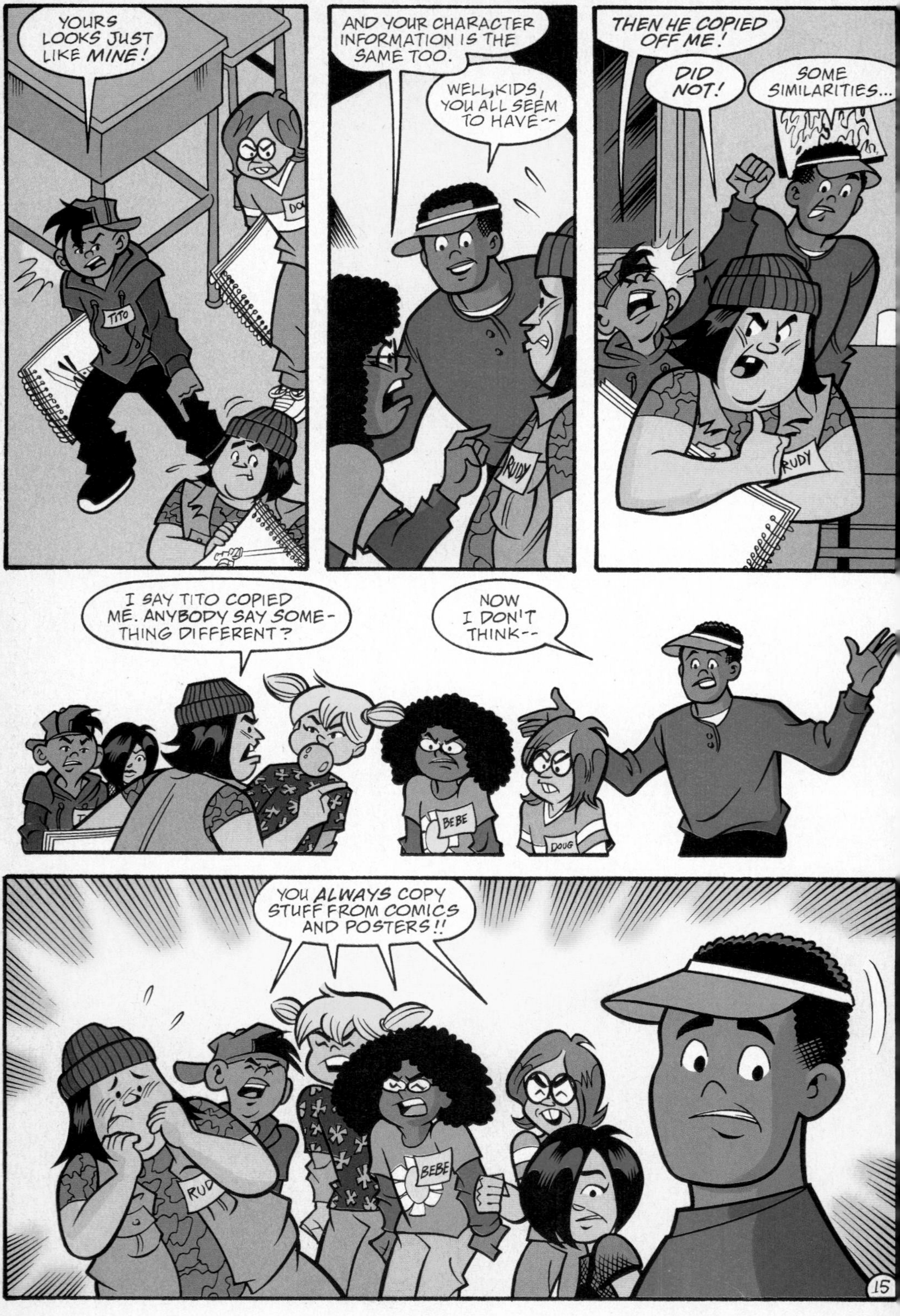
YOURS LOOKS JUST LIKE MINE!
TITO
AND YOUR CHARACTER INFORMATION IS THE SAME TOO.
WELL, KIDS, YOU ALL SEEM TO HAVE--
RUDY
THEN HE COPIED OFF ME!
DID NOT!
SOME SIMILARITIES...
RUDY
I SAY TITO COPIED ME. ANYBODY SAY SOME-THING DIFFERENT?
NOW I DON'T THINK--
BEBE
DOUG
YOU ALWAYS COPY STUFF FROM COMICS AND POSTERS!!
RUD
BEBE
15

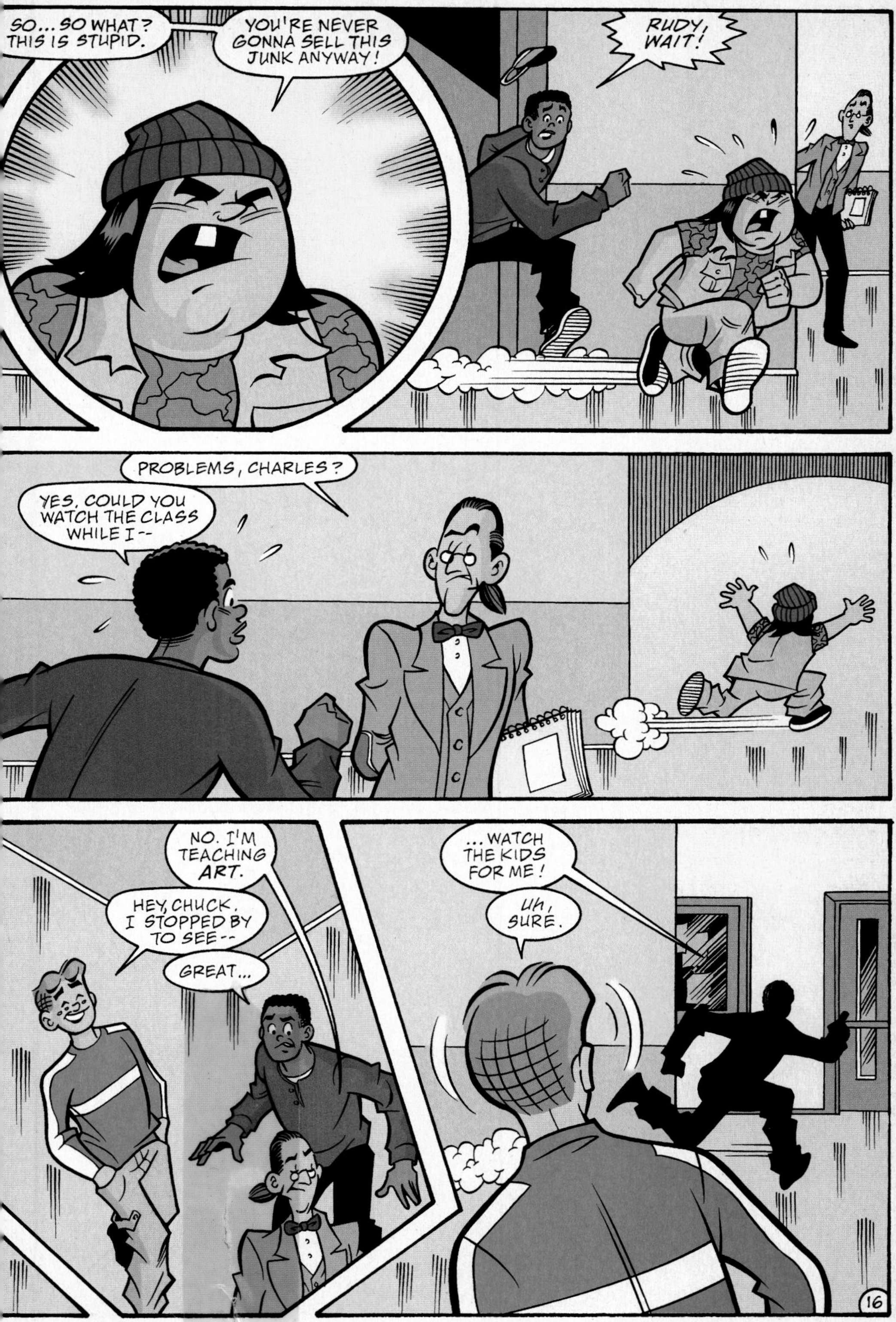
SO... SO WHAT? THIS IS STUPID.
YOU'RE NEVER GONNA SELL THIS JUNK ANYWAY!
RUDY, WAIT!
PROBLEMS, CHARLES?
YES, COULD YOU WATCH THE CLASS WHILE I--
NO. I'M TEACHING ART.
HEY, CHUCK, I STOPPED BY TO SEE--
GREAT...
...WATCH THE KIDS FOR ME!
UH, SURE.

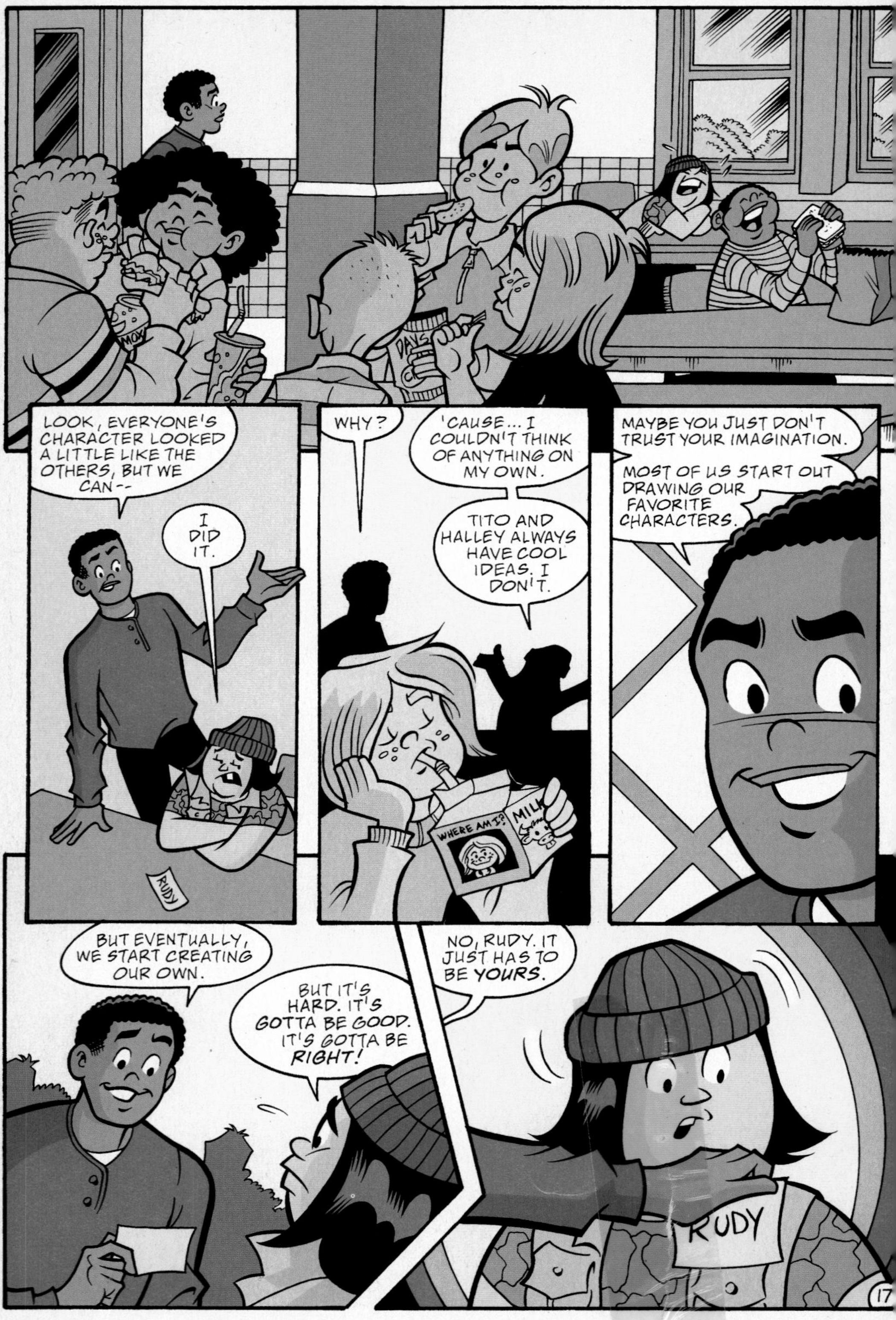
MOX
DAYS
LOOK, EVERYONE'S CHARACTER LOOKED A LITTLE LIKE THE OTHERS, BUT WE CAN--
I DID IT.
RUDY
WHY?
'CAUSE... I COULDN'T THINK OF ANYTHING ON MY OWN.
TITO AND HALLEY ALWAYS HAVE COOL IDEAS. I DON'T.
WHERE AM I?
MILK
MAYBE YOU JUST DON'T TRUST YOUR IMAGINATION.
MOST OF US START OUT DRAWING OUR FAVORITE CHARACTERS.
BUT EVENTUALLY, WE START CREATING OUR OWN.
BUT IT'S HARD. IT'S GOTTA BE GOOD. IT'S GOTTA BE **RIGHT!**
NO, RUDY. IT JUST HAS TO BE **YOURS**.
RUDY
17

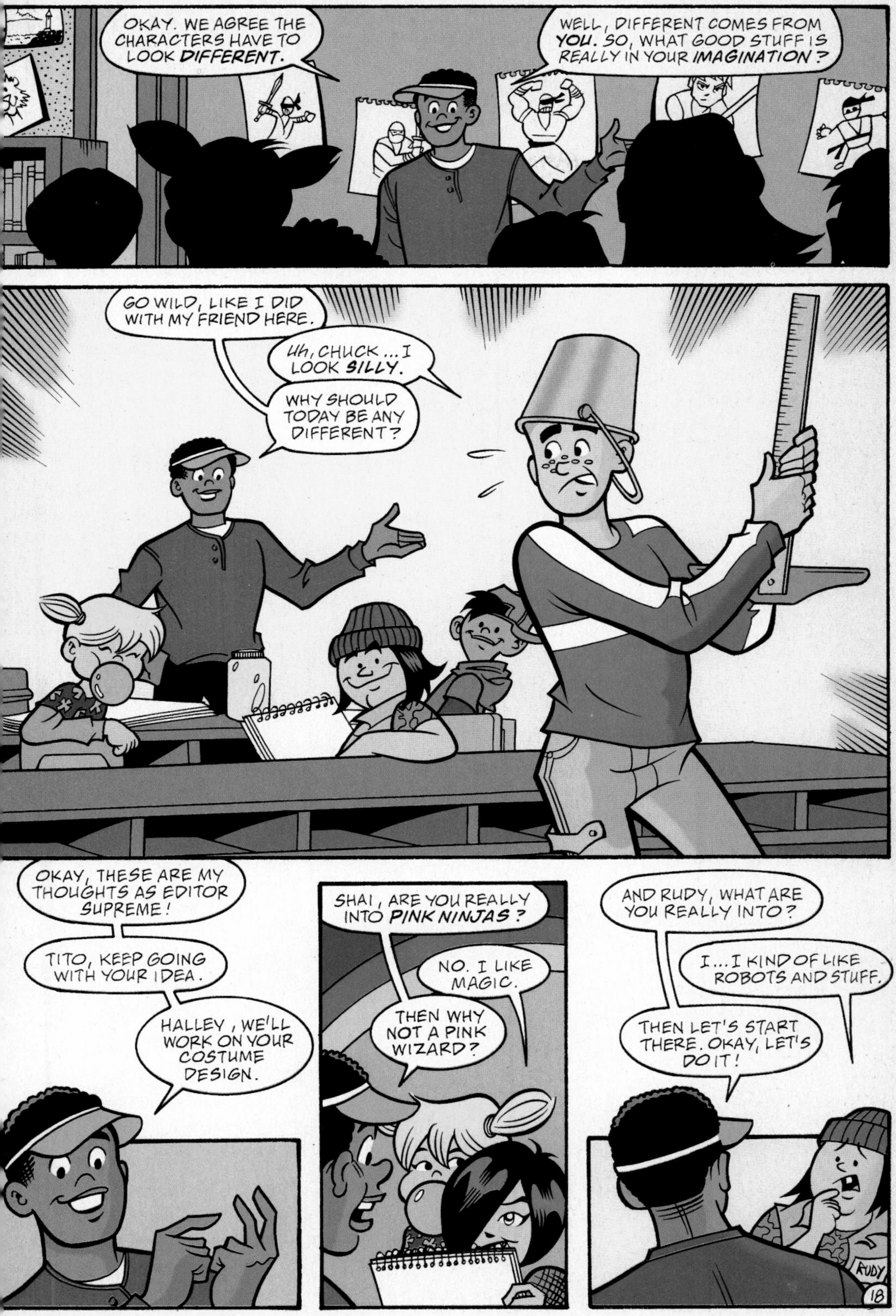
OKAY. WE AGREE THE CHARACTERS HAVE TO LOOK DIFFERENT.
WELL, DIFFERENT COMES FROM YOU. SO, WHAT GOOD STUFF IS REALLY IN YOUR IMAGINATION?
GO WILD, LIKE I DID WITH MY FRIEND HERE.
Uh, CHUCK ... I LOOK SILLY.
WHY SHOULD TODAY BE ANY DIFFERENT?
OKAY, THESE ARE MY THOUGHTS AS EDITOR SUPREME!
TITO, KEEP GOING WITH YOUR IDEA.
HALLEY, WE'LL WORK ON YOUR COSTUME DESIGN.
SHAI, ARE YOU REALLY INTO PINK NINJAS?
NO. I LIKE MAGIC.
THEN WHY NOT A PINK WIZARD?
AND RUDY, WHAT ARE YOU REALLY INTO?
I... I KIND OF LIKE ROBOTS AND STUFF.
THEN LET'S START THERE. OKAY, LET'S DO IT!
RUDY
18

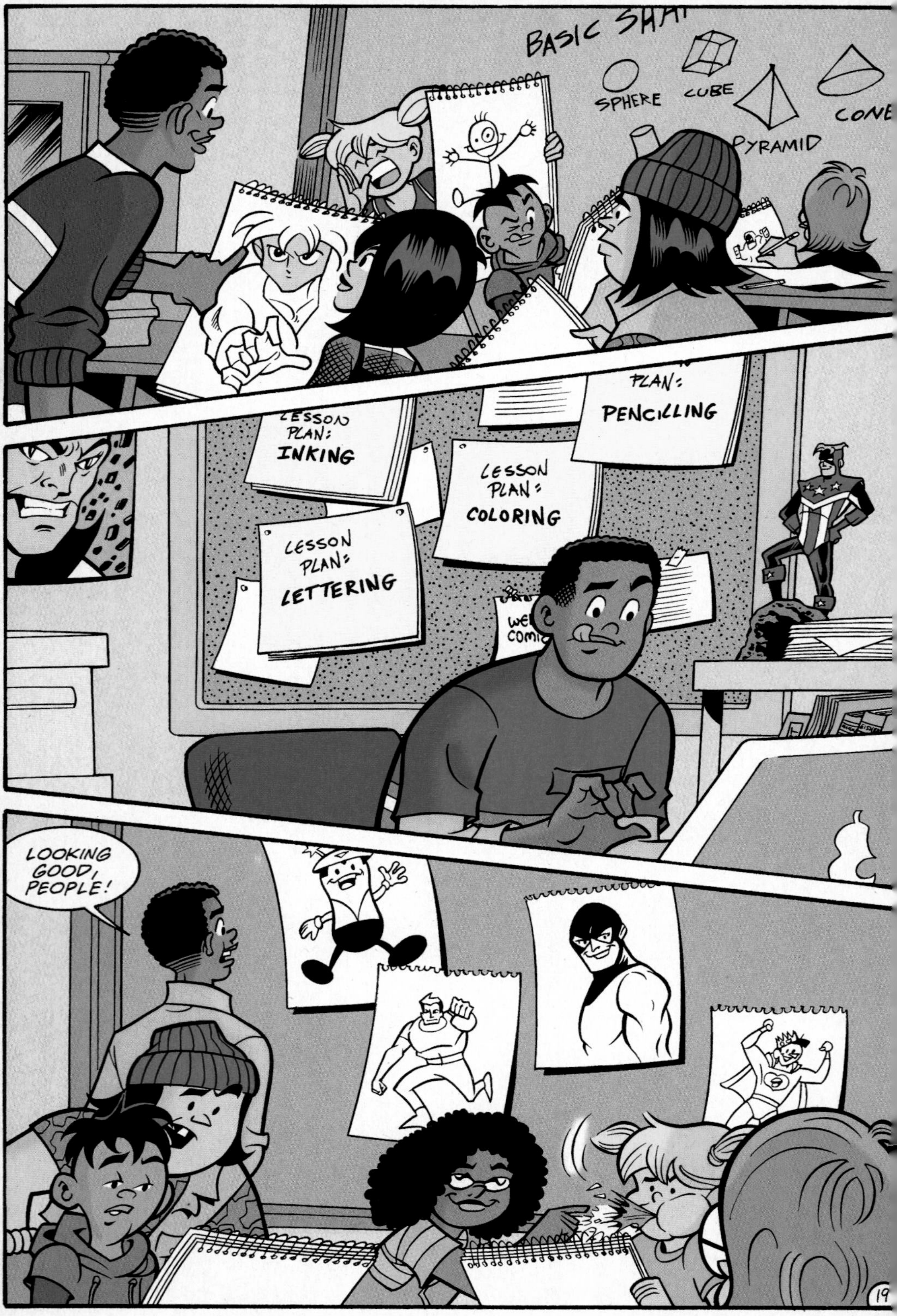
BASIC SHA
SPHERE
CUBE
PYRAMID
CONE
LESSON PLAN: INKING
PLAN: PENCILLING
LESSON PLAN: COLORING
LESSON PLAN: LETTERING
LOOKING GOOD, PEOPLE!

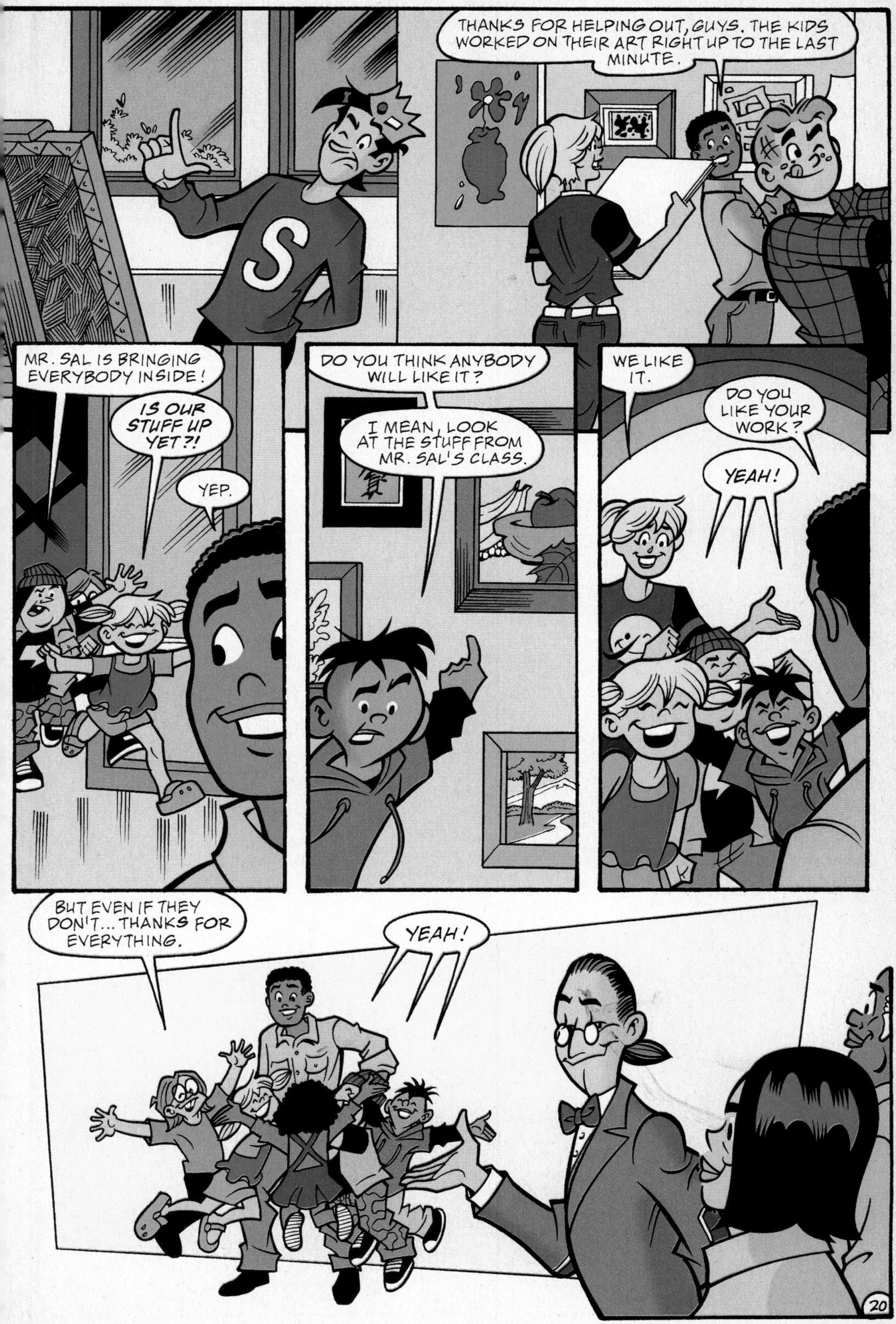
THANKS FOR HELPING OUT, GUYS. THE KIDS WORKED ON THEIR ART RIGHT UP TO THE LAST MINUTE.
MR. SAL IS BRINGING EVERYBODY INSIDE!
IS OUR STUFF UP YET?!
YEP.
DO YOU THINK ANYBODY WILL LIKE IT?
I MEAN, LOOK AT THE STUFF FROM MR. SAL'S CLASS.
WE LIKE IT.
DO YOU LIKE YOUR WORK?
YEAH!
BUT EVEN IF THEY DON'T... THANKS FOR EVERYTHING.
YEAH!
20

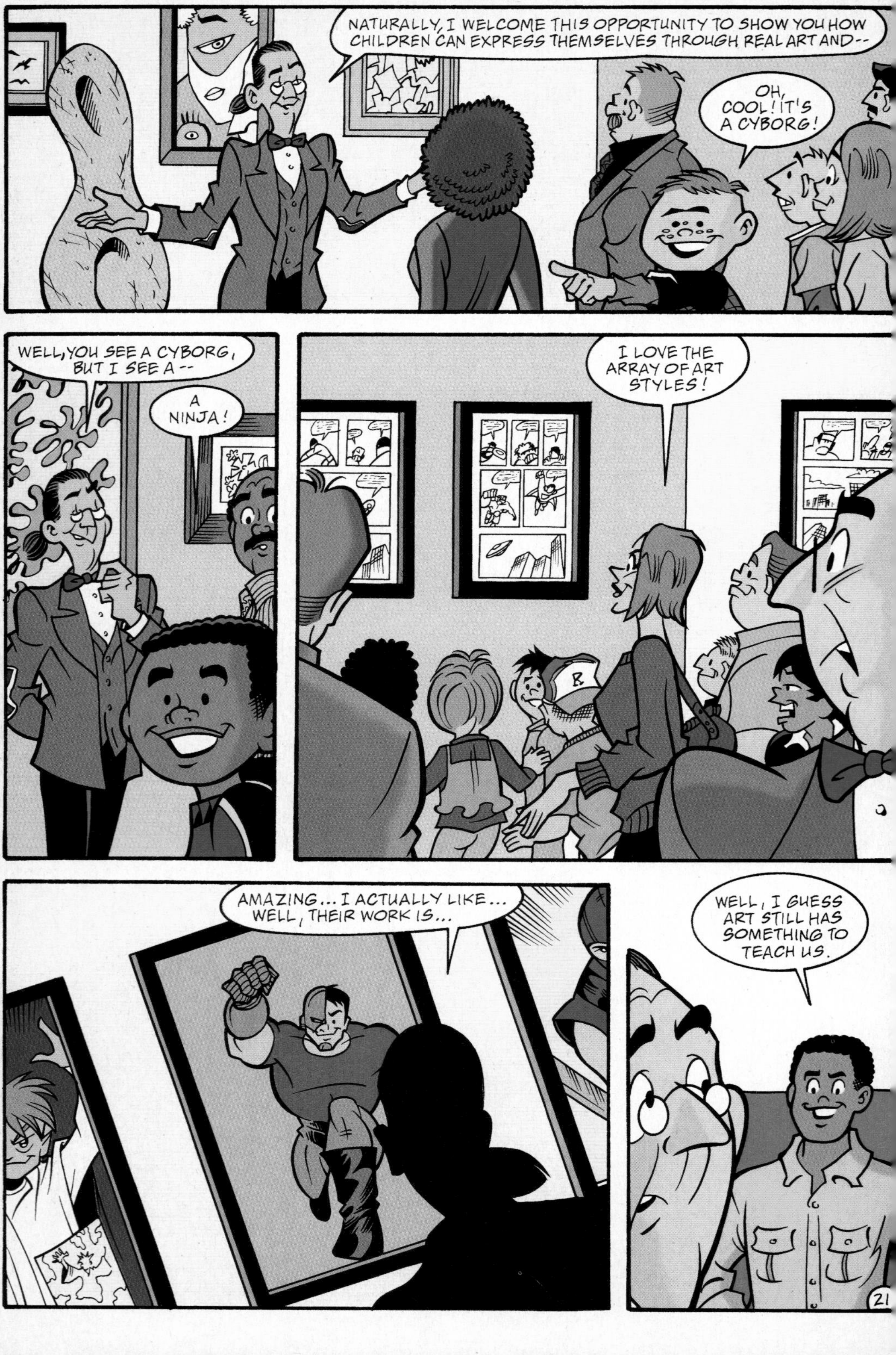
NATURALLY, I WELCOME THIS OPPORTUNITY TO SHOW YOU HOW CHILDREN CAN EXPRESS THEMSELVES THROUGH REAL ART AND--
OH, COOL! IT'S A CYBORG!
WELL, YOU SEE A CYBORG, BUT I SEE A --
A NINJA!
I LOVE THE ARRAY OF ART STYLES!
AMAZING... I ACTUALLY LIKE... WELL, THEIR WORK IS...
WELL, I GUESS ART STILL HAS SOMETHING TO TEACH US.
21

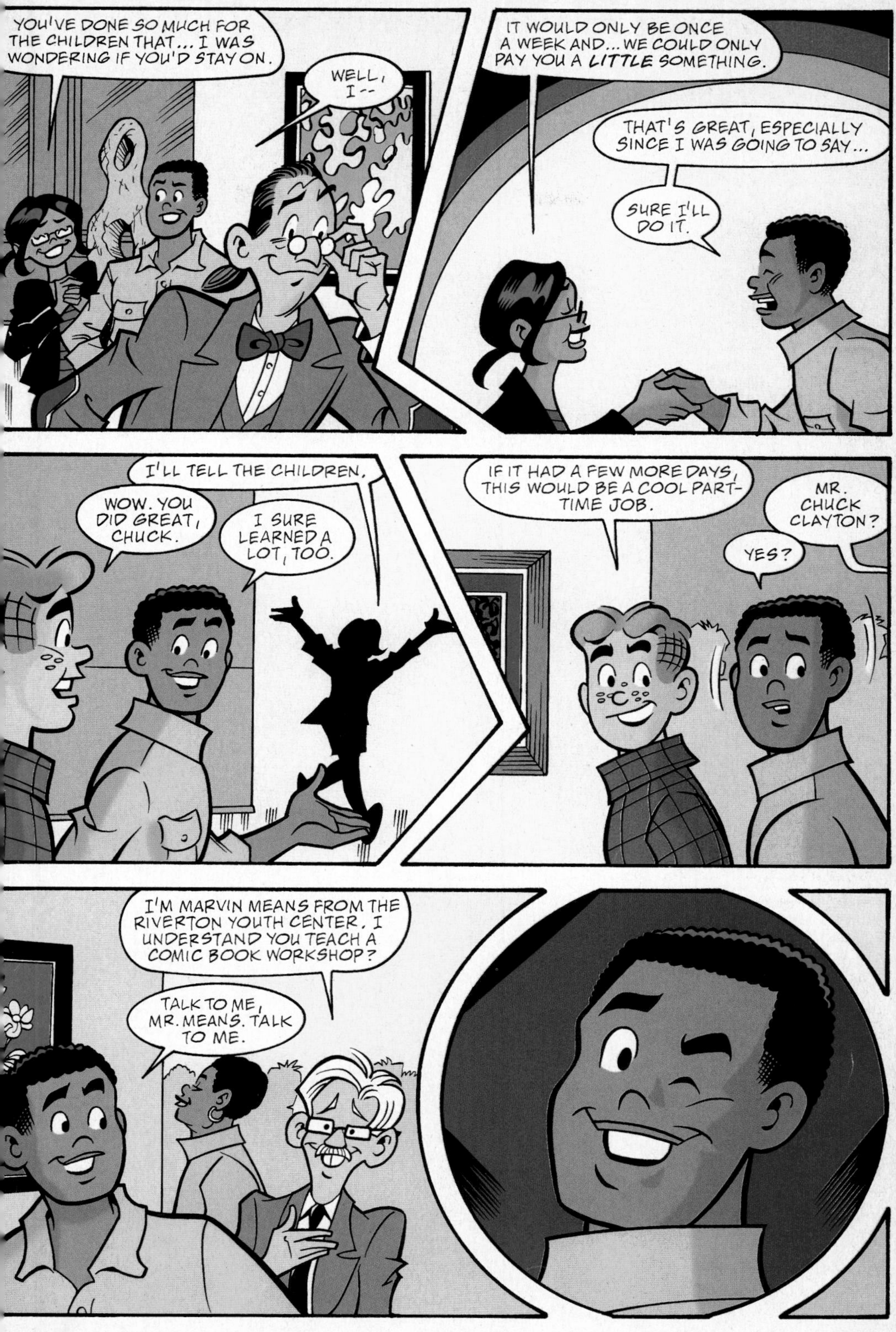
YOU'VE DONE SO MUCH FOR THE CHILDREN THAT... I WAS WONDERING IF YOU'D STAY ON.
WELL, I --
IT WOULD ONLY BE ONCE A WEEK AND... WE COULD ONLY PAY YOU A LITTLE SOMETHING.
THAT'S GREAT, ESPECIALLY SINCE I WAS GOING TO SAY...
SURE I'LL DO IT.
I'LL TELL THE CHILDREN.
WOW. YOU DID GREAT, CHUCK.
I SURE LEARNED A LOT, TOO.
IF IT HAD A FEW MORE DAYS, THIS WOULD BE A COOL PART-TIME JOB.
MR. CHUCK CLAYTON?
YES?
I'M MARVIN MEANS FROM THE RIVERTON YOUTH CENTER. I UNDERSTAND YOU TEACH A COMIC BOOK WORKSHOP?
TALK TO ME, MR. MEANS. TALK TO ME.

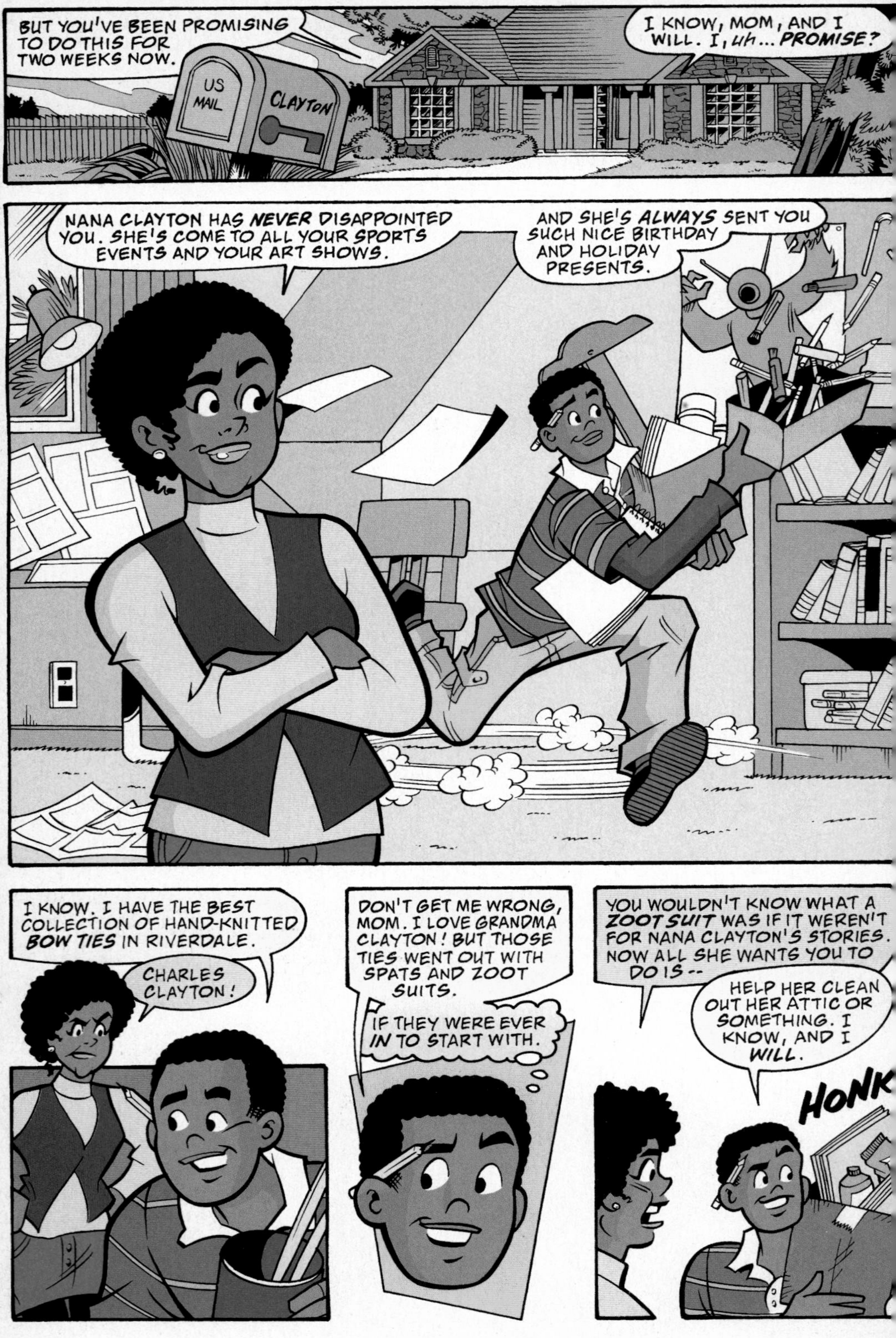

BUT YOU'VE BEEN PROMISING TO DO THIS FOR TWO WEEKS NOW.
US MAIL
CLAYTON
I KNOW, MOM, AND I WILL. I, *uh*... ***PROMISE?***
NANA CLAYTON HAS ***NEVER*** DISAPPOINTED YOU. SHE'S COME TO ALL YOUR ***SPORTS*** EVENTS AND YOUR ***ART SHOWS***.
AND SHE'S ***ALWAYS*** SENT YOU SUCH NICE BIRTHDAY AND HOLIDAY PRESENTS.
I KNOW. I HAVE THE ***BEST*** COLLECTION OF HAND-KNITTED ***BOW TIES*** IN RIVERDALE.
CHARLES CLAYTON!
DON'T GET ME WRONG, MOM. I LOVE GRANDMA CLAYTON! BUT THOSE TIES WENT OUT WITH SPATS AND ZOOT SUITS.
IF THEY WERE EVER ***IN*** TO START WITH.
YOU WOULDN'T KNOW WHAT A ***ZOOT SUIT*** WAS IF IT WEREN'T FOR NANA CLAYTON'S STORIES. NOW ALL SHE WANTS YOU TO DO IS --
HELP HER CLEAN OUT HER ATTIC OR SOMETHING. I KNOW, AND I ***WILL***.
HONK

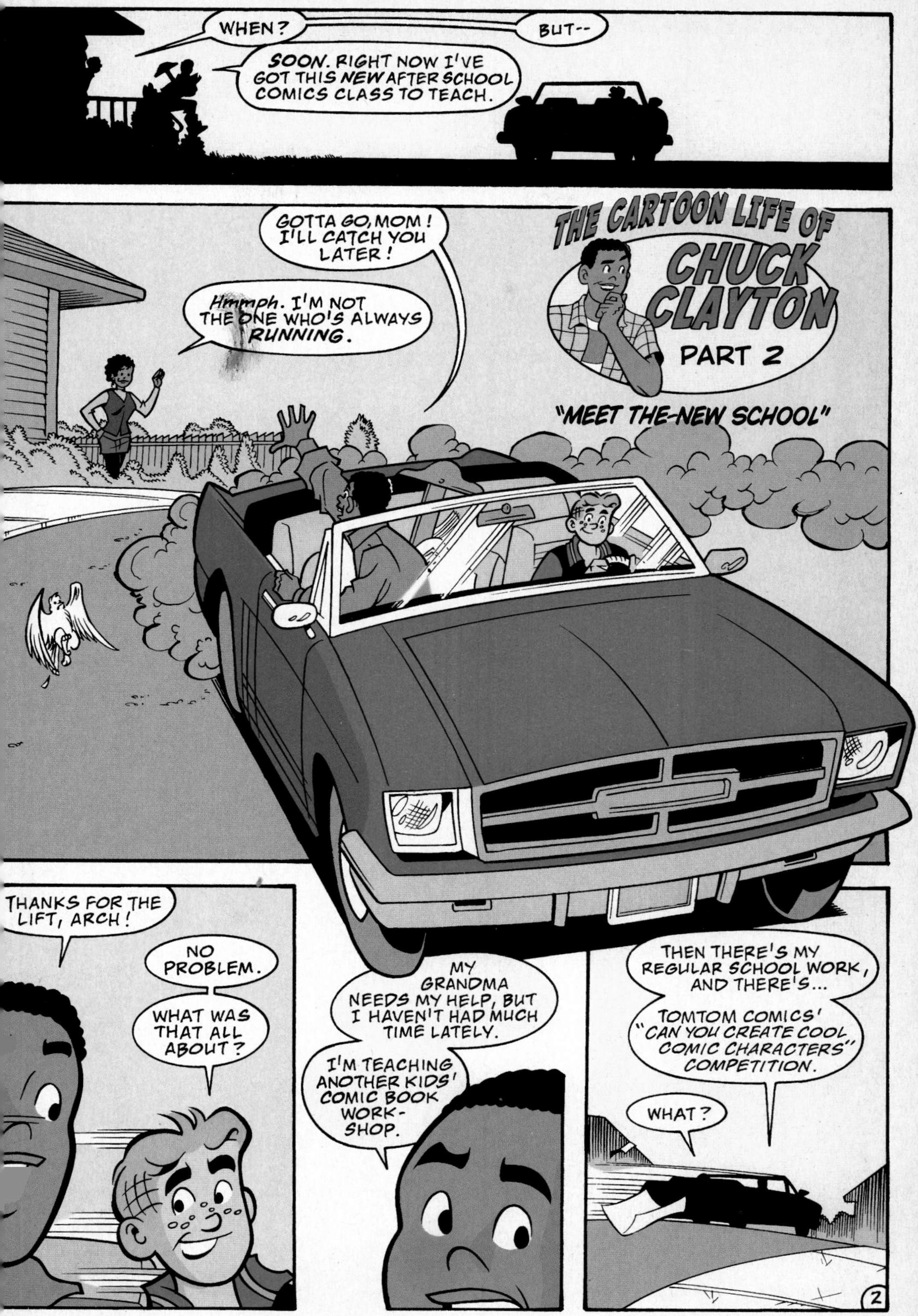
WHEN?
BUT--
SOON. RIGHT NOW I'VE GOT THIS NEW AFTER SCHOOL COMICS CLASS TO TEACH.
THE CARTOON LIFE OF
CHUCK CLAYTON
PART 2
"MEET THE-NEW SCHOOL"
GOTTA GO, MOM! I'LL CATCH YOU LATER!
Hmmph. I'M NOT THE ONE WHO'S ALWAYS RUNNING.
THANKS FOR THE LIFT, ARCH!
NO PROBLEM.
WHAT WAS THAT ALL ABOUT?
MY GRANDMA NEEDS MY HELP, BUT I HAVEN'T HAD MUCH TIME LATELY.
I'M TEACHING ANOTHER KIDS' COMIC BOOK WORK-SHOP.
THEN THERE'S MY REGULAR SCHOOL WORK, AND THERE'S...
TOMTOM COMICS' "CAN YOU CREATE COOL COMIC CHARACTERS" COMPETITION.
WHAT?
2

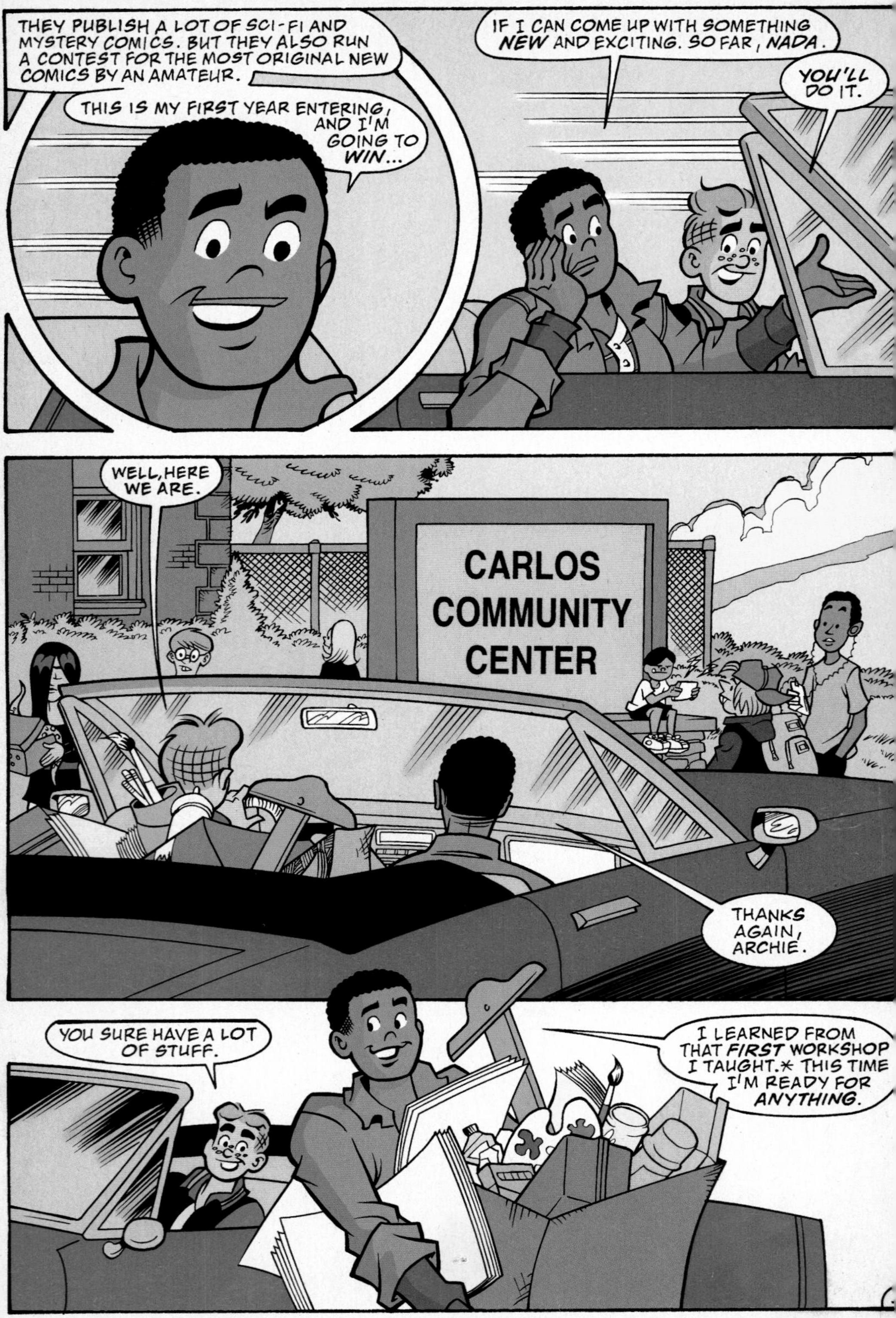
THEY PUBLISH A LOT OF SCI-FI AND MYSTERY COMICS. BUT THEY ALSO RUN A CONTEST FOR THE MOST ORIGINAL NEW COMICS BY AN AMATEUR.
THIS IS MY FIRST YEAR ENTERING, AND I'M GOING TO *WIN*...
IF I CAN COME UP WITH SOMETHING *NEW* AND EXCITING. SO FAR, *NADA*.
YOU'LL DO IT.
WELL, HERE WE ARE.
CARLOS COMMUNITY CENTER
THANKS AGAIN, ARCHIE.
YOU SURE HAVE A LOT OF STUFF.
I LEARNED FROM THAT *FIRST* WORKSHOP I TAUGHT.* THIS TIME I'M READY FOR *ANYTHING*.

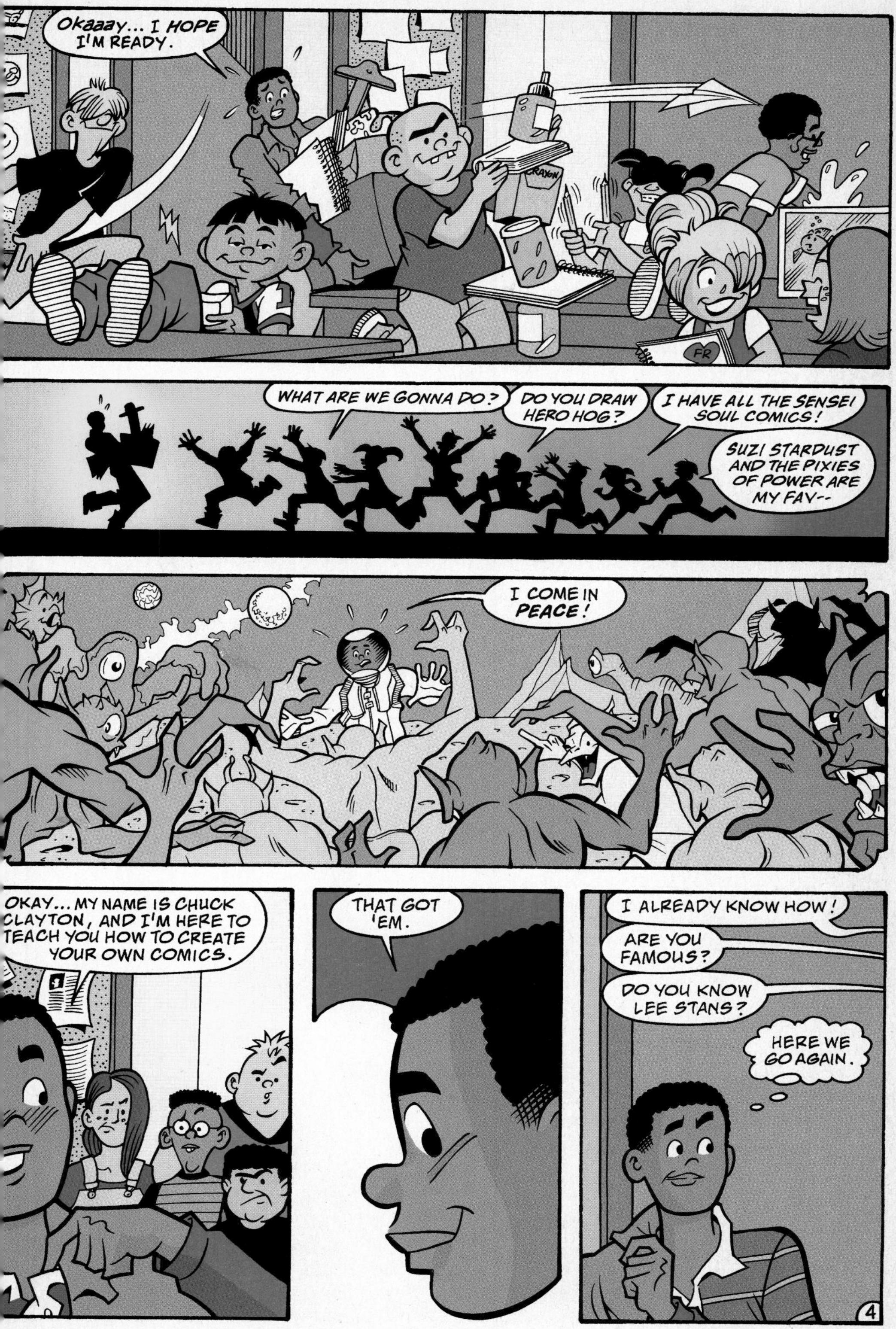

Okaaay... I HOPE I'M READY.
CRAYON
WHAT ARE WE GONNA DO?
DO YOU DRAW HERO HOG?
I HAVE ALL THE SENSEI SOUL COMICS!
SUZI STARDUST AND THE PIXIES OF POWER ARE MY FAV--
I COME IN PEACE!
OKAY... MY NAME IS CHUCK CLAYTON, AND I'M HERE TO TEACH YOU HOW TO CREATE YOUR OWN COMICS.
THAT GOT 'EM.
I ALREADY KNOW HOW!
ARE YOU FAMOUS?
DO YOU KNOW LEE STANS?
HERE WE GO AGAIN.
4

LATER.

THIS IS GREAT WORK. YOUR PENCIL SKETCHES ARE--

HOW COME WE CAN'T COLOR THEM?

BECAUSE THEY'RE NOT FINISHED YET.

YOURS IS A ROBOT, RIGHT? HOW DOES HE SPEAK, OR HEAR?

RICKY

THROUGH HIS MOUTH AND EARS.

WHERE ARE THEY?

Oh.

TINA...

YOUR CHARACTER IS A LITTLE GIRL?

YEAH.

HOW OLD IS SHE? WHERE DOES SHE LIVE? WHAT IS SHE LIKE? WHO ARE HER FRIENDS?

UH... WELL... UH...

SEE, THE MORE YOU KNOW ABOUT YOUR CHARACTERS, THE EASIER IT IS TO WRIT A STORY ABOUT THEM.

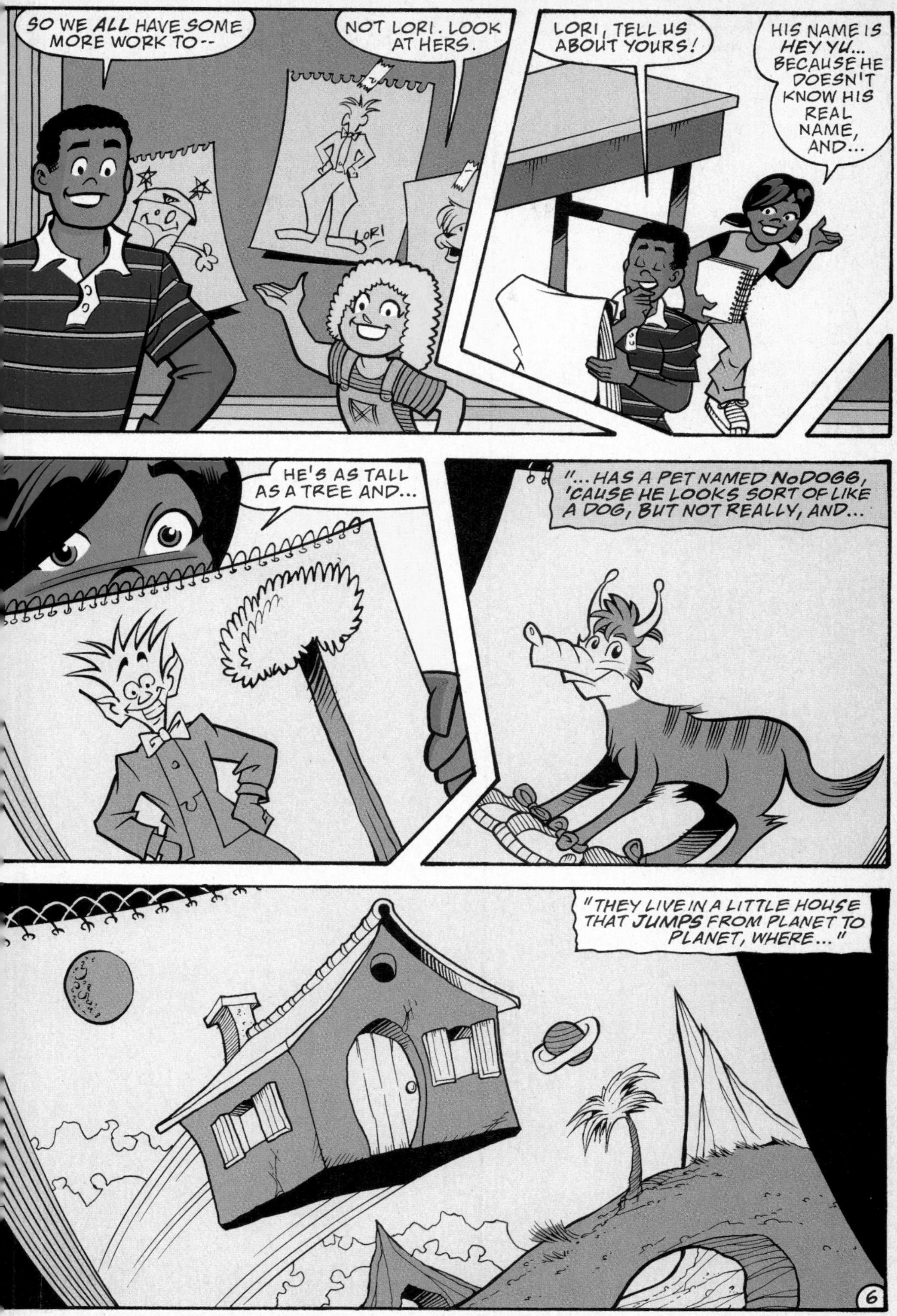
SO WE ALL HAVE SOME MORE WORK TO--
NOT LORI. LOOK AT HERS.
LORI
LORI, TELL US ABOUT YOURS!
HIS NAME IS HEY YU... BECAUSE HE DOESN'T KNOW HIS REAL NAME, AND...
HE'S AS TALL AS A TREE AND...
"...HAS A PET NAMED NoDOGG, 'CAUSE HE LOOKS SORT OF LIKE A DOG, BUT NOT REALLY, AND...
"THEY LIVE IN A LITTLE HOUSE THAT JUMPS FROM PLANET TO PLANET, WHERE..."
6

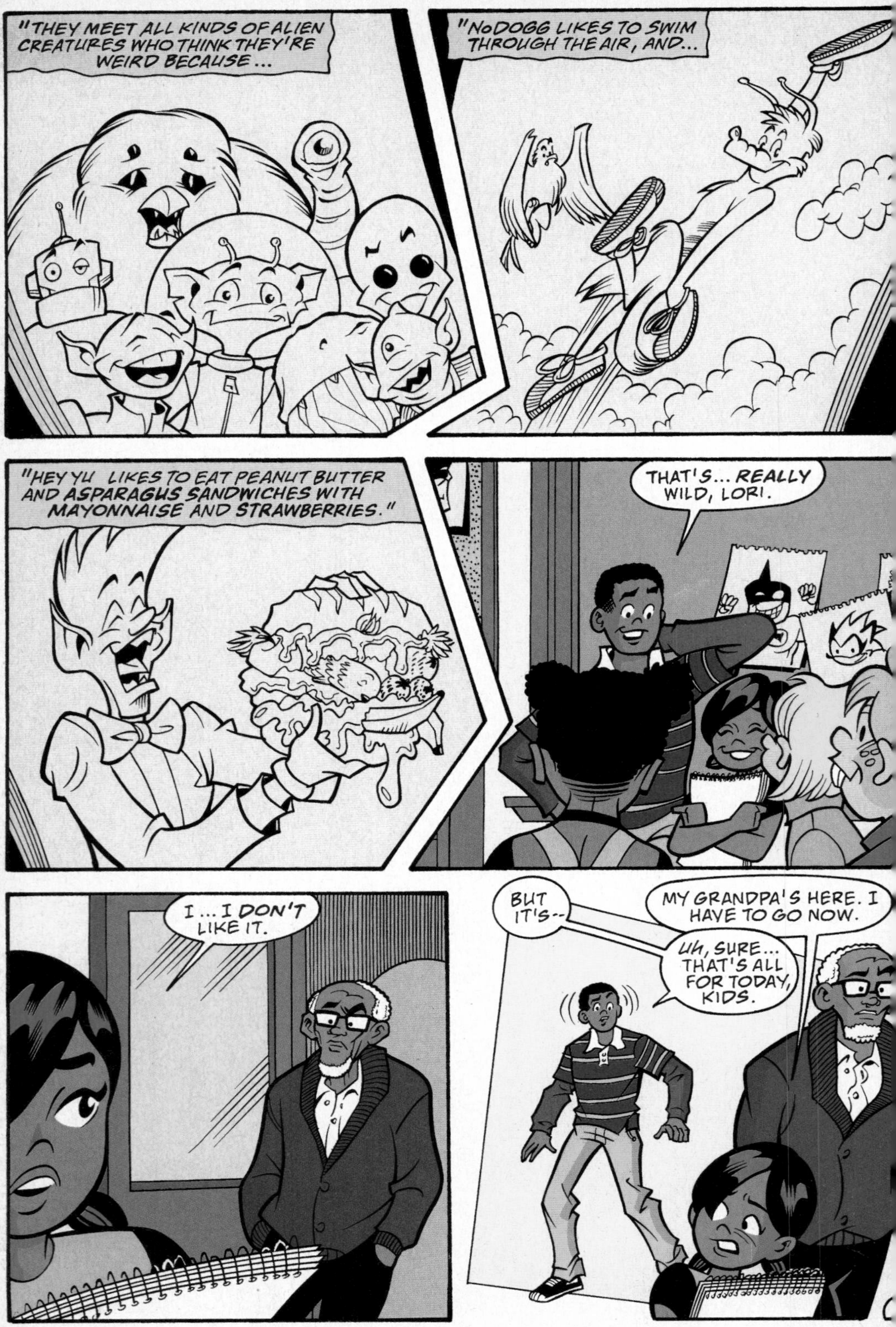
"THEY MEET ALL KINDS OF ALIEN CREATURES WHO THINK THEY'RE WEIRD BECAUSE ...
"NoDOGG LIKES TO SWIM THROUGH THE AIR, AND...
"HEY YU LIKES TO EAT PEANUT BUTTER AND ASPARAGUS SANDWICHES WITH MAYONNAISE AND STRAWBERRIES."
THAT'S... REALLY WILD, LORI.
I ... I DON'T LIKE IT.
BUT IT'S--
MY GRANDPA'S HERE. I HAVE TO GO NOW.
UH, SURE... THAT'S ALL FOR TODAY, KIDS.

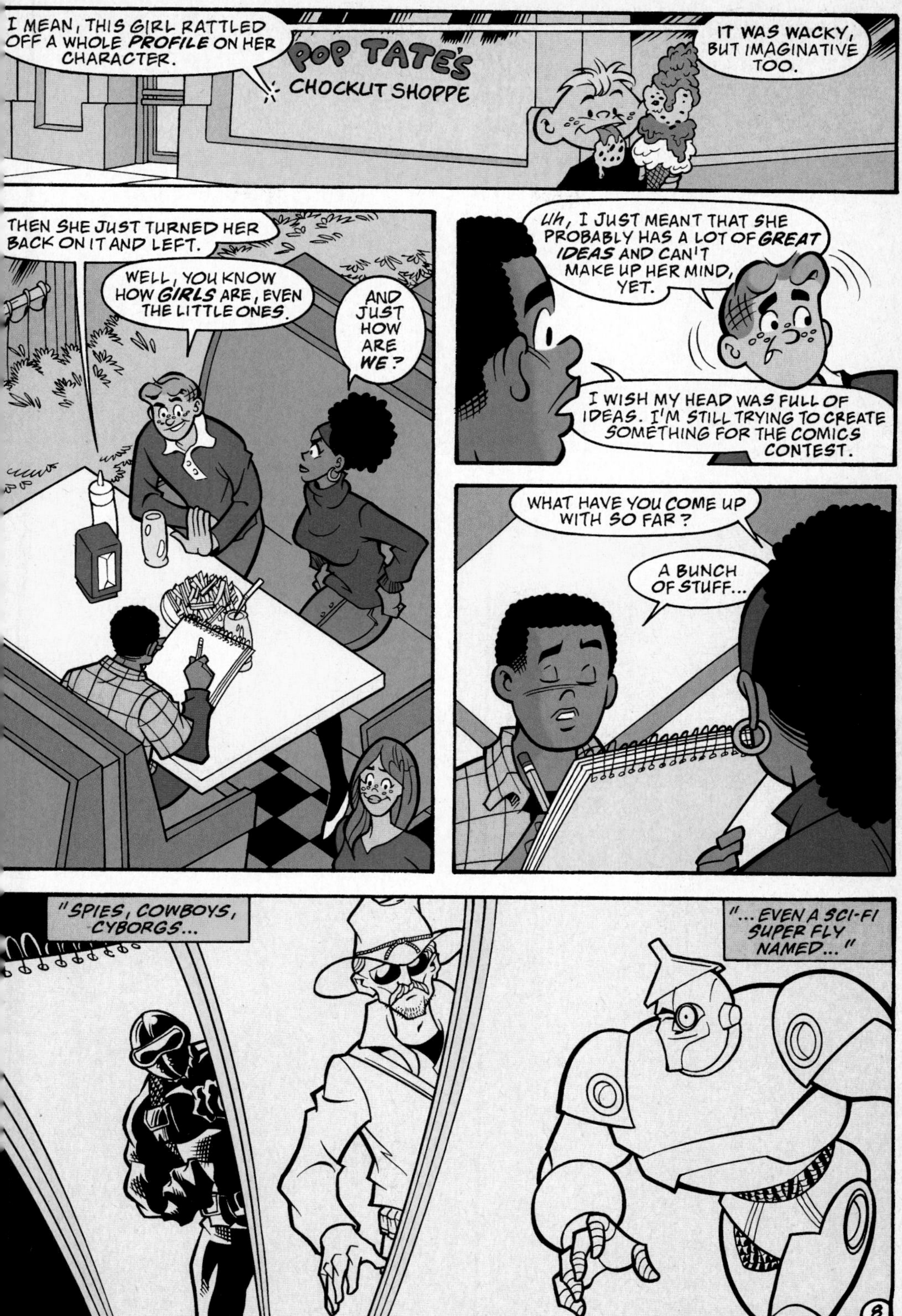
I MEAN, THIS GIRL RATTLED OFF A WHOLE PROFILE ON HER CHARACTER.
POP TATE'S CHOCKLIT SHOPPE
IT WAS WACKY, BUT IMAGINATIVE TOO.
THEN SHE JUST TURNED HER BACK ON IT AND LEFT.
WELL, YOU KNOW HOW GIRLS ARE, EVEN THE LITTLE ONES.
AND JUST HOW ARE WE?
UH, I JUST MEANT THAT SHE PROBABLY HAS A LOT OF GREAT IDEAS AND CAN'T MAKE UP HER MIND, YET.
I WISH MY HEAD WAS FULL OF IDEAS. I'M STILL TRYING TO CREATE SOMETHING FOR THE COMICS CONTEST.
WHAT HAVE YOU COME UP WITH SO FAR?
A BUNCH OF STUFF...
"SPIES, COWBOYS, CYBORGS...
"...EVEN A SCI-FI SUPER FLY NAMED..."
8

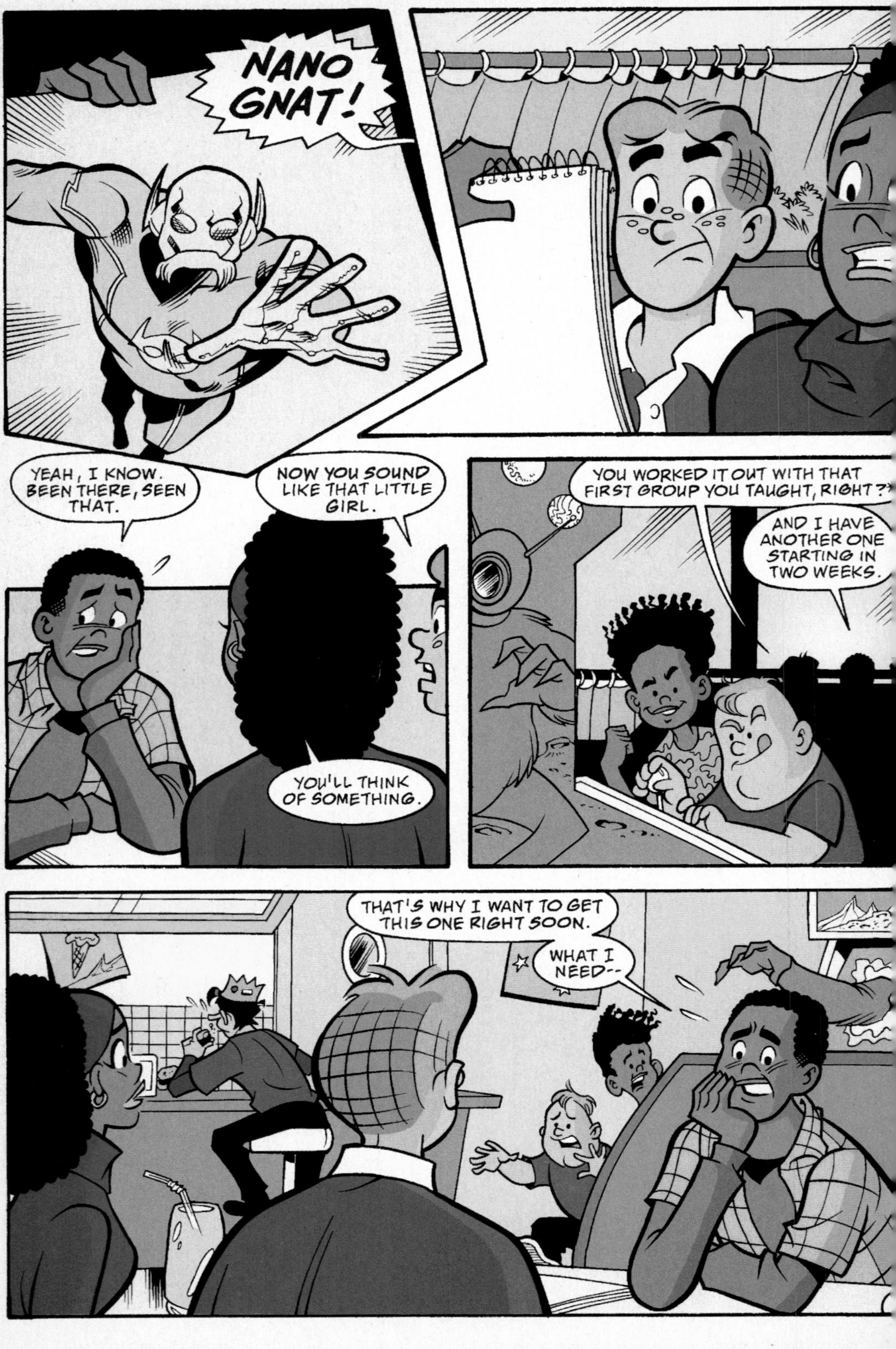
NANO GNAT!
YEAH, I KNOW. BEEN THERE, SEEN THAT.
NOW YOU SOUND LIKE THAT LITTLE GIRL.
YOU'LL THINK OF SOMETHING.
YOU WORKED IT OUT WITH THAT FIRST GROUP YOU TAUGHT, RIGHT?
AND I HAVE ANOTHER ONE STARTING IN TWO WEEKS.
THAT'S WHY I WANT TO GET THIS ONE RIGHT SOON.
WHAT I NEED--

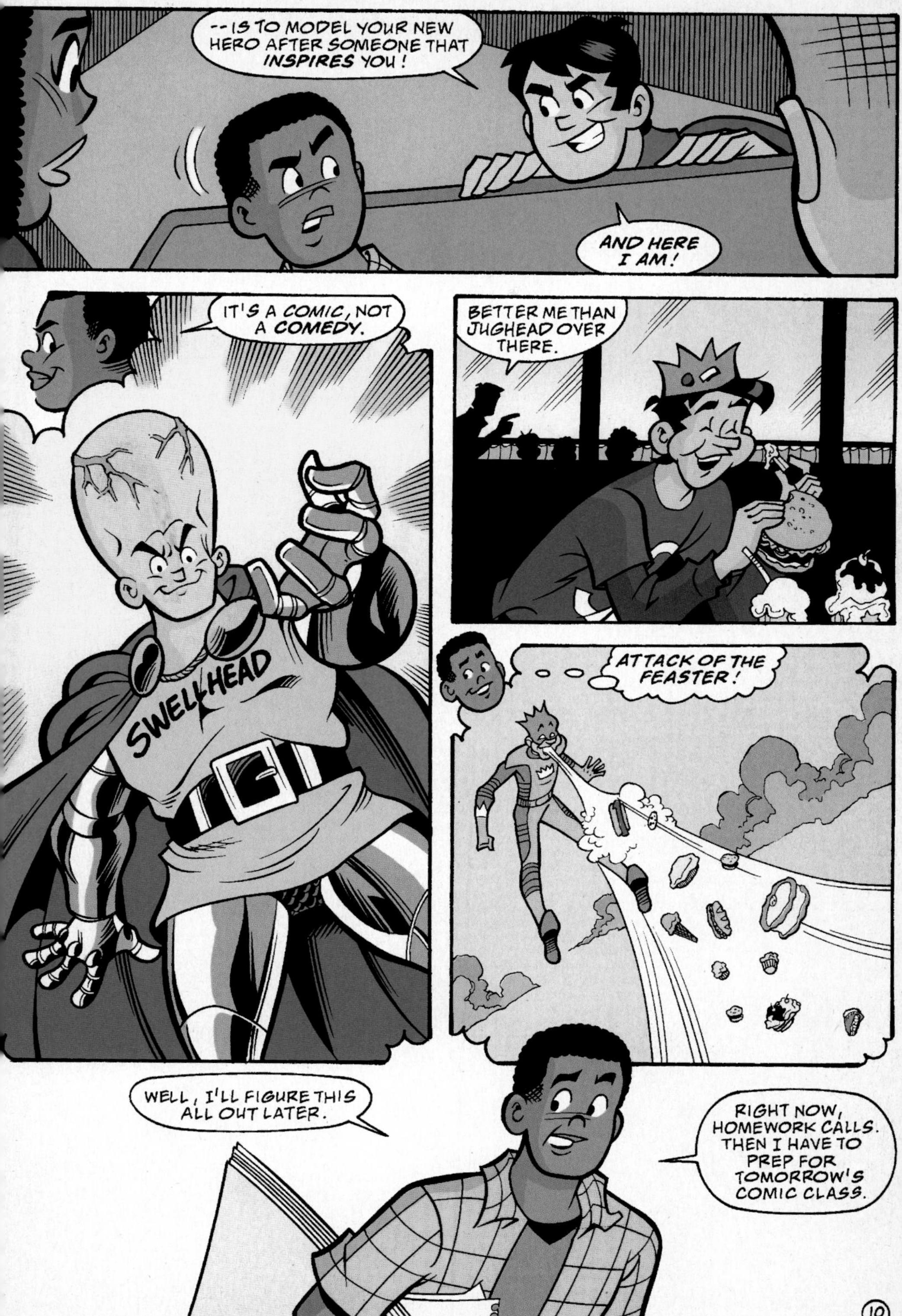
--IS TO MODEL YOUR NEW HERO AFTER SOMEONE THAT *INSPIRES* YOU!
AND HERE I AM!
IT'S A *COMIC*, NOT A *COMEDY*.
SWELLHEAD
BETTER ME THAN JUGHEAD OVER THERE.
ATTACK OF THE FEASTER!
WELL, I'LL FIGURE THIS ALL OUT LATER.
RIGHT NOW, HOMEWORK CALLS. THEN I HAVE TO PREP FOR TOMORROW'S COMIC CLASS.

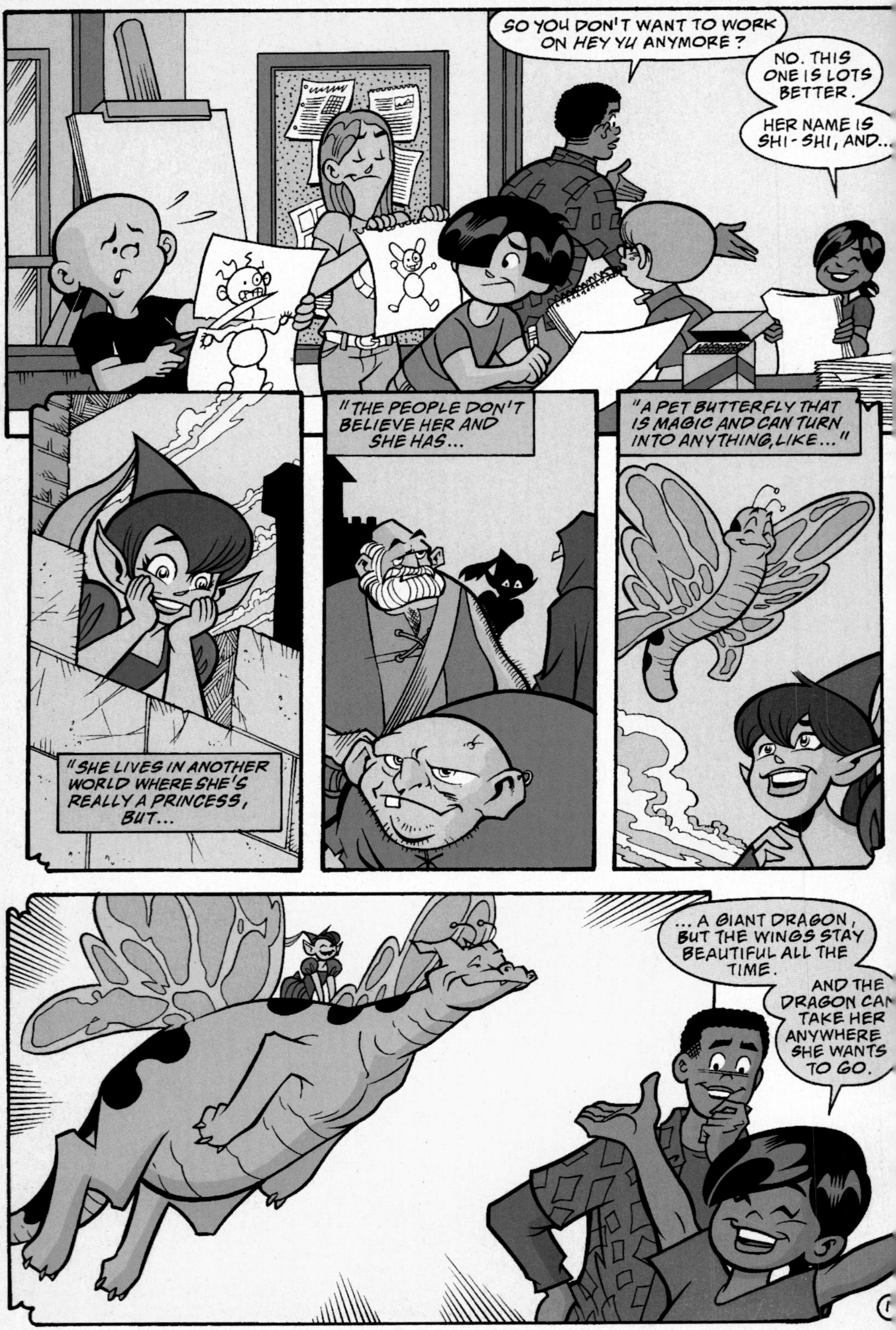
SO YOU DON'T WANT TO WORK ON HEY YU ANYMORE?
NO. THIS ONE IS LOTS BETTER.
HER NAME IS SHI-SHI, AND...
"SHE LIVES IN ANOTHER WORLD WHERE SHE'S REALLY A PRINCESS, BUT...
"THE PEOPLE DON'T BELIEVE HER AND SHE HAS...
"A PET BUTTERFLY THAT IS MAGIC AND CAN TURN INTO ANYTHING, LIKE..."
... A GIANT DRAGON, BUT THE WINGS STAY BEAUTIFUL ALL THE TIME.
AND THE DRAGON CAN TAKE HER ANYWHERE SHE WANTS TO GO.

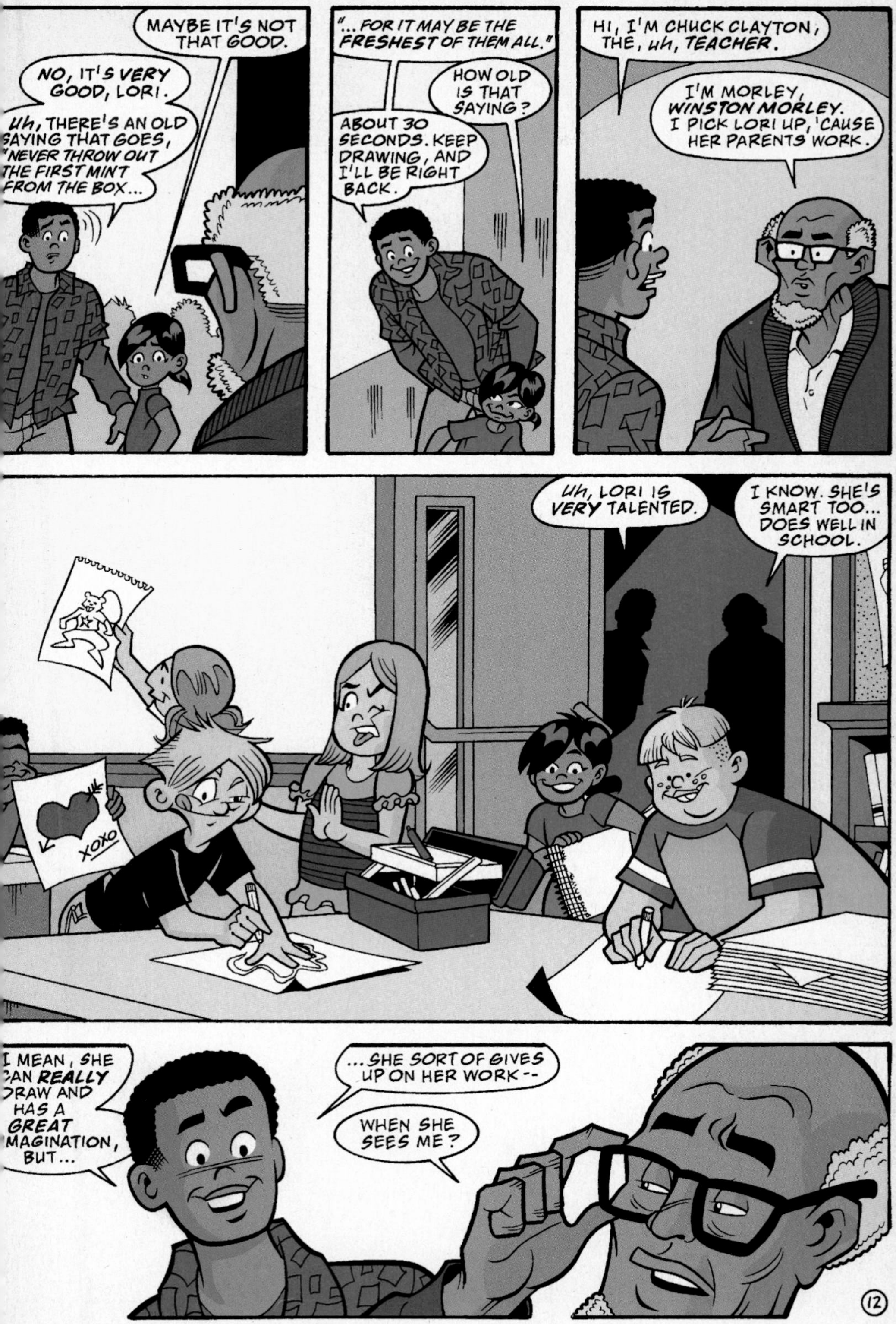
MAYBE IT'S NOT THAT GOOD.
NO, IT'S VERY GOOD, LORI.
uh, THERE'S AN OLD SAYING THAT GOES, "NEVER THROW OUT THE FIRST MINT FROM THE BOX...
"...FOR IT MAY BE THE FRESHEST OF THEM ALL."
HOW OLD IS THAT SAYING?
ABOUT 30 SECONDS. KEEP DRAWING, AND I'LL BE RIGHT BACK.
HI, I'M CHUCK CLAYTON, THE, uh, TEACHER.
I'M MORLEY, WINSTON MORLEY. I PICK LORI UP, 'CAUSE HER PARENTS WORK.
XOXO
uh, LORI IS VERY TALENTED.
I KNOW. SHE'S SMART TOO... DOES WELL IN SCHOOL.
I MEAN, SHE CAN REALLY DRAW AND HAS A GREAT IMAGINATION, BUT...
...SHE SORT OF GIVES UP ON HER WORK--
WHEN SHE SEES ME?
12

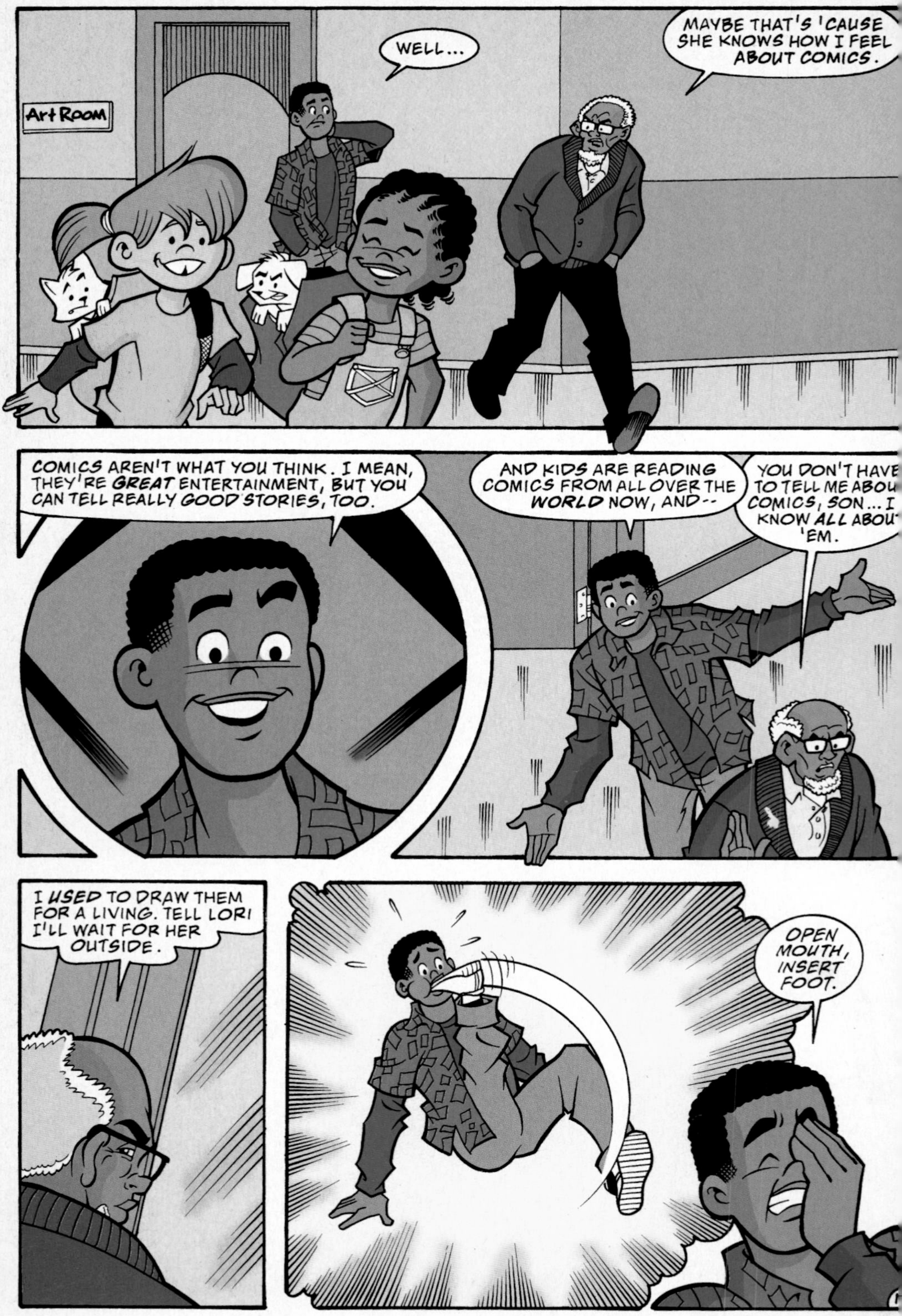
Art Room
WELL...
MAYBE THAT'S 'CAUSE SHE KNOWS HOW I FEEL ABOUT COMICS.
COMICS AREN'T WHAT YOU THINK. I MEAN, THEY'RE GREAT ENTERTAINMENT, BUT YOU CAN TELL REALLY GOOD STORIES, TOO.
AND KIDS ARE READING COMICS FROM ALL OVER THE WORLD NOW, AND--
YOU DON'T HAVE TO TELL ME ABOUT COMICS, SON... I KNOW ALL ABOUT 'EM.
I USED TO DRAW THEM FOR A LIVING. TELL LORI I'LL WAIT FOR HER OUTSIDE.
OPEN MOUTH, INSERT FOOT.

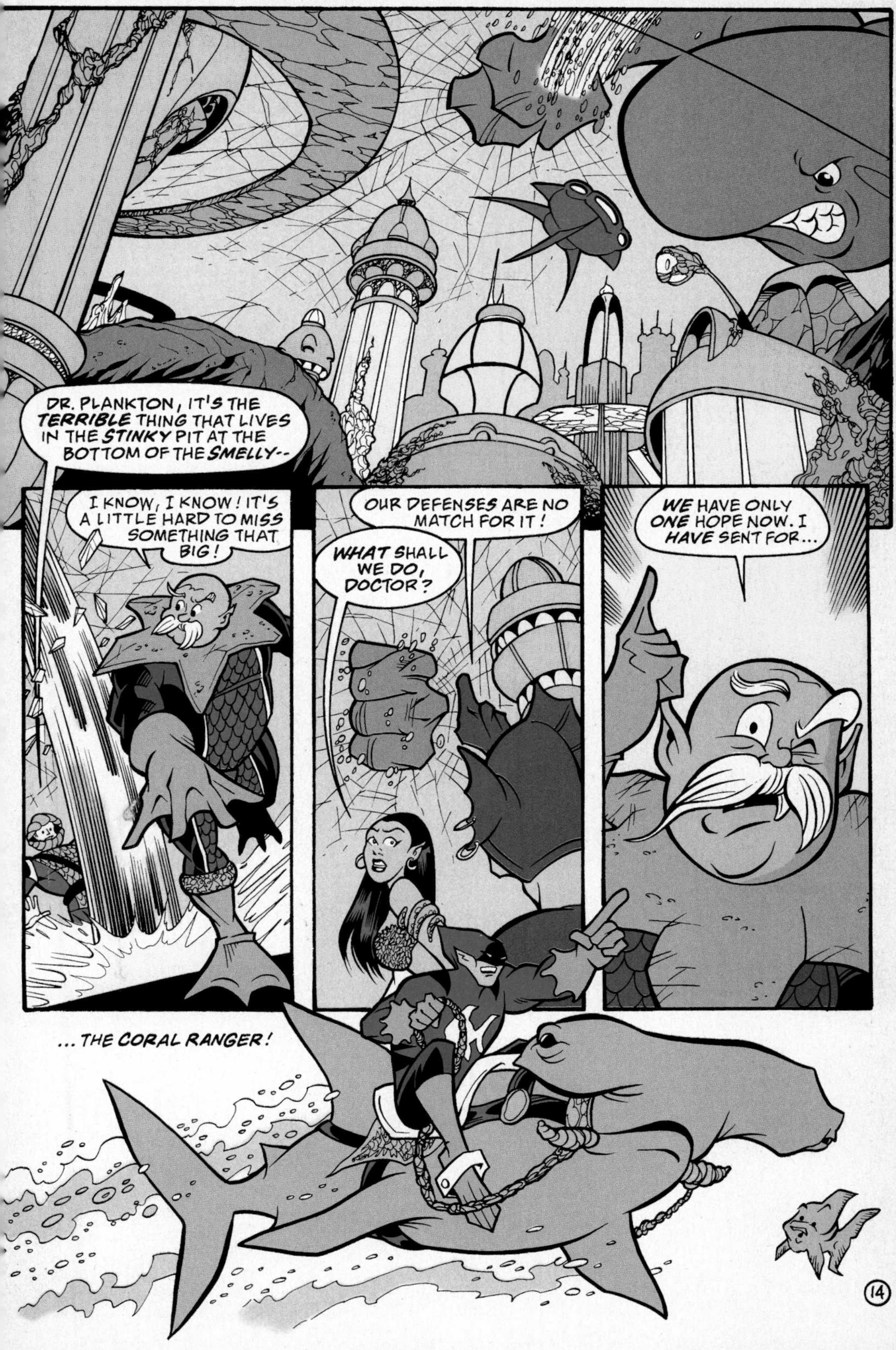
DR. PLANKTON, IT'S THE TERRIBLE THING THAT LIVES IN THE STINKY PIT AT THE BOTTOM OF THE SMELLY--
I KNOW, I KNOW! IT'S A LITTLE HARD TO MISS SOMETHING THAT BIG!
OUR DEFENSES ARE NO MATCH FOR IT!
WHAT SHALL WE DO, DOCTOR?
WE HAVE ONLY ONE HOPE NOW. I HAVE SENT FOR...
...THE CORAL RANGER!
14

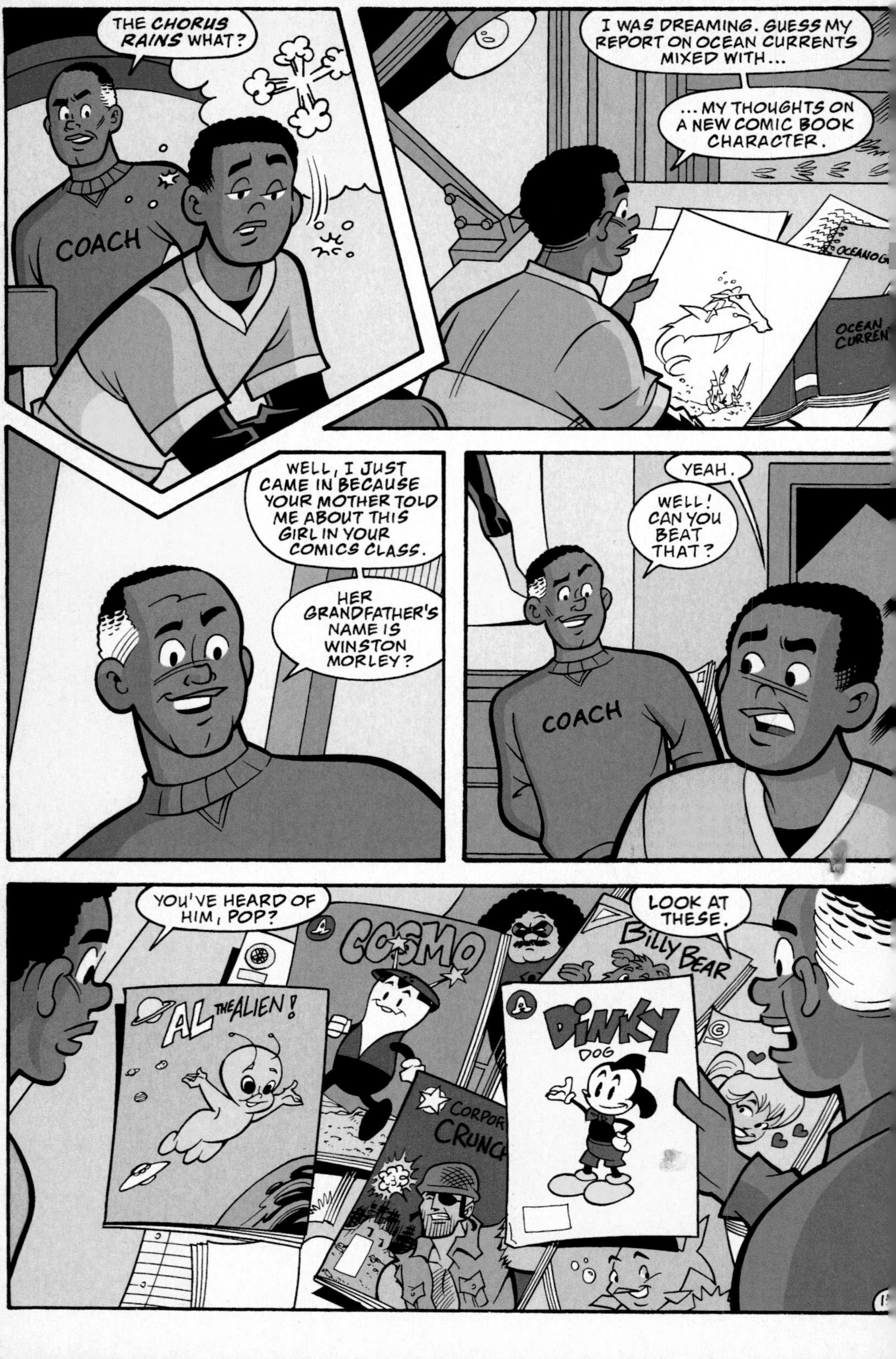
THE CHORUS RAINS WHAT?
COACH
I WAS DREAMING. GUESS MY REPORT ON OCEAN CURRENTS MIXED WITH...
...MY THOUGHTS ON A NEW COMIC BOOK CHARACTER.
OCEAN CURRENTS
WELL, I JUST CAME IN BECAUSE YOUR MOTHER TOLD ME ABOUT THIS GIRL IN YOUR COMICS CLASS.
HER GRANDFATHER'S NAME IS WINSTON MORLEY?
YEAH.
WELL! CAN YOU BEAT THAT?
COACH
YOU'VE HEARD OF HIM, POP?
LOOK AT THESE.
COSMO
BILLY BEAR
AL THE ALIEN!
DINKY DOG

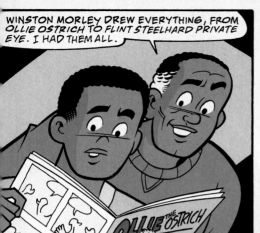

WINSTON MORLEY DREW EVERYTHING, FROM OLLIE OSTRICH TO FLINT STEELHARD PRIVATE EYE. I HAD THEM ALL.

WAIT A MINUTE. IF HE WAS SUCH A *BIG TIME* ARTIST, HOW COME I NEVER HEARD OF HIM?

HE *WASN'T* BIG TIME.

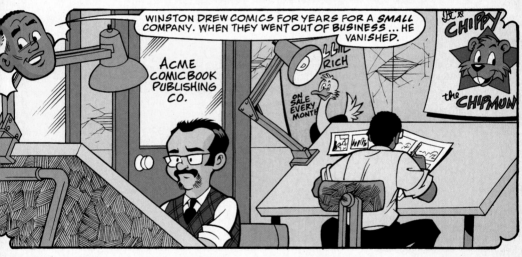

WINSTON DREW COMICS FOR YEARS FOR A *SMALL* COMPANY. WHEN THEY WENT OUT OF BUSINESS ... HE VANISHED.

ACME COMIC BOOK PUBLISHING CO.

ON SALE EVERY MONTH

CHIPPY THE CHIPMUN

WHY DIDN'T HE JUST GO WORK FOR THE OTHER COMPANIES -- YOU KNOW, THE BIG ONES?

I HAVE NO IDEA.

BET I KNOW WHO *DOES*.

16

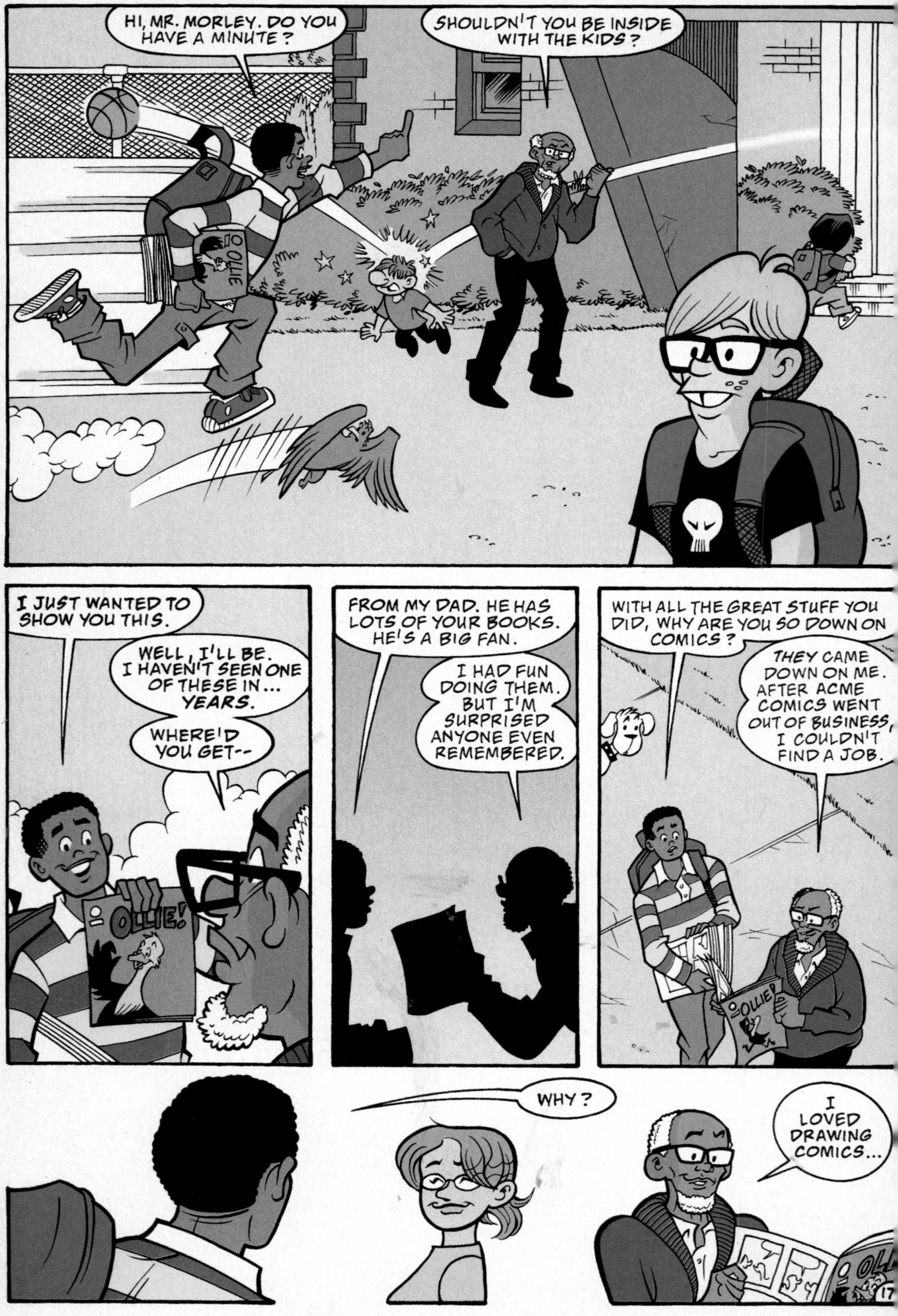
HI, MR. MORLEY. DO YOU HAVE A MINUTE?
SHOULDN'T YOU BE INSIDE WITH THE KIDS?
OLLIE
I JUST WANTED TO SHOW YOU THIS.
WELL, I'LL BE. I HAVEN'T SEEN ONE OF THESE IN... YEARS.
WHERE'D YOU GET--
OLLIE!
FROM MY DAD. HE HAS LOTS OF YOUR BOOKS. HE'S A BIG FAN.
I HAD FUN DOING THEM. BUT I'M SURPRISED ANYONE EVEN REMEMBERED.
WITH ALL THE GREAT STUFF YOU DID, WHY ARE YOU SO DOWN ON COMICS?
THEY CAME DOWN ON ME. AFTER ACME COMICS WENT OUT OF BUSINESS, I COULDN'T FIND A JOB.
OLLIE
WHY?
I LOVED DRAWING COMICS...

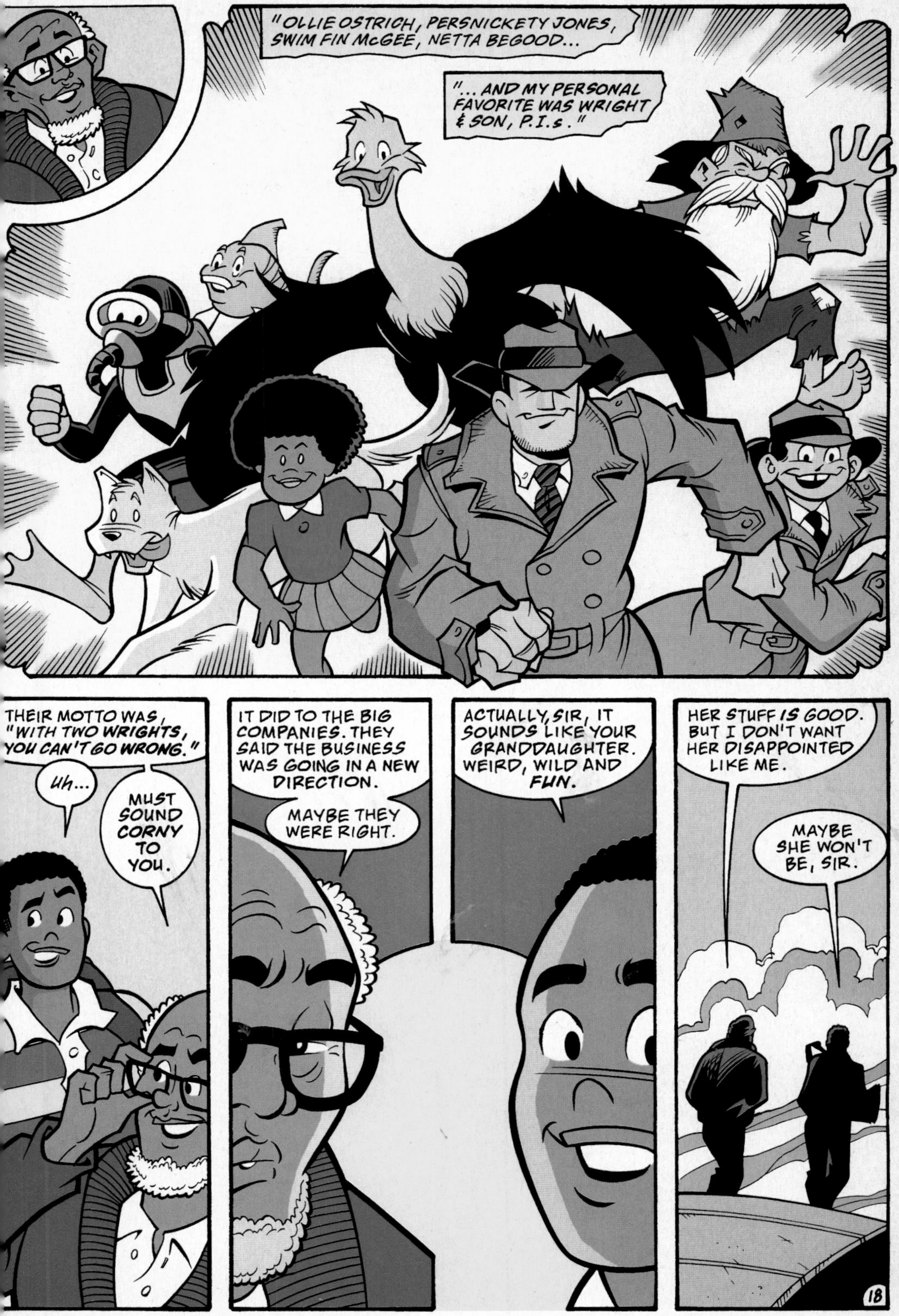

"OLLIE OSTRICH, PERSNICKETY JONES, SWIM FIN McGEE, NETTA BEGOOD...
"... AND MY PERSONAL FAVORITE WAS WRIGHT & SON, P.I.s."
THEIR MOTTO WAS, "WITH TWO WRIGHTS, YOU CAN'T GO WRONG."
uh...
MUST SOUND CORNY TO YOU.
IT DID TO THE BIG COMPANIES. THEY SAID THE BUSINESS WAS GOING IN A NEW DIRECTION.
MAYBE THEY WERE RIGHT.
ACTUALLY, SIR, IT SOUNDS LIKE YOUR GRANDDAUGHTER. WEIRD, WILD AND FUN.
HER STUFF IS GOOD. BUT I DON'T WANT HER DISAPPOINTED LIKE ME.
MAYBE SHE WON'T BE, SIR.
18

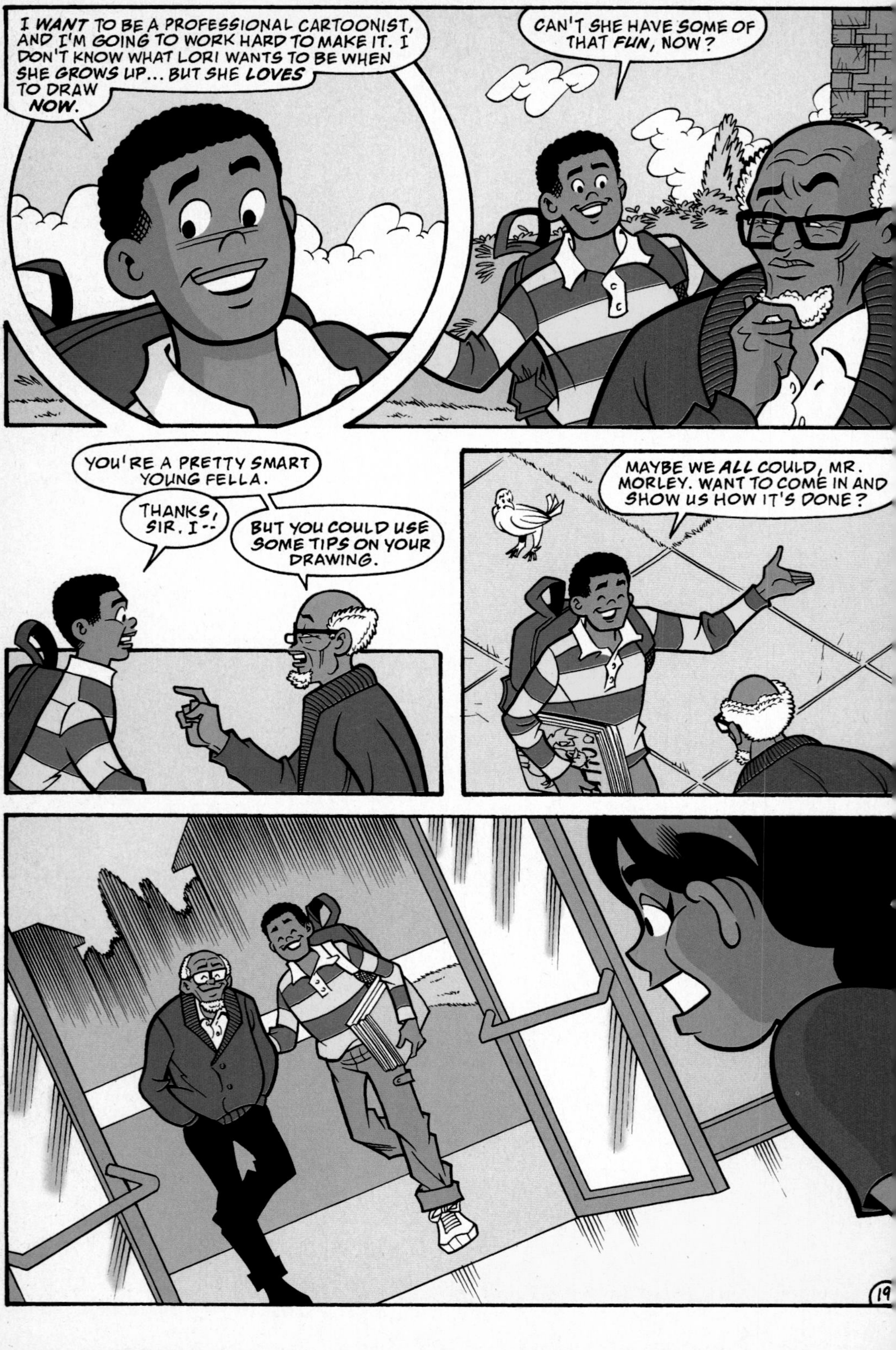
I WANT TO BE A PROFESSIONAL CARTOONIST, AND I'M GOING TO WORK HARD TO MAKE IT. I DON'T KNOW WHAT LORI WANTS TO BE WHEN SHE GROWS UP... BUT SHE LOVES TO DRAW NOW.
CAN'T SHE HAVE SOME OF THAT FUN, NOW?
YOU'RE A PRETTY SMART YOUNG FELLA.
THANKS, SIR. I--
BUT YOU COULD USE SOME TIPS ON YOUR DRAWING.
MAYBE WE ALL COULD, MR. MORLEY. WANT TO COME IN AND SHOW US HOW IT'S DONE?
19

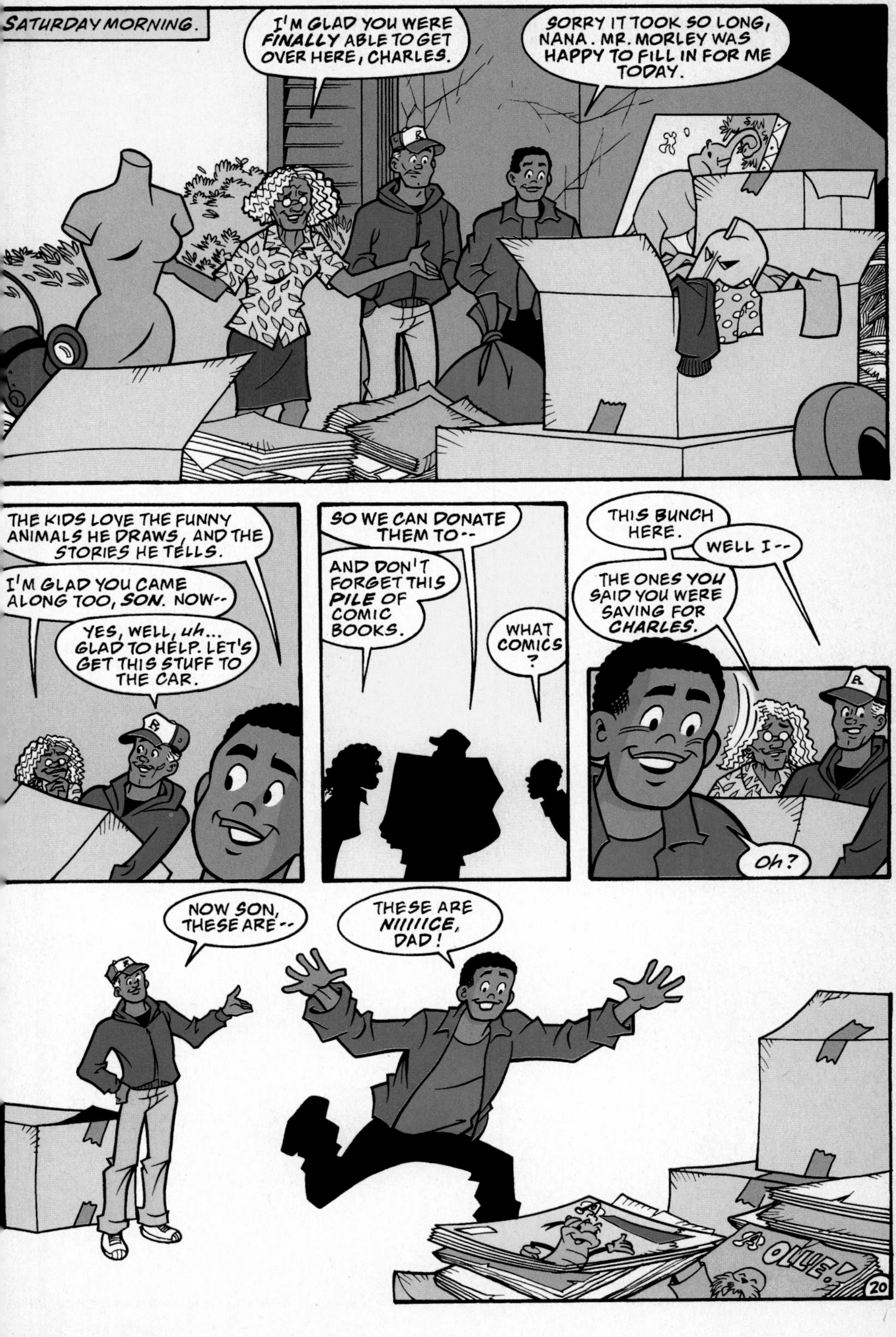
SATURDAY MORNING.
I'M GLAD YOU WERE FINALLY ABLE TO GET OVER HERE, CHARLES.
SORRY IT TOOK SO LONG, NANA. MR. MORLEY WAS HAPPY TO FILL IN FOR ME TODAY.
THE KIDS LOVE THE FUNNY ANIMALS HE DRAWS, AND THE STORIES HE TELLS.
I'M GLAD YOU CAME ALONG TOO, SON. NOW--
YES, WELL, uh... GLAD TO HELP. LET'S GET THIS STUFF TO THE CAR.
SO WE CAN DONATE THEM TO--
AND DON'T FORGET THIS PILE OF COMIC BOOKS.
WHAT COMICS?
THIS BUNCH HERE.
WELL I--
THE ONES YOU SAID YOU WERE SAVING FOR CHARLES.
Oh?
NOW SON, THESE ARE--
THESE ARE NIIIIICE, DAD!
OLLIE!
20

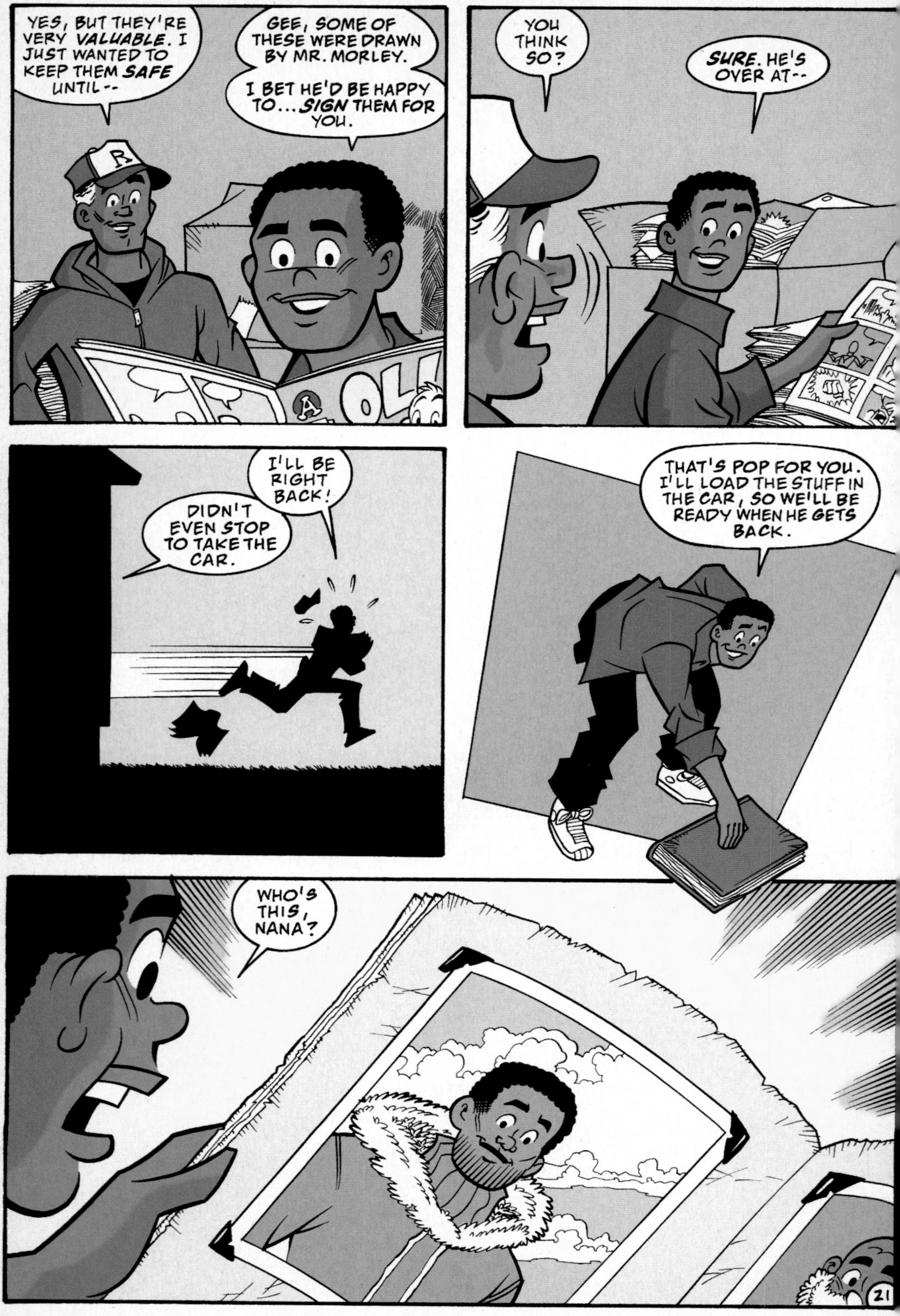
YES, BUT THEY'RE VERY VALUABLE. I JUST WANTED TO KEEP THEM SAFE UNTIL--
GEE, SOME OF THESE WERE DRAWN BY MR. MORLEY.
I BET HE'D BE HAPPY TO... SIGN THEM FOR YOU.
YOU THINK SO?
SURE. HE'S OVER AT--
I'LL BE RIGHT BACK!
DIDN'T EVEN STOP TO TAKE THE CAR.
THAT'S POP FOR YOU. I'LL LOAD THE STUFF IN THE CAR, SO WE'LL BE READY WHEN HE GETS BACK.
WHO'S THIS, NANA?
21

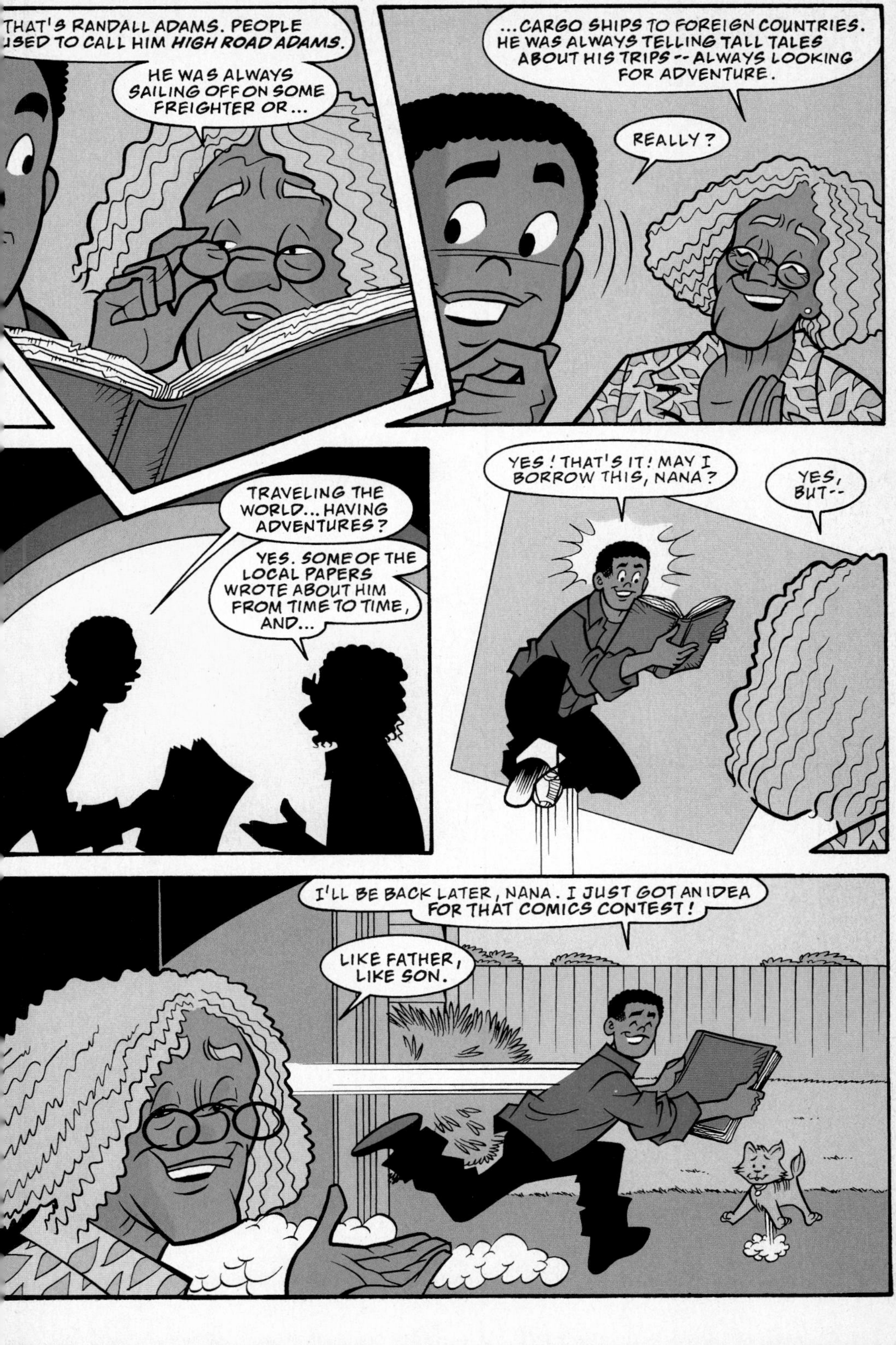
THAT'S RANDALL ADAMS. PEOPLE USED TO CALL HIM *HIGH ROAD ADAMS*.
HE WAS ALWAYS SAILING OFF ON SOME FREIGHTER OR...
...CARGO SHIPS TO FOREIGN COUNTRIES. HE WAS ALWAYS TELLING TALL TALES ABOUT HIS TRIPS -- ALWAYS LOOKING FOR ADVENTURE.
REALLY?
TRAVELING THE WORLD... HAVING ADVENTURES?
YES. SOME OF THE LOCAL PAPERS WROTE ABOUT HIM FROM TIME TO TIME, AND...
YES! THAT'S IT! MAY I BORROW THIS, NANA?
YES, BUT--
I'LL BE BACK LATER, NANA. I JUST GOT AN IDEA FOR THAT COMICS CONTEST!
LIKE FATHER, LIKE SON.

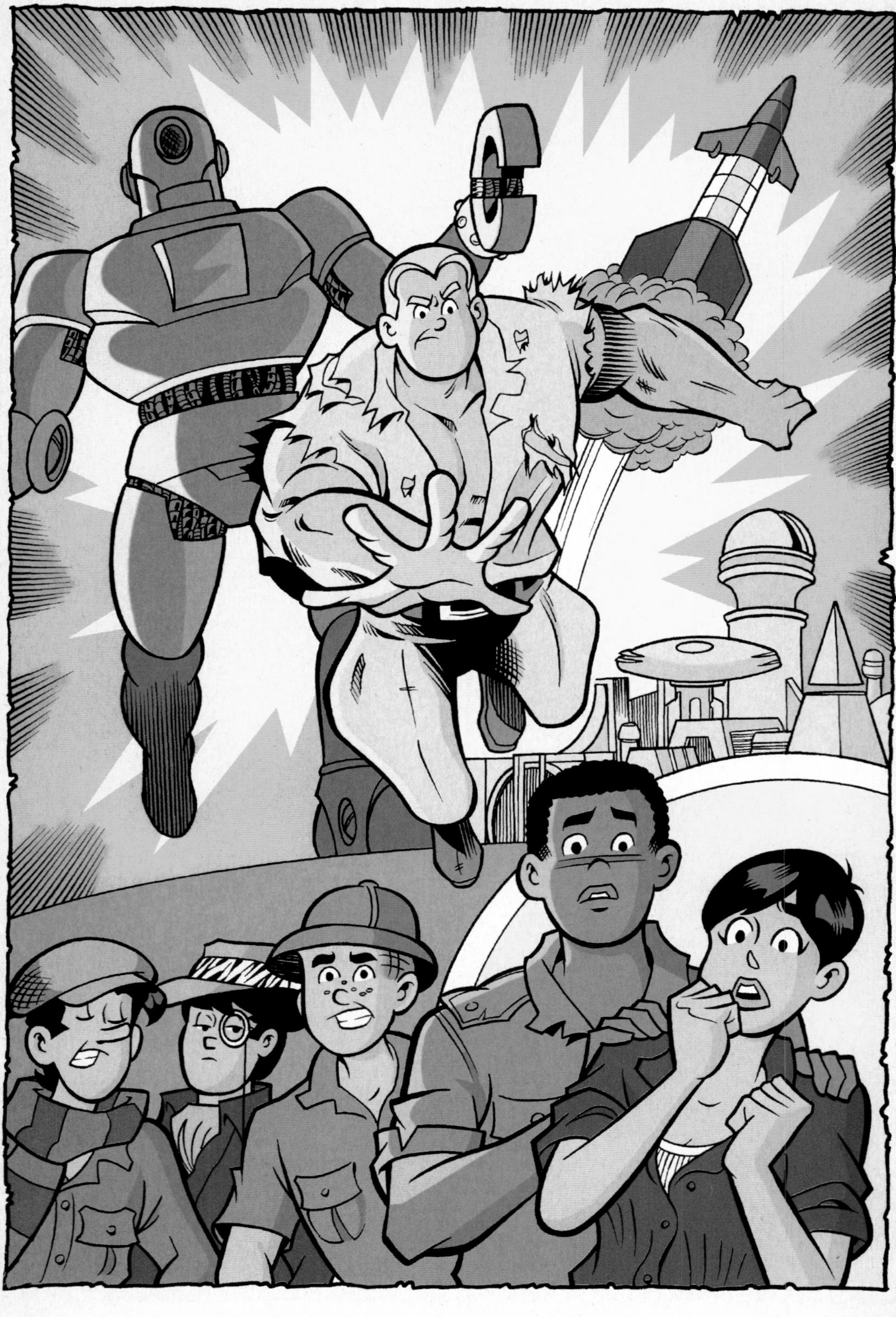

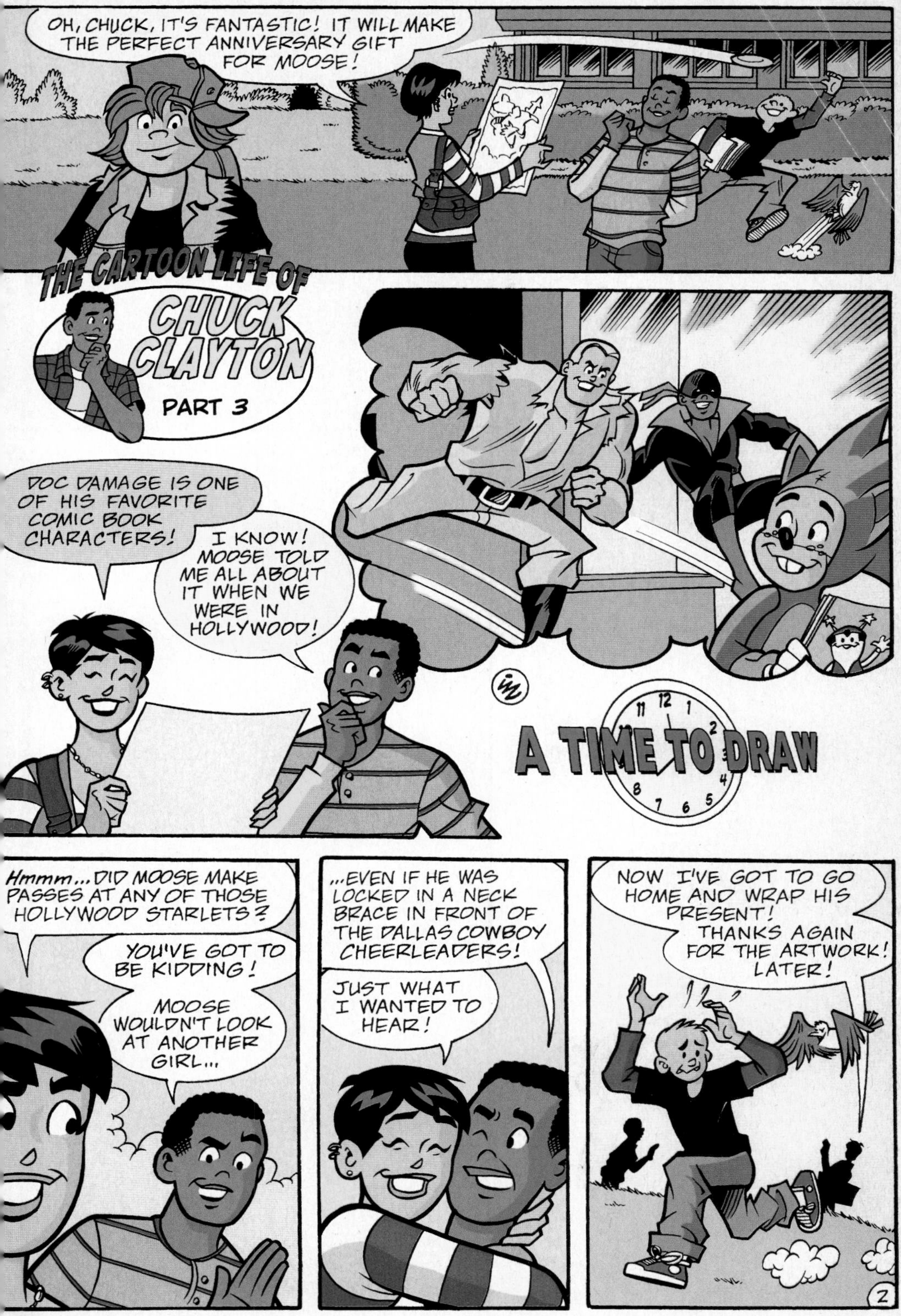
OH, CHUCK, IT'S FANTASTIC! IT WILL MAKE THE PERFECT ANNIVERSARY GIFT FOR MOOSE!
THE CARTOON LIFE OF
CHUCK CLAYTON
PART 3
DOC DAMAGE IS ONE OF HIS FAVORITE COMIC BOOK CHARACTERS!
I KNOW! MOOSE TOLD ME ALL ABOUT IT WHEN WE WERE IN HOLLYWOOD!
A TIME TO DRAW
Hmmm... DID MOOSE MAKE PASSES AT ANY OF THOSE HOLLYWOOD STARLETS?
YOU'VE GOT TO BE KIDDING!
MOOSE WOULDN'T LOOK AT ANOTHER GIRL...
...EVEN IF HE WAS LOCKED IN A NECK BRACE IN FRONT OF THE DALLAS COWBOY CHEERLEADERS!
JUST WHAT I WANTED TO HEAR!
NOW I'VE GOT TO GO HOME AND WRAP HIS PRESENT!
THANKS AGAIN FOR THE ARTWORK! LATER!
2

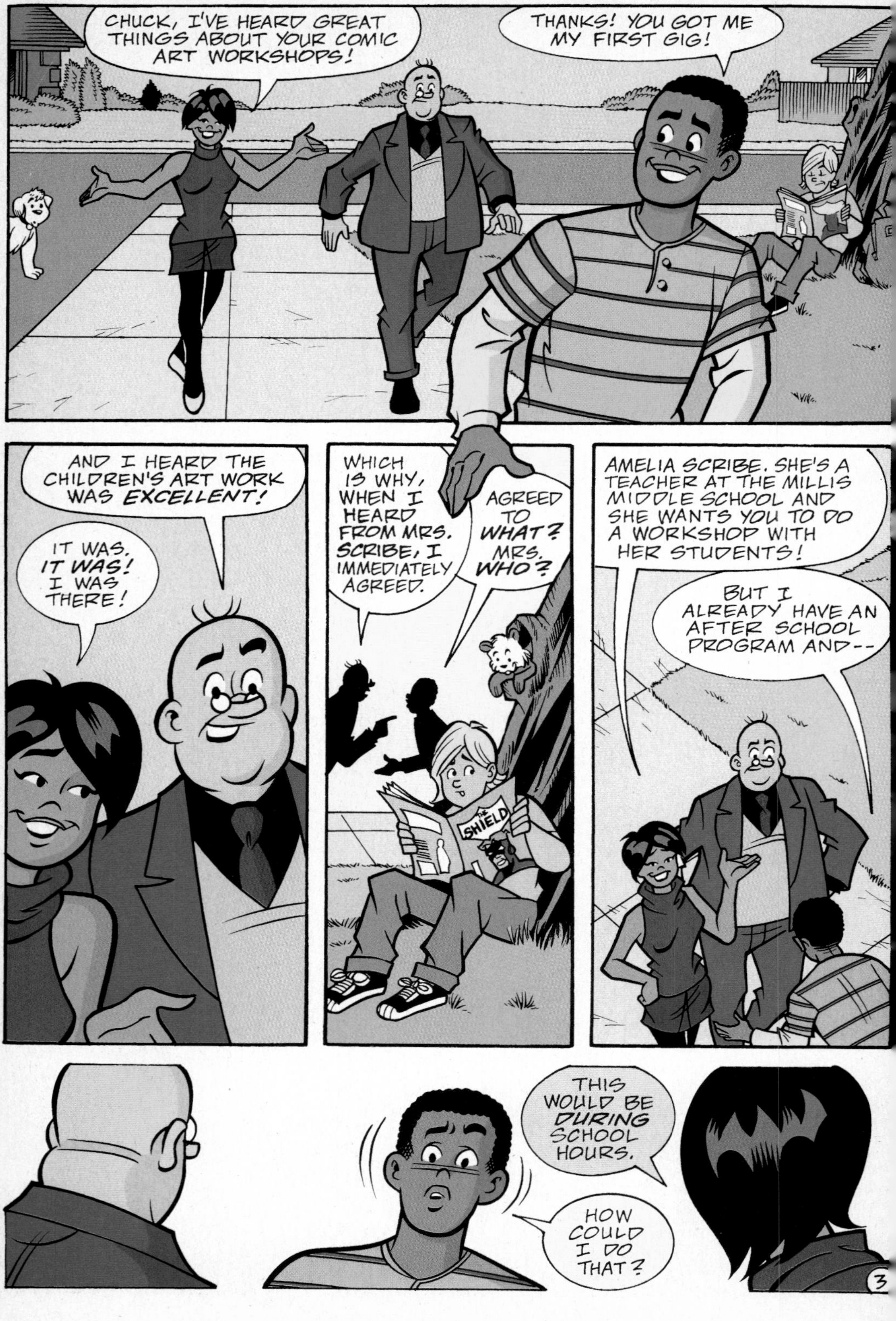
CHUCK, I'VE HEARD GREAT THINGS ABOUT YOUR COMIC ART WORKSHOPS!
THANKS! YOU GOT ME MY FIRST GIG!
AND I HEARD THE CHILDREN'S ART WORK WAS *EXCELLENT!*
IT WAS, *IT WAS!* I WAS THERE!
WHICH IS WHY, WHEN I HEARD FROM MRS. SCRIBE, I IMMEDIATELY AGREED.
AGREED TO *WHAT?* MRS. *WHO?*
THE SHIELD
AMELIA SCRIBE. SHE'S A TEACHER AT THE MILLIS MIDDLE SCHOOL AND SHE WANTS YOU TO DO A WORKSHOP WITH HER STUDENTS!
BUT I ALREADY HAVE AN AFTER SCHOOL PROGRAM AND--
THIS WOULD BE *DURING* SCHOOL HOURS.
HOW COULD I DO THAT?
3

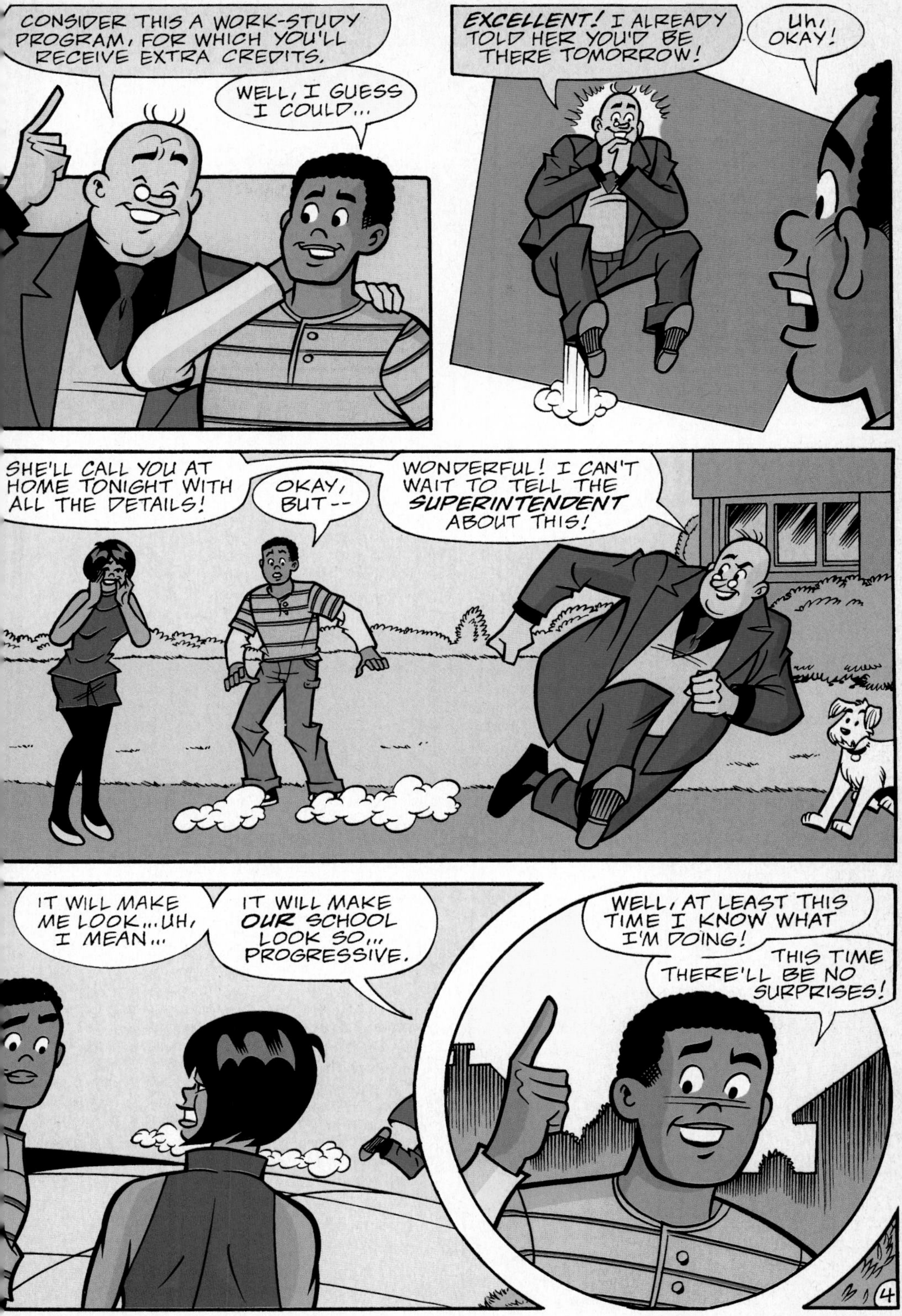
CONSIDER THIS A WORK-STUDY PROGRAM, FOR WHICH YOU'LL RECEIVE EXTRA CREDITS.
WELL, I GUESS I COULD...
EXCELLENT! I ALREADY TOLD HER YOU'D BE THERE TOMORROW!
UH, OKAY!
SHE'LL CALL YOU AT HOME TONIGHT WITH ALL THE DETAILS!
OKAY, BUT--
WONDERFUL! I CAN'T WAIT TO TELL THE SUPERINTENDENT ABOUT THIS!
IT WILL MAKE ME LOOK...UH, I MEAN...
IT WILL MAKE OUR SCHOOL LOOK SO... PROGRESSIVE.
WELL, AT LEAST THIS TIME I KNOW WHAT I'M DOING!
THIS TIME THERE'LL BE NO SURPRISES!
4

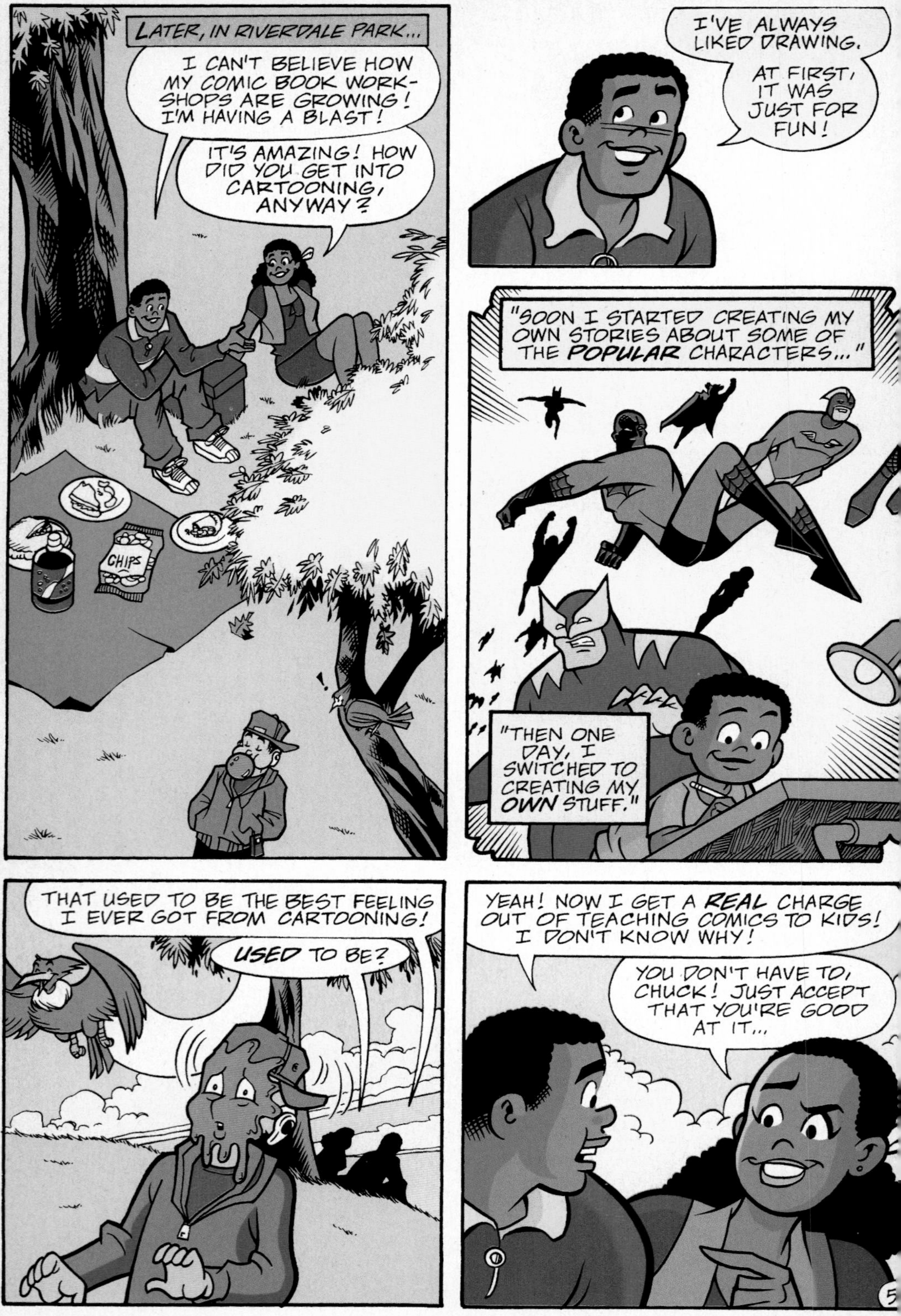
LATER, IN RIVERDALE PARK...
I CAN'T BELIEVE HOW MY COMIC BOOK WORK-SHOPS ARE GROWING! I'M HAVING A BLAST!
IT'S AMAZING! HOW DID YOU GET INTO CARTOONING, ANYWAY?
CHIPS
I'VE ALWAYS LIKED DRAWING.
AT FIRST, IT WAS JUST FOR FUN!
"SOON I STARTED CREATING MY OWN STORIES ABOUT SOME OF THE POPULAR CHARACTERS..."
"THEN ONE DAY, I SWITCHED TO CREATING MY OWN STUFF."
THAT USED TO BE THE BEST FEELING I EVER GOT FROM CARTOONING!
USED TO BE?
YEAH! NOW I GET A REAL CHARGE OUT OF TEACHING COMICS TO KIDS! I DON'T KNOW WHY!
YOU DON'T HAVE TO, CHUCK! JUST ACCEPT THAT YOU'RE GOOD AT IT...

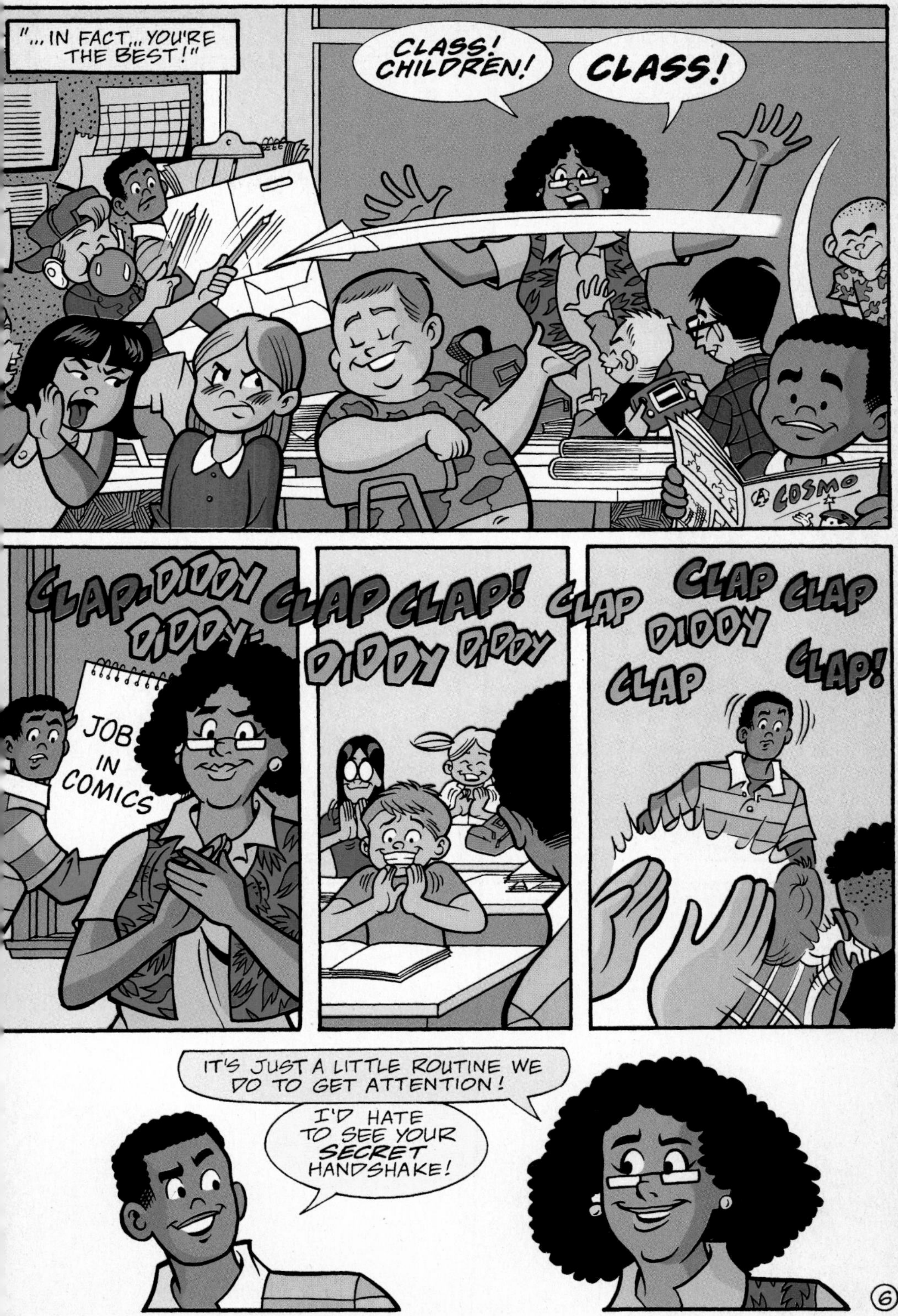
"... IN FACT... YOU'RE THE BEST!"
CLASS! CHILDREN!
CLASS!
COSMO
CLAP-DIDDY DIDDY-
JOB IN COMICS
CLAP CLAP!
DIDDY DIDDY
CLAP
CLAP CLAP
DIDDY
CLAP
CLAP!
IT'S JUST A LITTLE ROUTINE WE DO TO GET ATTENTION!
I'D HATE TO SEE YOUR SECRET HANDSHAKE!
6

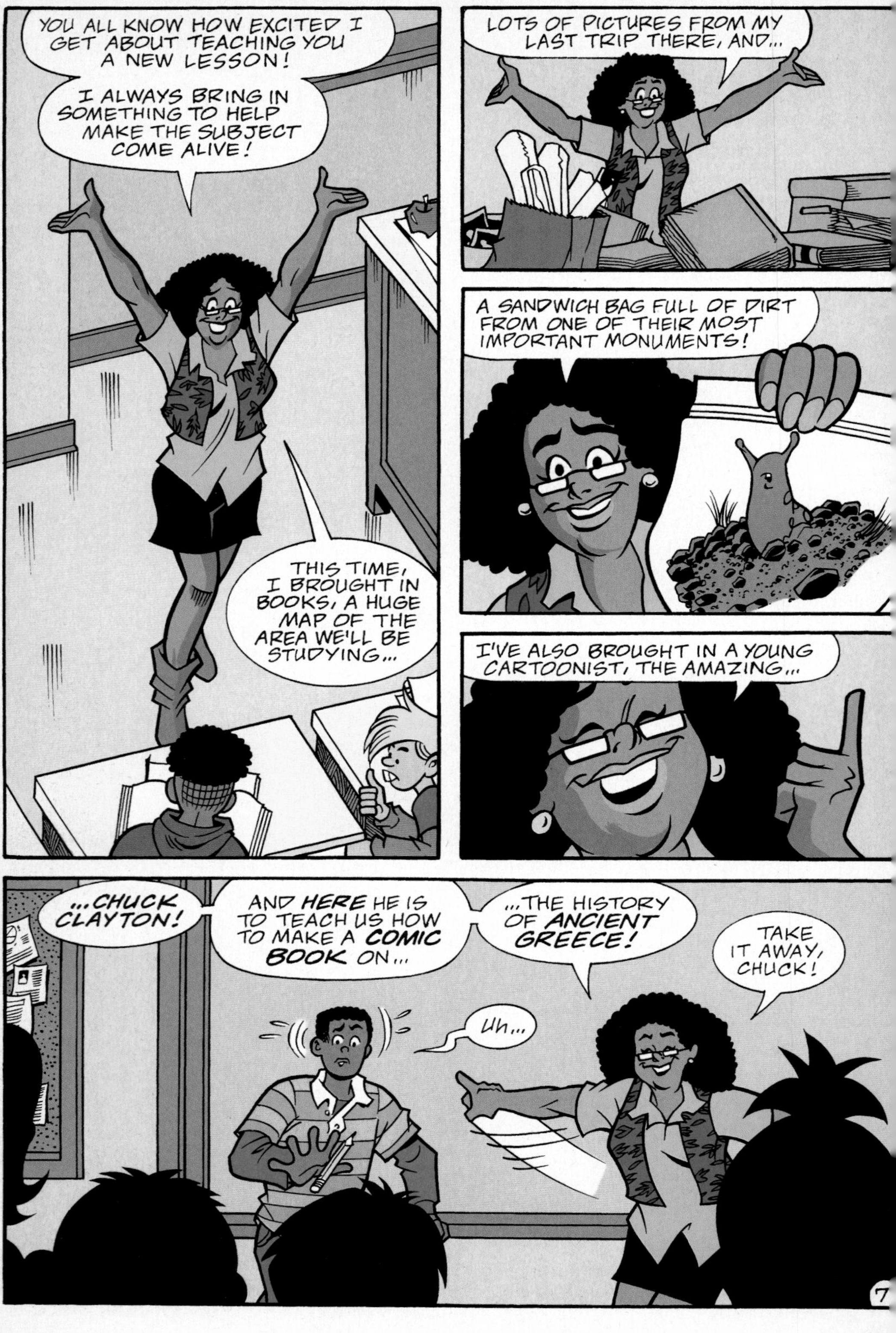
YOU ALL KNOW HOW EXCITED I GET ABOUT TEACHING YOU A NEW LESSON!
I ALWAYS BRING IN SOMETHING TO HELP MAKE THE SUBJECT COME ALIVE!
THIS TIME, I BROUGHT IN BOOKS, A HUGE MAP OF THE AREA WE'LL BE STUDYING...
LOTS OF PICTURES FROM MY LAST TRIP THERE, AND...
A SANDWICH BAG FULL OF DIRT FROM ONE OF THEIR MOST IMPORTANT MONUMENTS!
I'VE ALSO BROUGHT IN A YOUNG CARTOONIST, THE AMAZING...
...CHUCK CLAYTON!
AND HERE HE IS TO TEACH US HOW TO MAKE A COMIC BOOK ON...
...THE HISTORY OF ANCIENT GREECE!
TAKE IT AWAY, CHUCK!
Uh...
7

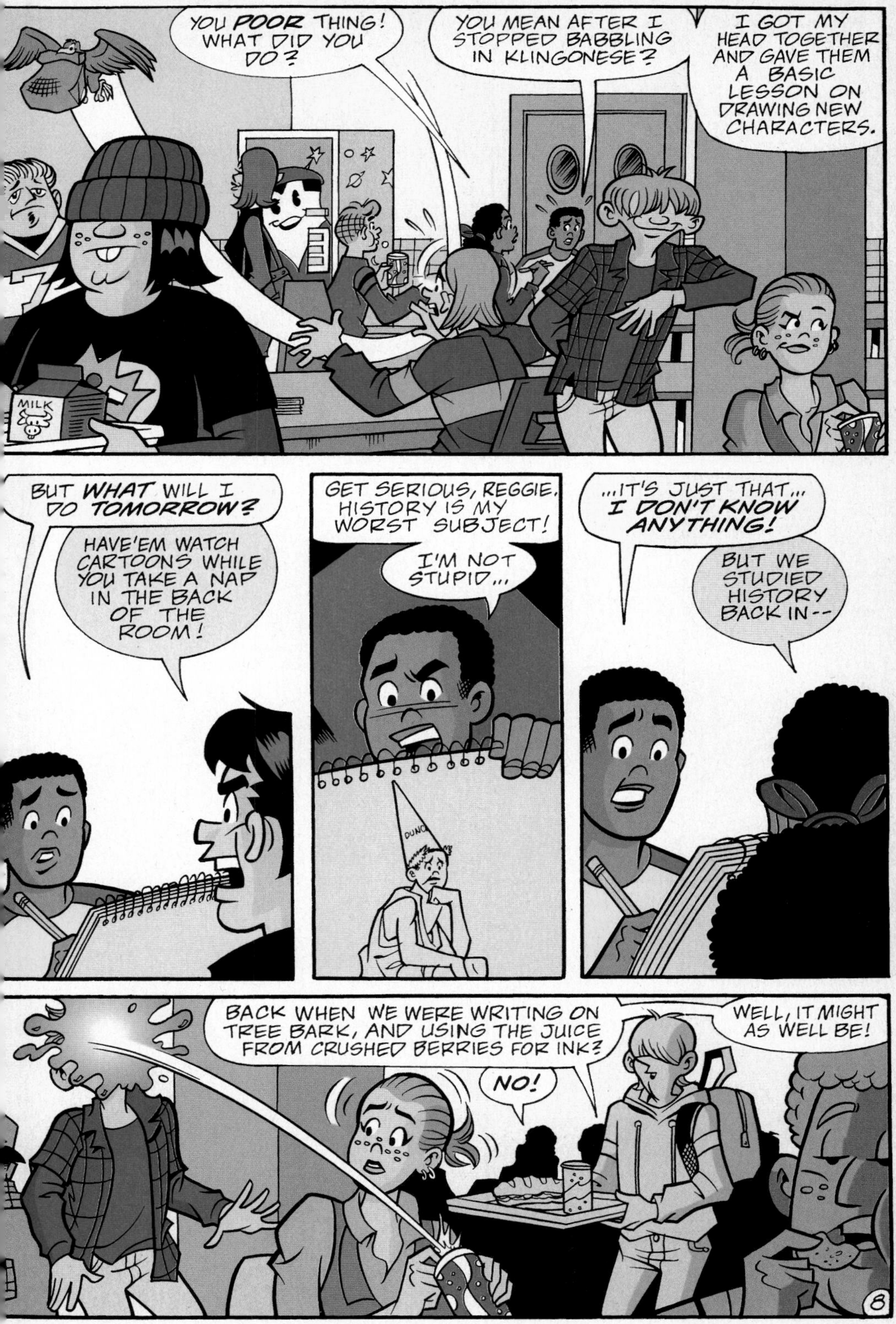
YOU **POOR** THING! WHAT DID YOU DO?
YOU MEAN AFTER I STOPPED BABBLING IN KLINGONESE?
I GOT MY HEAD TOGETHER AND GAVE THEM A BASIC LESSON ON DRAWING NEW CHARACTERS.
MILK
BUT **WHAT** WILL I DO **TOMORROW?**
HAVE'EM WATCH CARTOONS WHILE YOU TAKE A NAP IN THE BACK OF THE ROOM!
GET SERIOUS, REGGIE. HISTORY IS MY WORST SUBJECT!
I'M NOT STUPID...
...IT'S JUST THAT... ***I DON'T KNOW ANYTHING!***
BUT WE STUDIED HISTORY BACK IN--
BACK WHEN WE WERE WRITING ON TREE BARK, AND USING THE JUICE FROM CRUSHED BERRIES FOR INK?
NO!
WELL, IT MIGHT AS WELL BE!
8

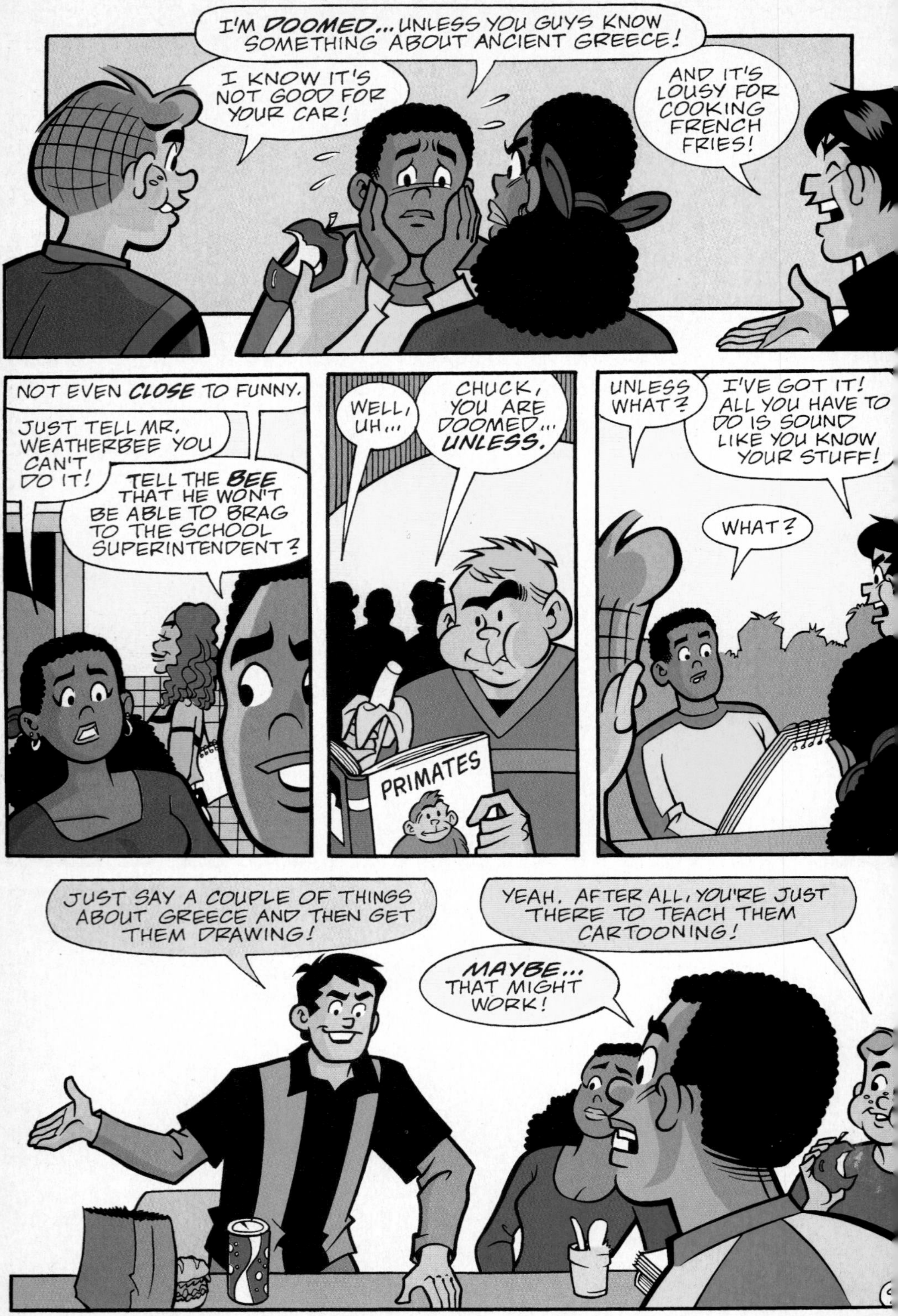
I'M DOOMED... UNLESS YOU GUYS KNOW SOMETHING ABOUT ANCIENT GREECE!
I KNOW IT'S NOT GOOD FOR YOUR CAR!
AND IT'S LOUSY FOR COOKING FRENCH FRIES!
NOT EVEN CLOSE TO FUNNY.
JUST TELL MR. WEATHERBEE YOU CAN'T DO IT!
TELL THE BEE THAT HE WON'T BE ABLE TO BRAG TO THE SCHOOL SUPERINTENDENT?
WELL, UH...
CHUCK, YOU ARE DOOMED... UNLESS.
PRIMATES
UNLESS WHAT?
I'VE GOT IT! ALL YOU HAVE TO DO IS SOUND LIKE YOU KNOW YOUR STUFF!
WHAT?
JUST SAY A COUPLE OF THINGS ABOUT GREECE AND THEN GET THEM DRAWING!
YEAH. AFTER ALL, YOU'RE JUST THERE TO TEACH THEM CARTOONING!
MAYBE... THAT MIGHT WORK!

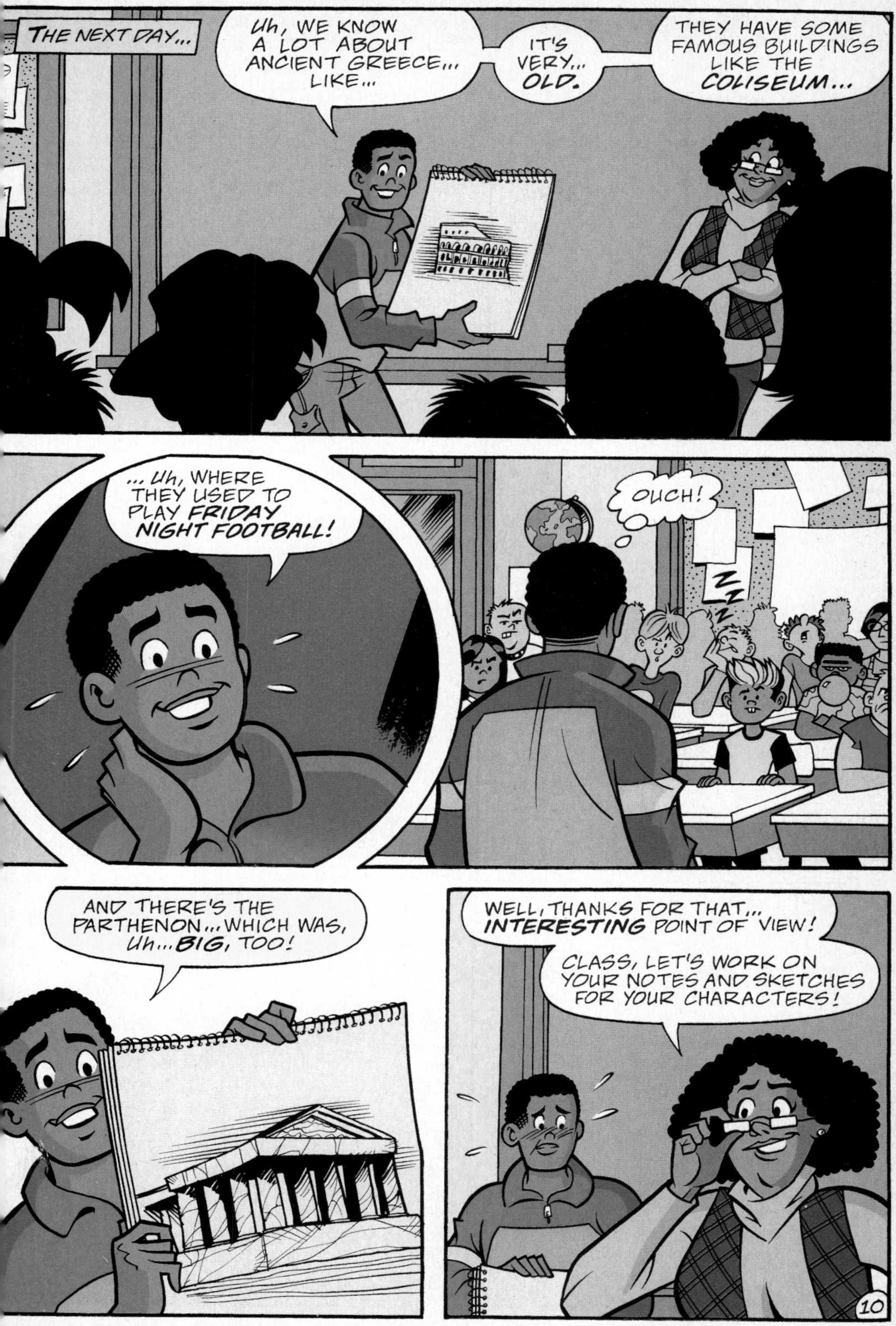
THE NEXT DAY...
Uh, WE KNOW A LOT ABOUT ANCIENT GREECE... LIKE...
IT'S VERY... OLD.
THEY HAVE SOME FAMOUS BUILDINGS LIKE THE COLISEUM...
... Uh, WHERE THEY USED TO PLAY FRIDAY NIGHT FOOTBALL!
OUCH!
Z Z Z
AND THERE'S THE PARTHENON... WHICH WAS, Uh... BIG, TOO!
WELL, THANKS FOR THAT... INTERESTING POINT OF VIEW!
CLASS, LET'S WORK ON YOUR NOTES AND SKETCHES FOR YOUR CHARACTERS!
10

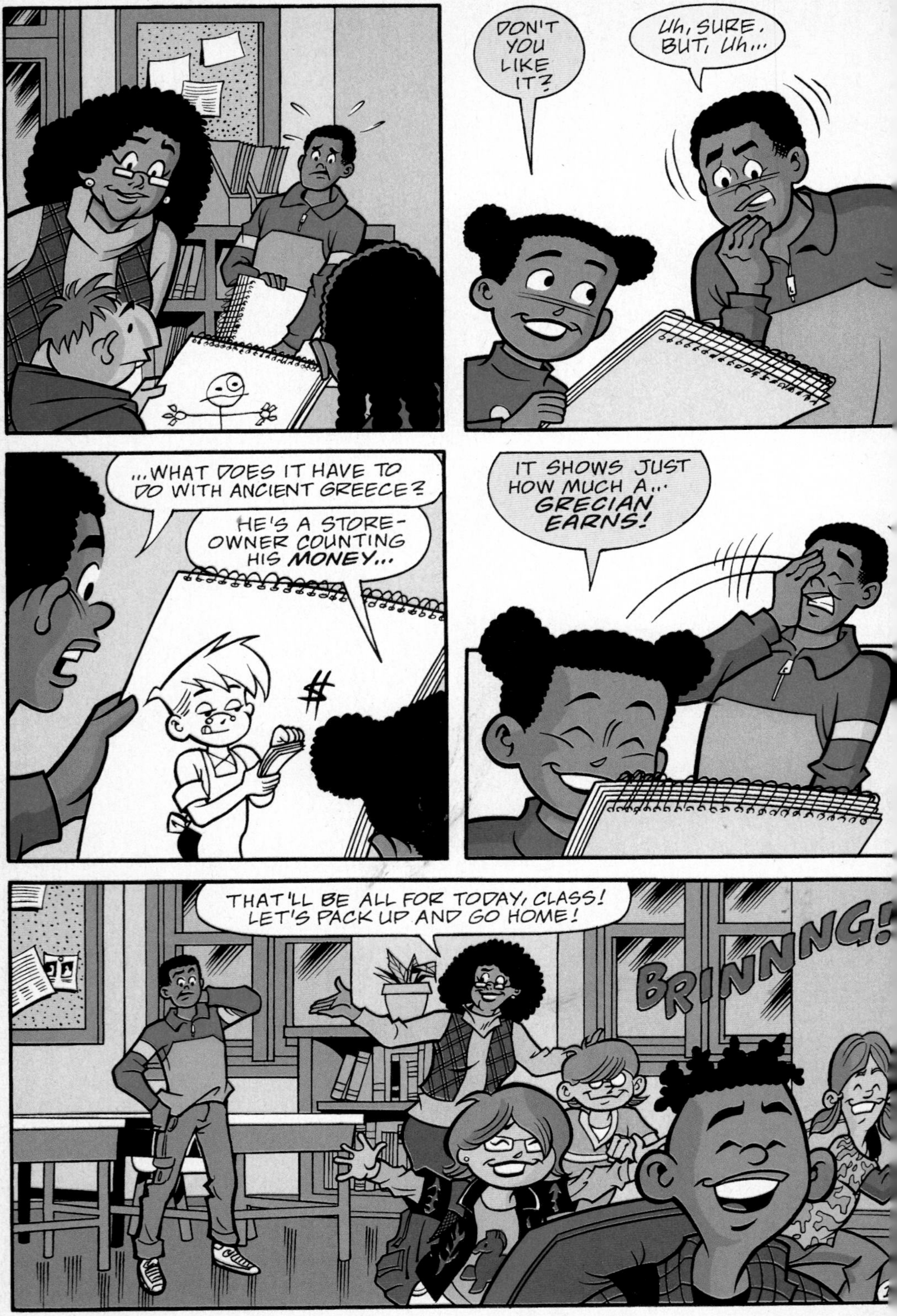
DON'T YOU LIKE IT?
UH, SURE. BUT, UH...
...WHAT DOES IT HAVE TO DO WITH ANCIENT GREECE?
HE'S A STORE-OWNER COUNTING HIS MONEY...
$
IT SHOWS JUST HOW MUCH A... GRECIAN EARNS!
THAT'LL BE ALL FOR TODAY, CLASS! LET'S PACK UP AND GO HOME!
BRINNNG!

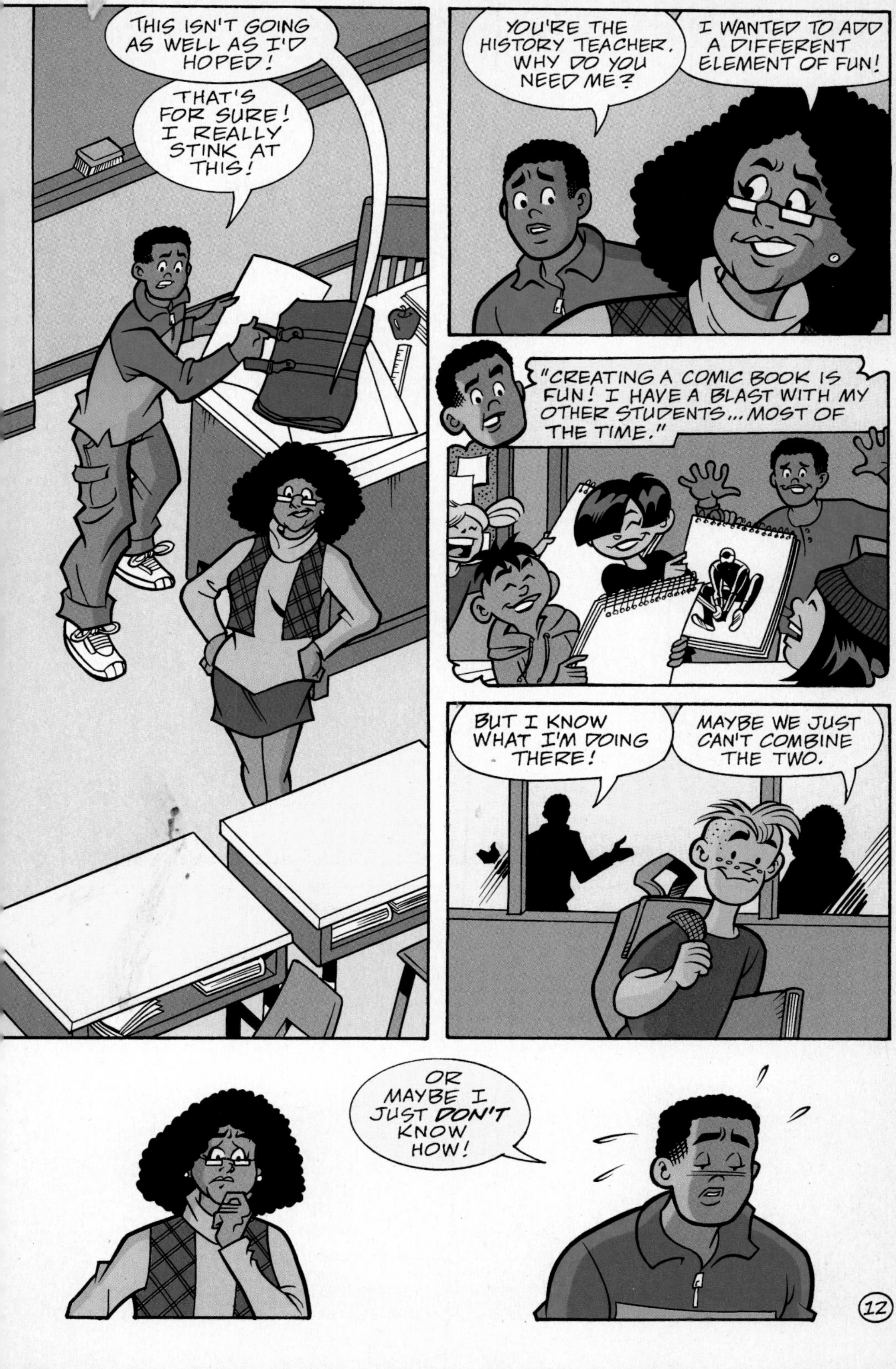
THIS ISN'T GOING AS WELL AS I'D HOPED!
THAT'S FOR SURE! I REALLY STINK AT THIS!
YOU'RE THE HISTORY TEACHER. WHY DO YOU NEED ME?
I WANTED TO ADD A DIFFERENT ELEMENT OF FUN!
"CREATING A COMIC BOOK IS FUN! I HAVE A BLAST WITH MY OTHER STUDENTS... MOST OF THE TIME."
BUT I KNOW WHAT I'M DOING THERE!
MAYBE WE JUST CAN'T COMBINE THE TWO.
OR MAYBE I JUST ***DON'T*** KNOW HOW!
12

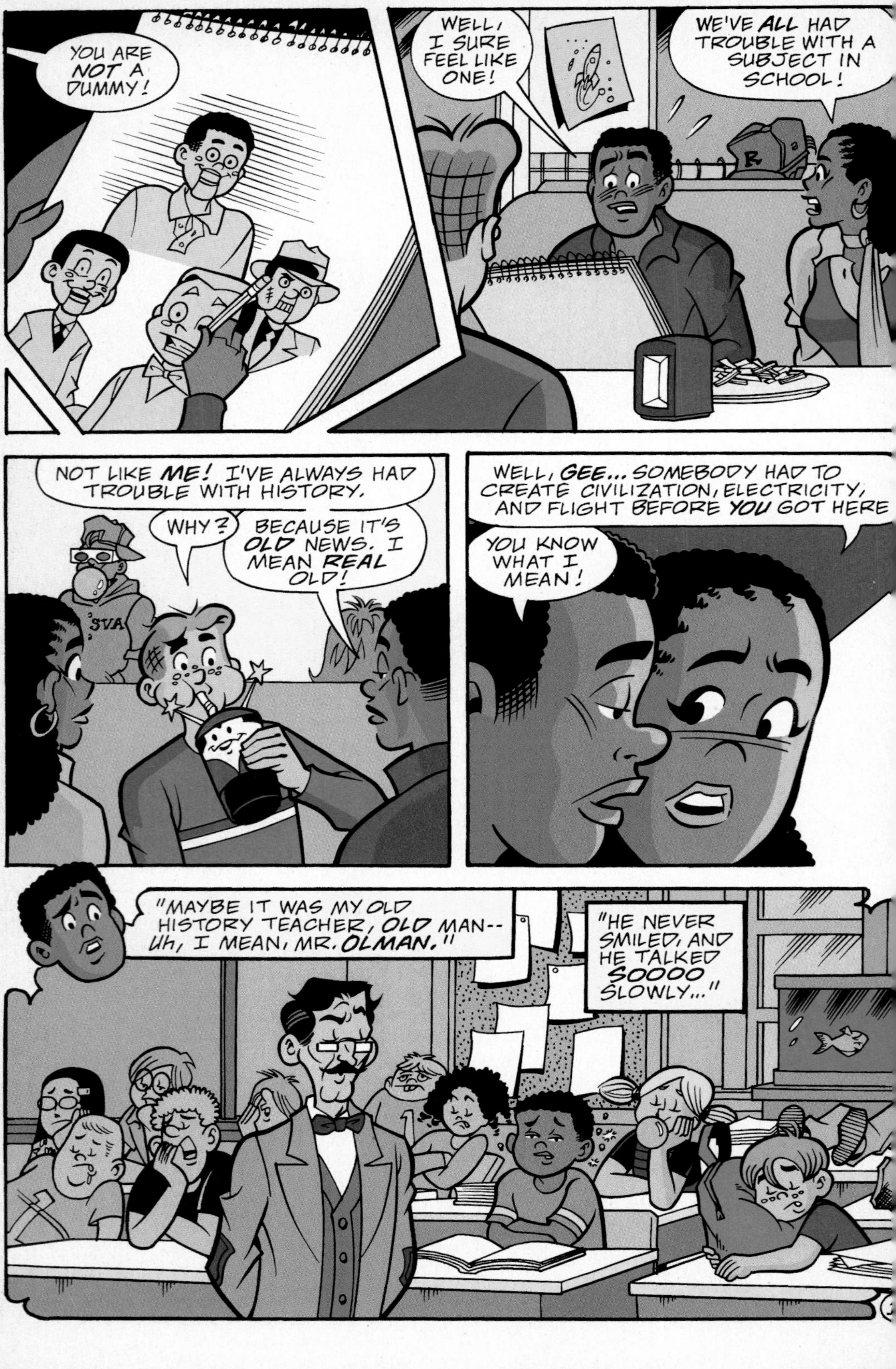
YOU ARE NOT A DUMMY!
WELL, I SURE FEEL LIKE ONE!
WE'VE ALL HAD TROUBLE WITH A SUBJECT IN SCHOOL!
NOT LIKE ME! I'VE ALWAYS HAD TROUBLE WITH HISTORY.
WHY?
BECAUSE IT'S OLD NEWS. I MEAN REAL OLD!
SVA
WELL, GEE... SOMEBODY HAD TO CREATE CIVILIZATION, ELECTRICITY, AND FLIGHT BEFORE YOU GOT HERE
YOU KNOW WHAT I MEAN!
"MAYBE IT WAS MY OLD HISTORY TEACHER, OLD MAN-- UH, I MEAN, MR. OLMAN."
"HE NEVER SMILED, AND HE TALKED SOOOO SLOWLY..."

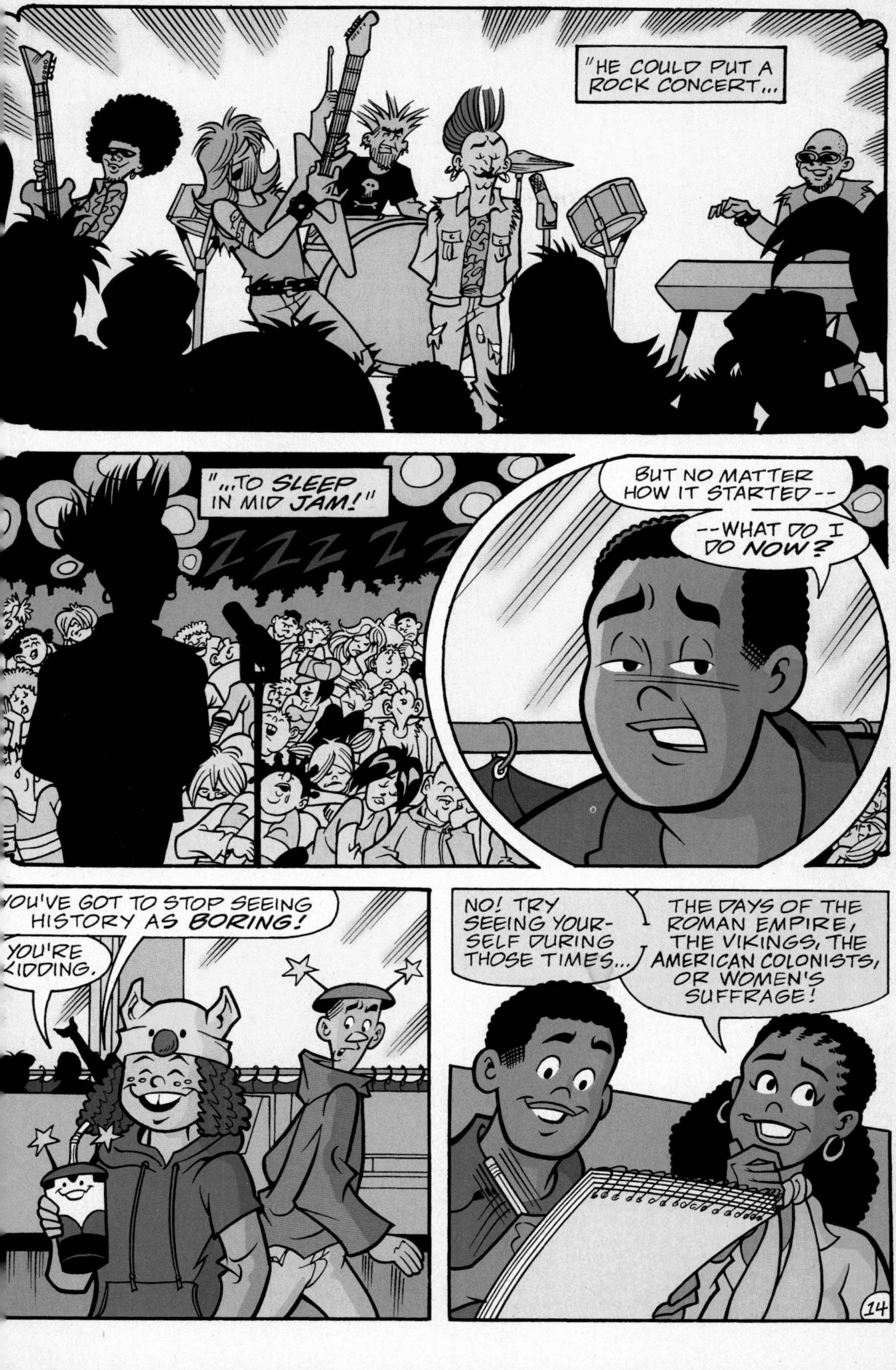
"HE COULD PUT A ROCK CONCERT...
"...TO SLEEP IN MID JAM!"
ZZZZZ
BUT NO MATTER HOW IT STARTED--
--WHAT DO I DO NOW?
YOU'VE GOT TO STOP SEEING HISTORY AS BORING!
YOU'RE KIDDING.
NO! TRY SEEING YOURSELF DURING THOSE TIMES...
THE DAYS OF THE ROMAN EMPIRE, THE VIKINGS, THE AMERICAN COLONISTS, OR WOMEN'S SUFFRAGE!
14

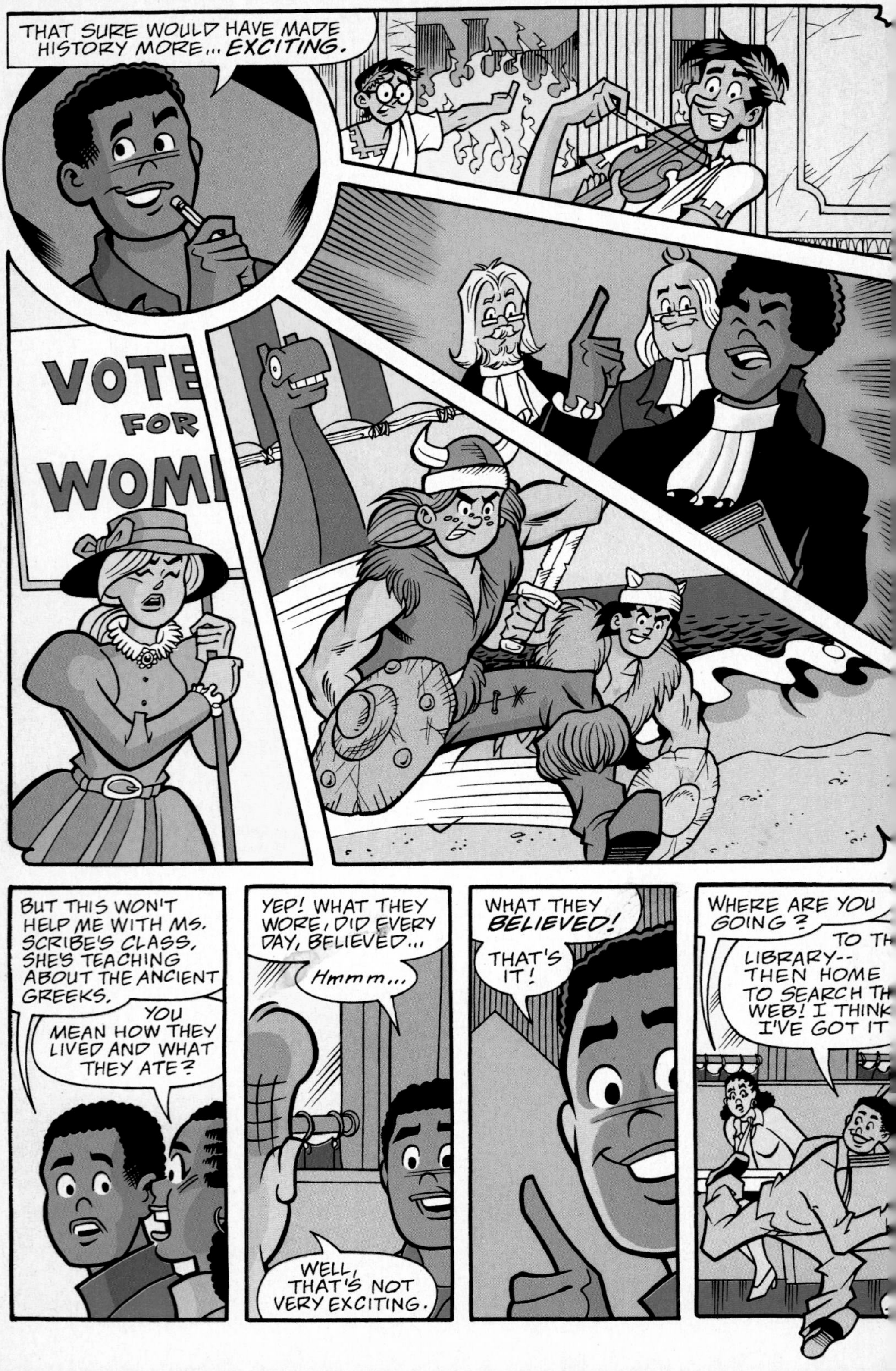
THAT SURE WOULD HAVE MADE HISTORY MORE... EXCITING.
VOTE FOR WOM
BUT THIS WON'T HELP ME WITH MS. SCRIBE'S CLASS. SHE'S TEACHING ABOUT THE ANCIENT GREEKS.
YOU MEAN HOW THEY LIVED AND WHAT THEY ATE?
YEP! WHAT THEY WORE, DID EVERY DAY, BELIEVED...
Hmmm...
WELL, THAT'S NOT VERY EXCITING.
WHAT THEY BELIEVED!
THAT'S IT!
WHERE ARE YOU GOING?
TO TH LIBRARY-- THEN HOME TO SEARCH TH WEB! I THINK I'VE GOT IT

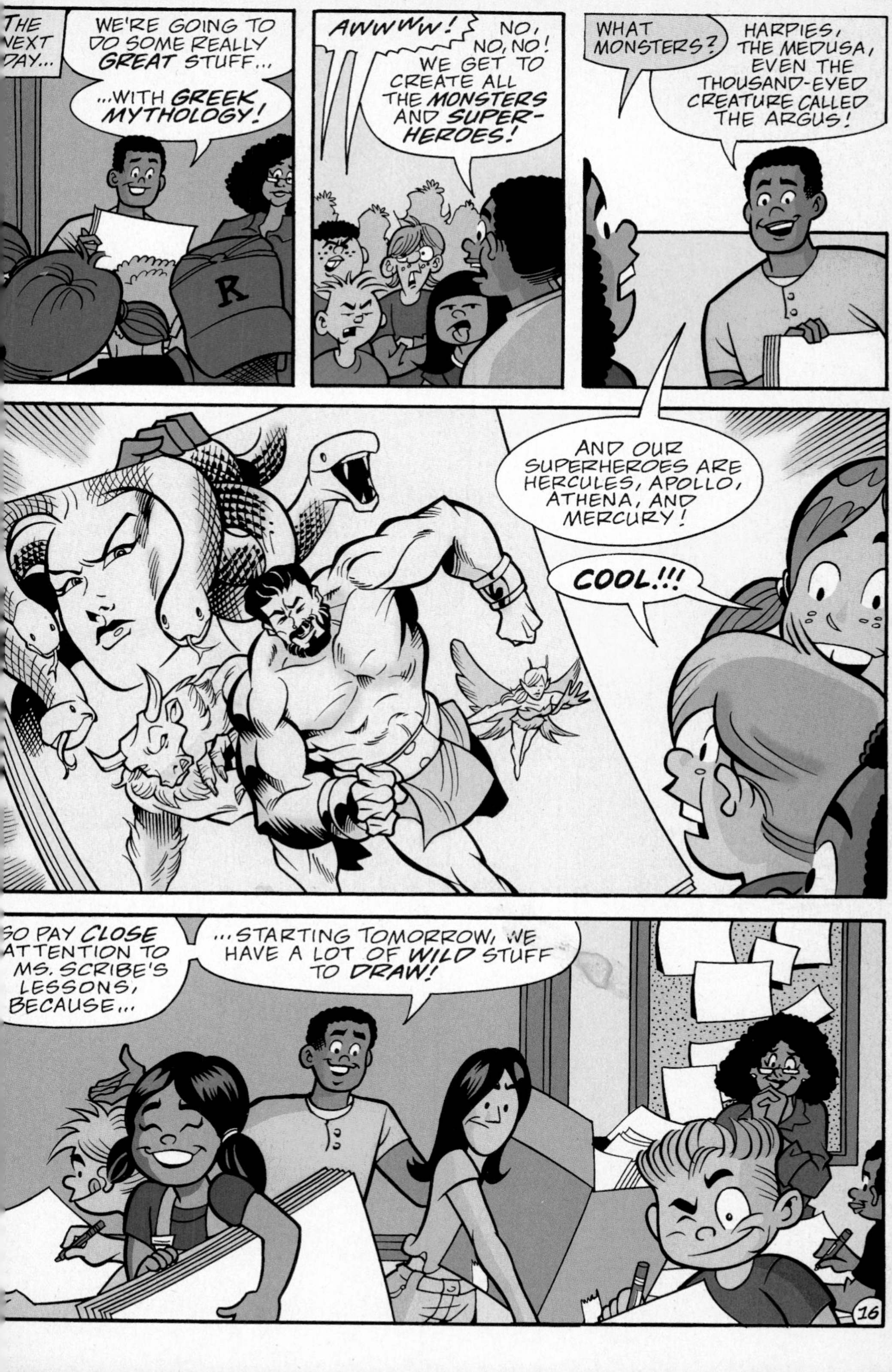
THE NEXT DAY...
WE'RE GOING TO DO SOME REALLY **GREAT** STUFF...
...WITH **GREEK MYTHOLOGY!**
AWWWW!
NO, NO, NO! WE GET TO CREATE ALL THE **MONSTERS** AND **SUPERHEROES!**
WHAT MONSTERS?
HARPIES, THE MEDUSA, EVEN THE THOUSAND-EYED CREATURE CALLED THE ARGUS!
AND OUR SUPERHEROES ARE HERCULES, APOLLO, ATHENA, AND MERCURY!
COOL!!!
SO PAY **CLOSE** ATTENTION TO MS. SCRIBE'S LESSONS, BECAUSE...
...STARTING TOMORROW, WE HAVE A LOT OF **WILD** STUFF TO **DRAW!**
16

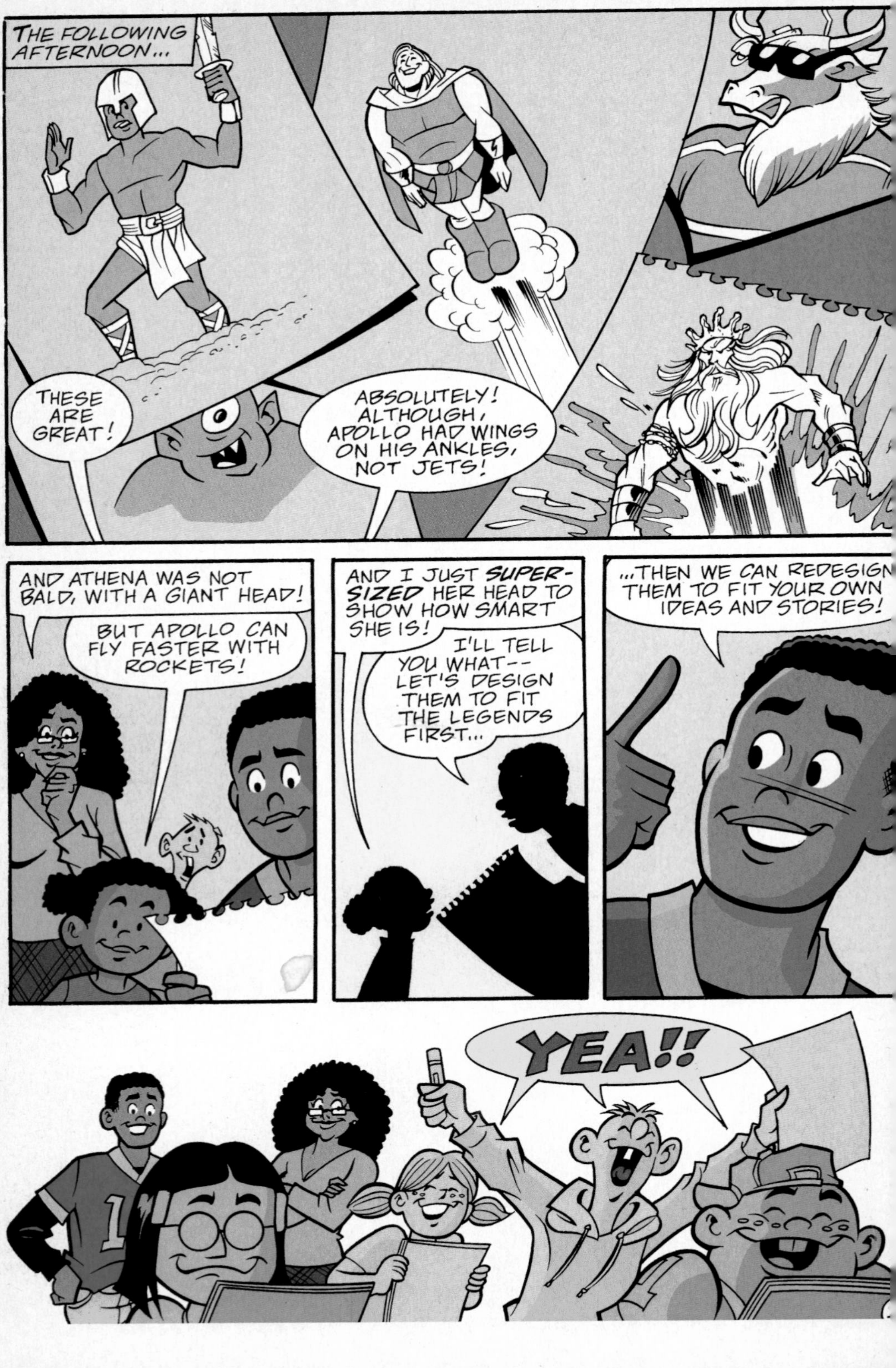
THE FOLLOWING AFTERNOON...
THESE ARE GREAT!
ABSOLUTELY! ALTHOUGH, APOLLO HAD WINGS ON HIS ANKLES, NOT JETS!
AND ATHENA WAS NOT BALD, WITH A GIANT HEAD!
BUT APOLLO CAN FLY FASTER WITH ROCKETS!
AND I JUST SUPER-SIZED HER HEAD TO SHOW HOW SMART SHE IS!
I'LL TELL YOU WHAT-- LET'S DESIGN THEM TO FIT THE LEGENDS FIRST...
...THEN WE CAN REDESIGN THEM TO FIT YOUR OWN IDEAS AND STORIES!
YEA!!

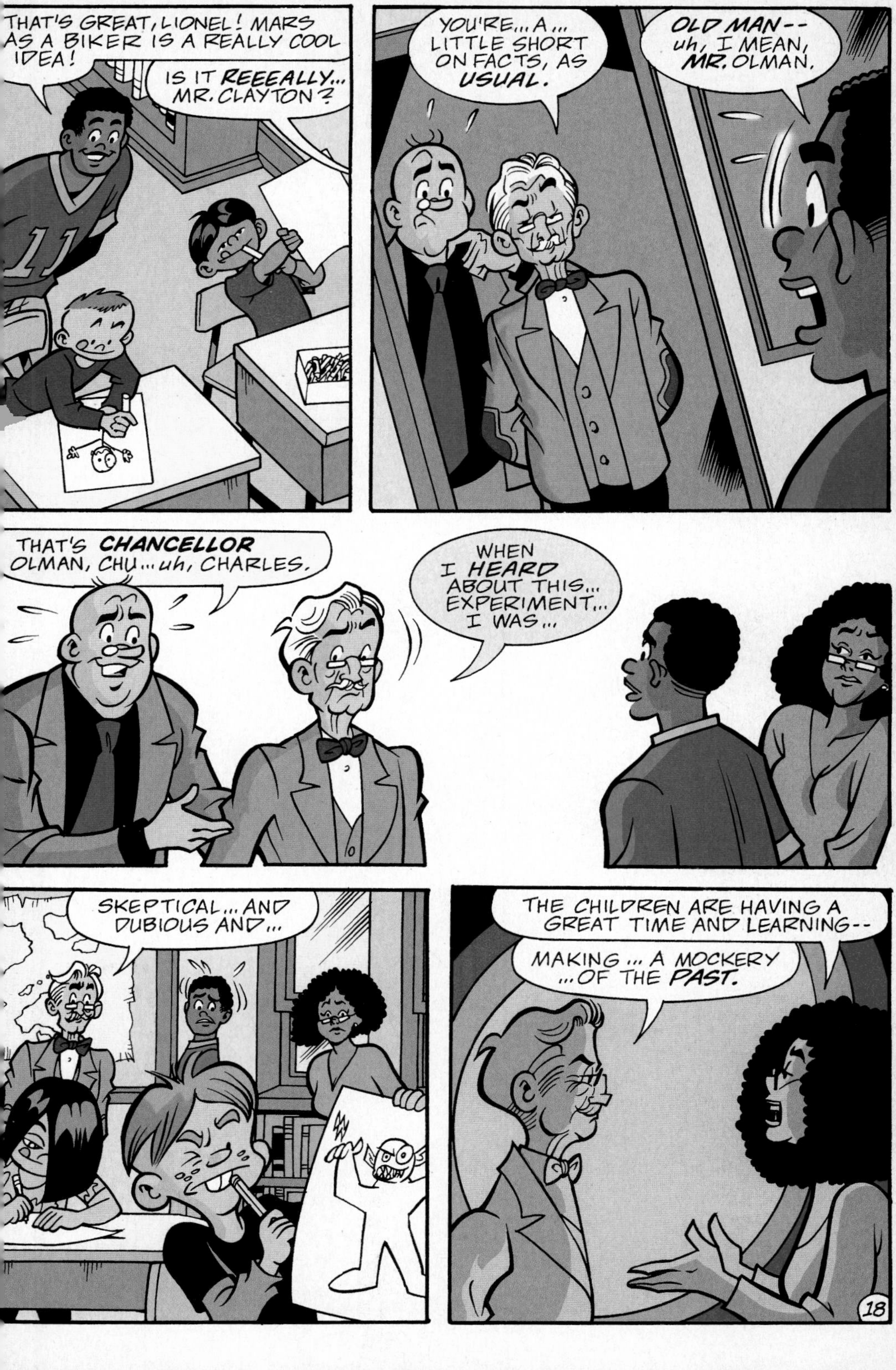
THAT'S GREAT, LIONEL! MARS AS A BIKER IS A REALLY COOL IDEA!
IS IT REEEALLY... MR. CLAYTON?
YOU'RE... A... LITTLE SHORT ON FACTS, AS USUAL.
OLD MAN-- uh, I MEAN, MR. OLMAN.
THAT'S CHANCELLOR OLMAN, CHU... uh, CHARLES.
WHEN I HEARD ABOUT THIS... EXPERIMENT... I WAS...
SKEPTICAL... AND DUBIOUS AND...
THE CHILDREN ARE HAVING A GREAT TIME AND LEARNING--
MAKING ... A MOCKERY ...OF THE PAST.
18

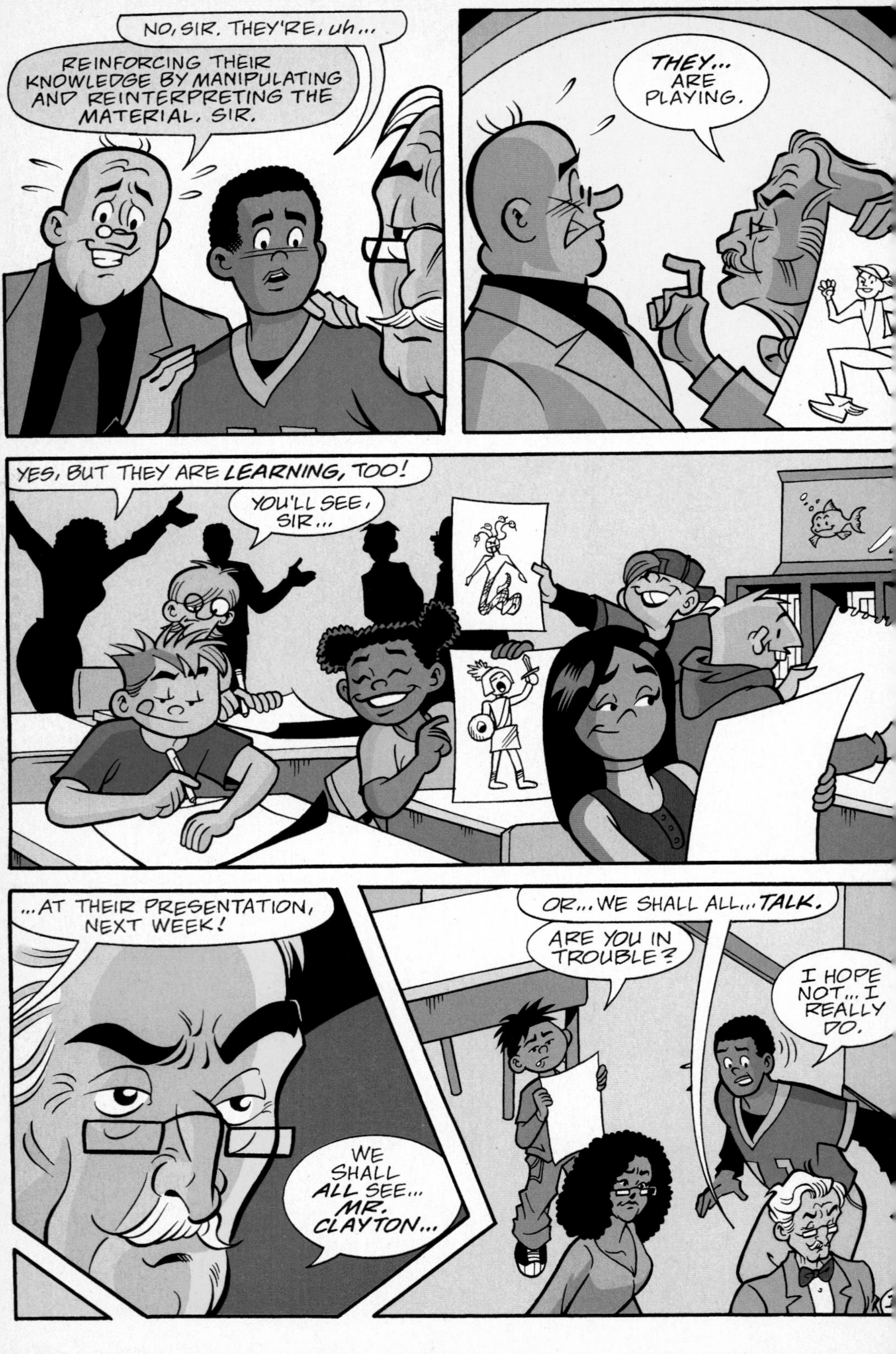
NO, SIR. THEY'RE, uh...
REINFORCING THEIR KNOWLEDGE BY MANIPULATING AND REINTERPRETING THE MATERIAL, SIR.
THEY... ARE PLAYING.
YES, BUT THEY ARE LEARNING, TOO!
YOU'LL SEE, SIR...
...AT THEIR PRESENTATION, NEXT WEEK!
WE SHALL ALL SEE... MR. CLAYTON...
OR... WE SHALL ALL... TALK.
ARE YOU IN TROUBLE?
I HOPE NOT... I REALLY DO.

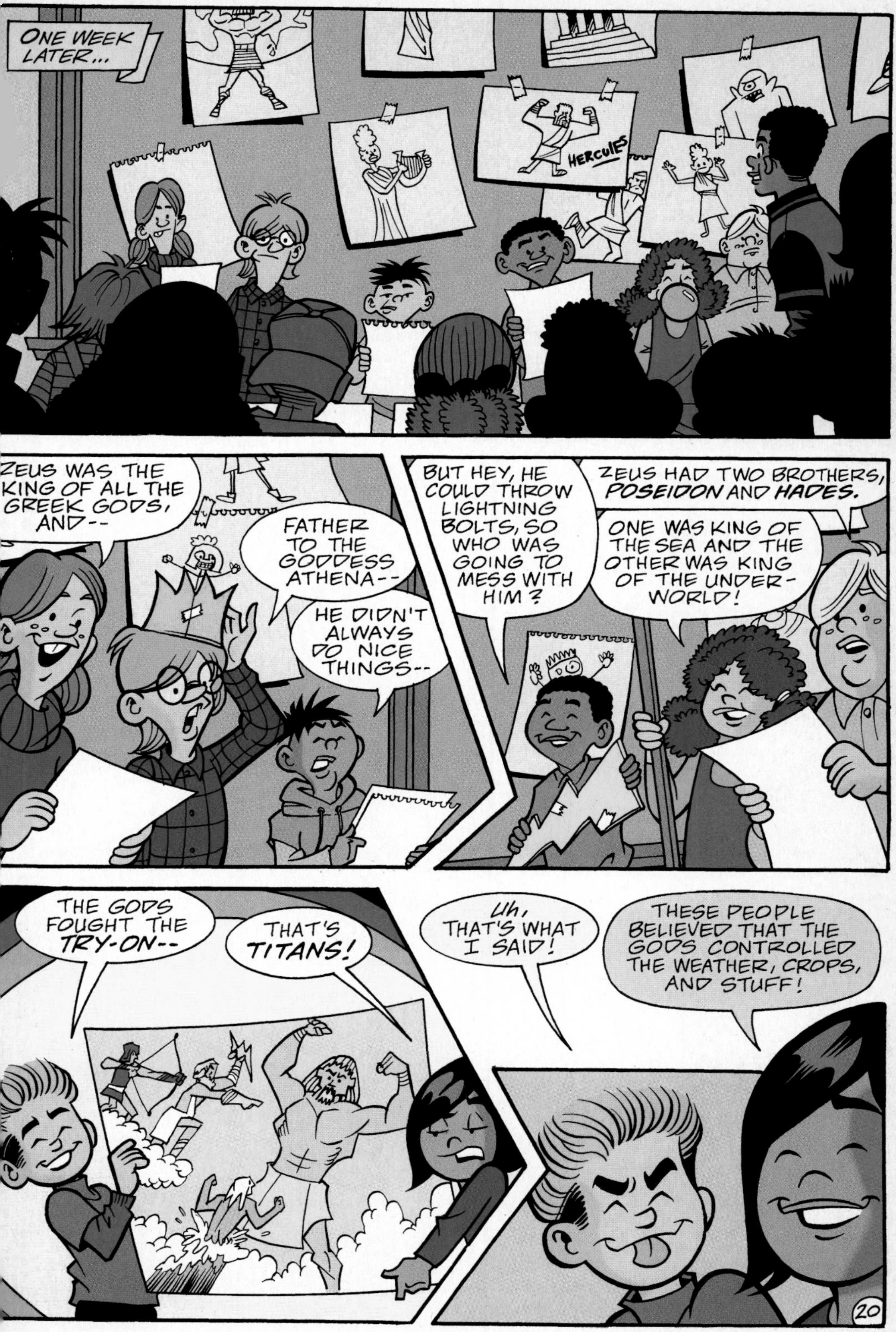
ONE WEEK LATER...
HERCULES
ZEUS WAS THE KING OF ALL THE GREEK GODS, AND--
FATHER TO THE GODDESS ATHENA--
HE DIDN'T ALWAYS DO NICE THINGS--
BUT HEY, HE COULD THROW LIGHTNING BOLTS, SO WHO WAS GOING TO MESS WITH HIM?
ZEUS HAD TWO BROTHERS, **POSEIDON** AND **HADES.**
ONE WAS KING OF THE SEA AND THE OTHER WAS KING OF THE UNDER-WORLD!
THE GODS FOUGHT THE *TRY-ON*--
THAT'S **TITANS!**
Uh, THAT'S WHAT I SAID!
THESE PEOPLE BELIEVED THAT THE GODS CONTROLLED THE WEATHER, CROPS, AND STUFF!
20

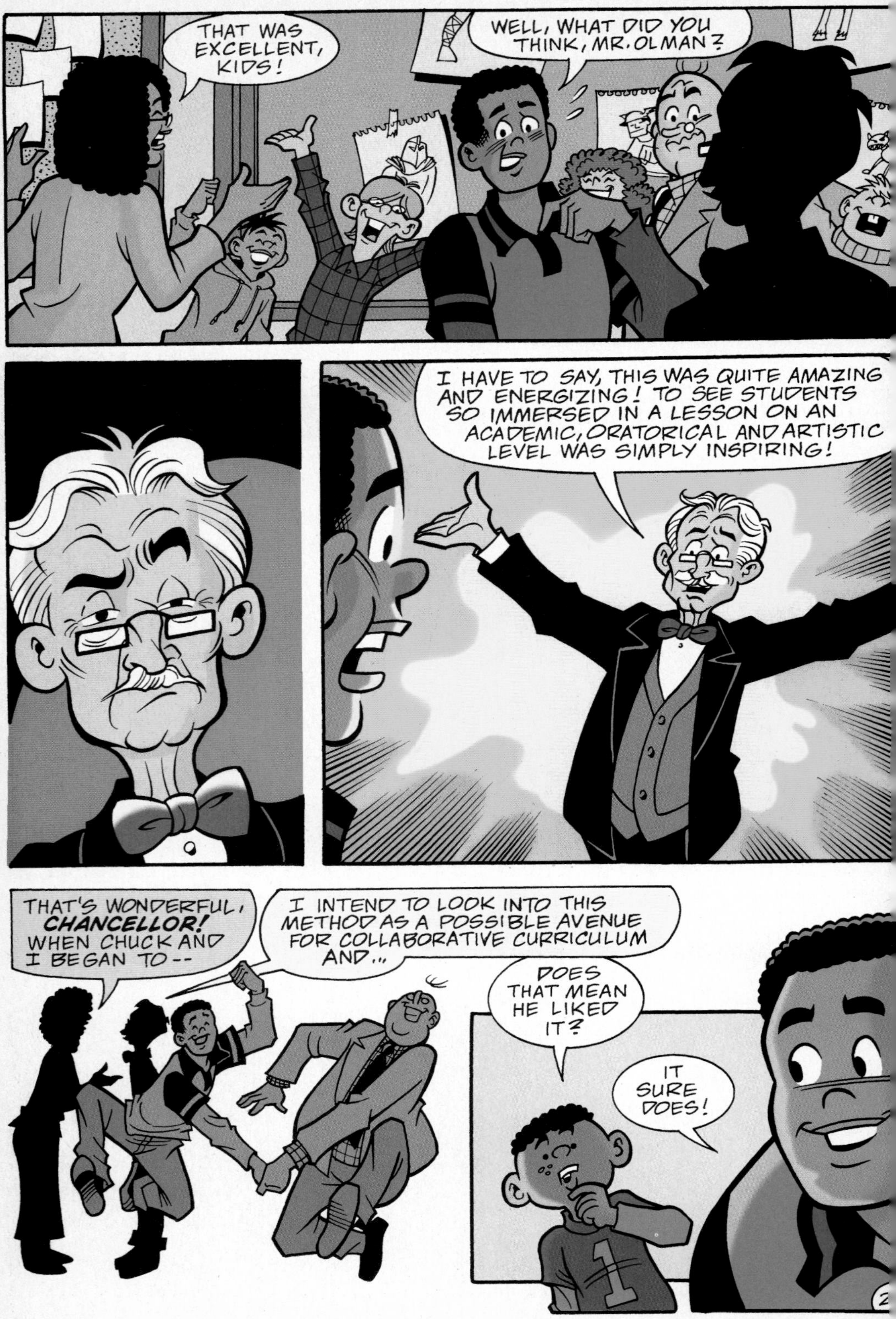
THAT WAS EXCELLENT, KIDS!
WELL, WHAT DID YOU THINK, MR. OLMAN?
I HAVE TO SAY, THIS WAS QUITE AMAZING AND ENERGIZING! TO SEE STUDENTS SO IMMERSED IN A LESSON ON AN ACADEMIC, ORATORICAL AND ARTISTIC LEVEL WAS SIMPLY INSPIRING!
THAT'S WONDERFUL, **CHANCELLOR!** WHEN CHUCK AND I BEGAN TO--
I INTEND TO LOOK INTO THIS METHOD AS A POSSIBLE AVENUE FOR COLLABORATIVE CURRICULUM AND...
DOES THAT MEAN HE LIKED IT?
IT SURE DOES!

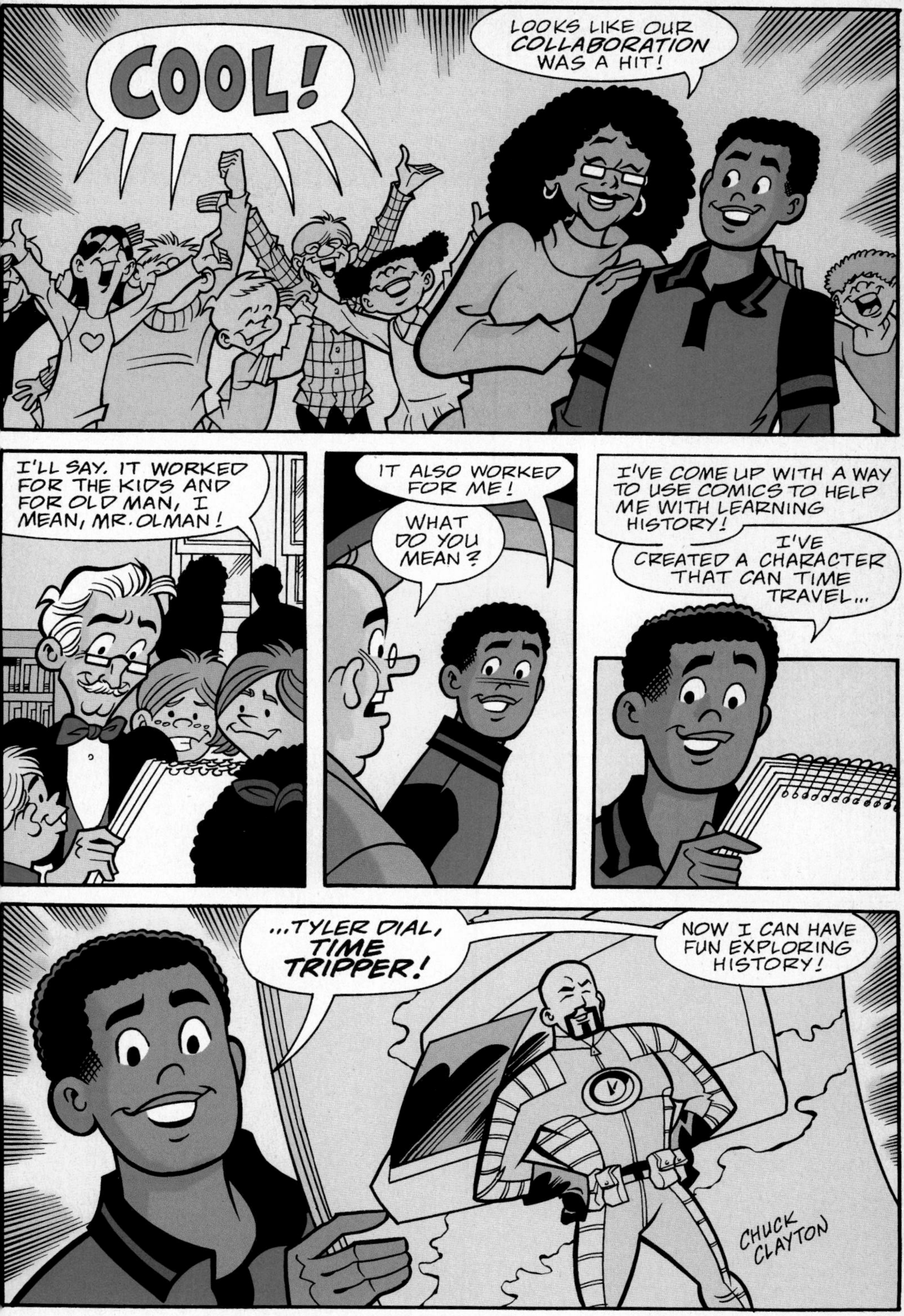
COOL!
LOOKS LIKE OUR COLLABORATION WAS A HIT!
I'LL SAY. IT WORKED FOR THE KIDS AND FOR OLD MAN, I MEAN, MR. OLMAN!
IT ALSO WORKED FOR ME!
WHAT DO YOU MEAN?
I'VE COME UP WITH A WAY TO USE COMICS TO HELP ME WITH LEARNING HISTORY!
I'VE CREATED A CHARACTER THAT CAN TIME TRAVEL...
...TYLER DIAL, TIME TRIPPER!
NOW I CAN HAVE FUN EXPLORING HISTORY!
CHUCK CLAYTON

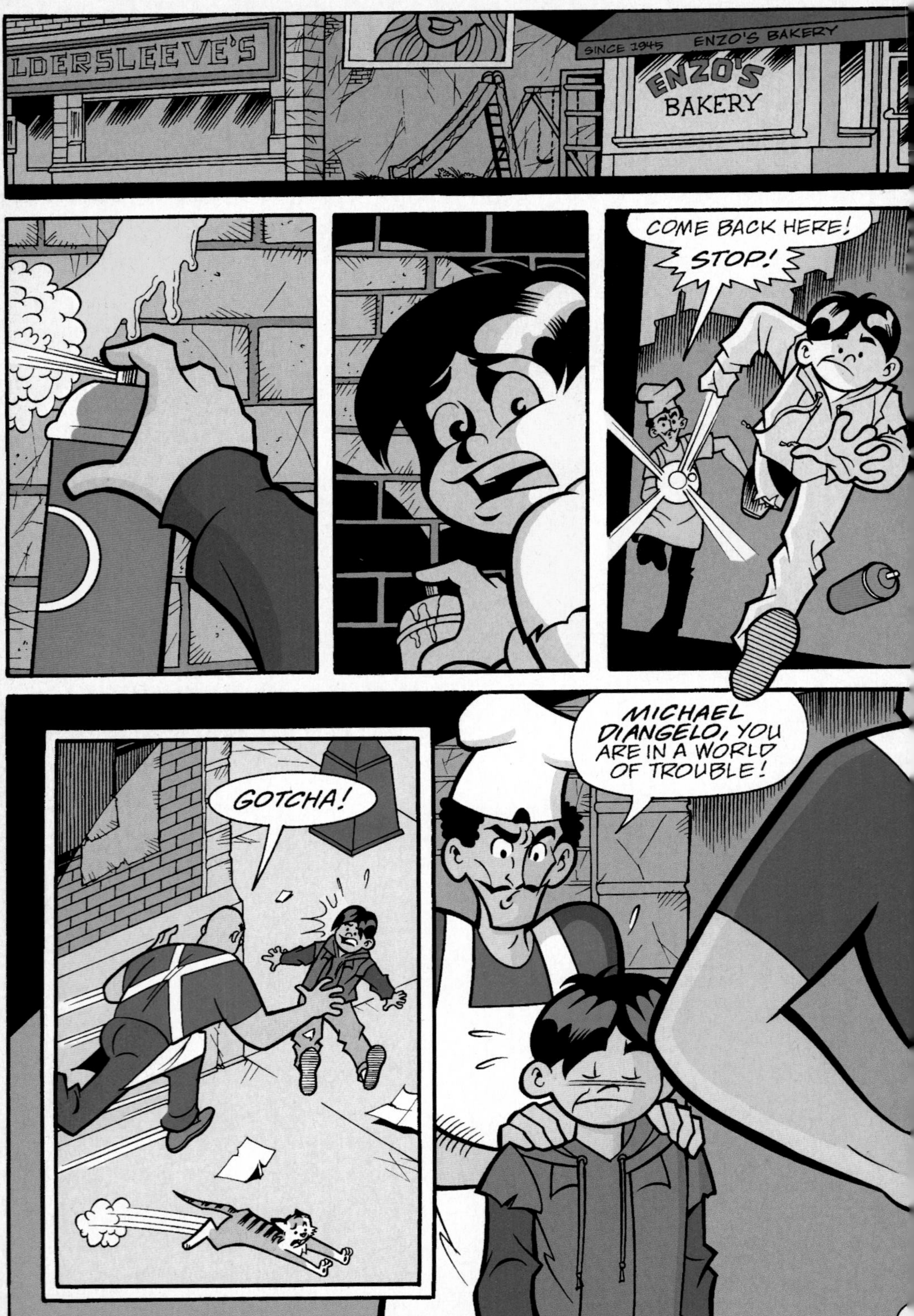
LDERSLEEVE'S
SINCE 1945
ENZO'S BAKERY
ENZO'S
BAKERY
COME BACK HERE!
STOP!
GOTCHA!
MICHAEL DIANGELO, YOU ARE IN A WORLD OF TROUBLE!

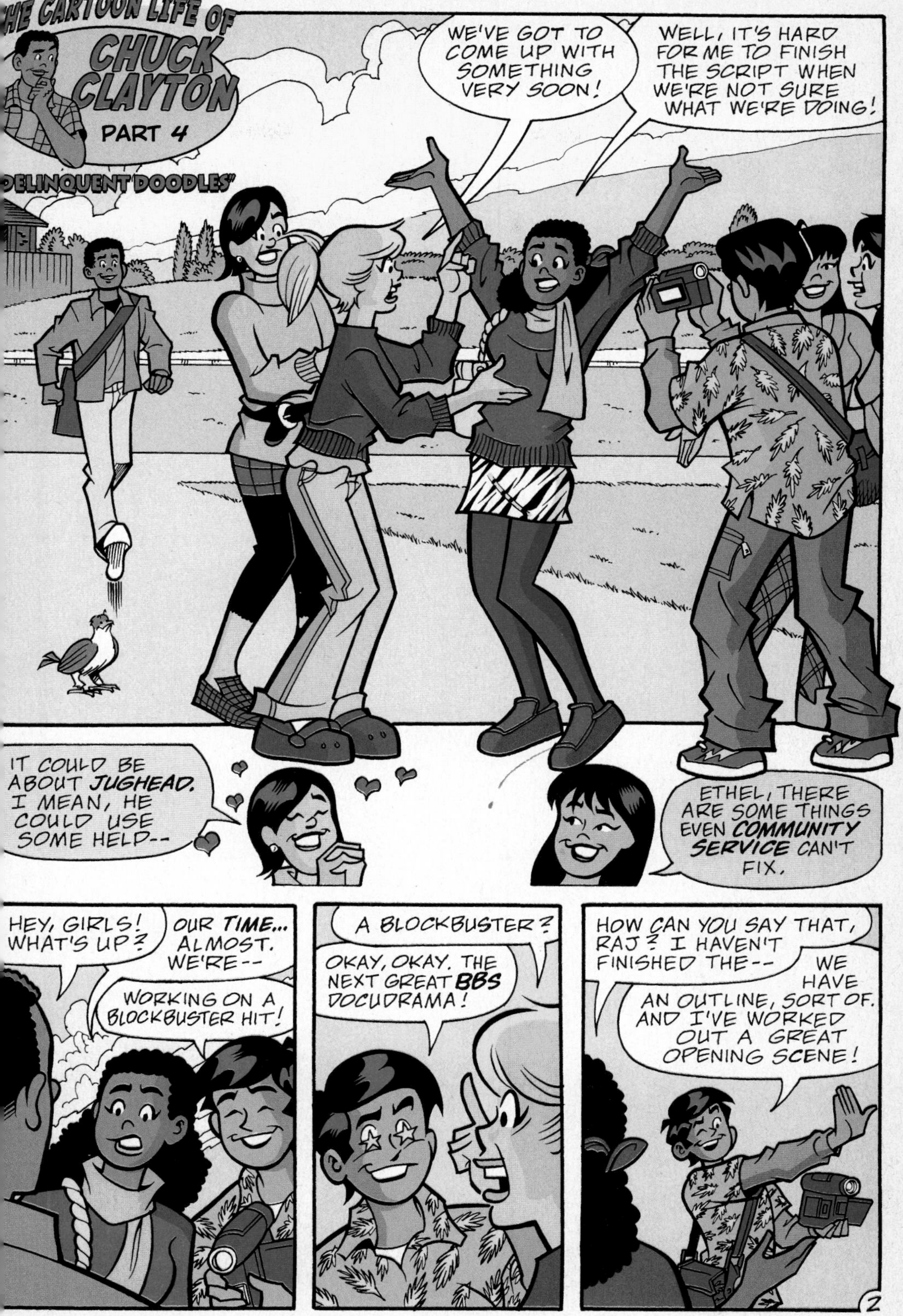
THE CARTOON LIFE OF
CHUCK CLAYTON
PART 4
"DELINQUENT DOODLES"
WE'VE GOT TO COME UP WITH SOMETHING VERY SOON!
WELL, IT'S HARD FOR ME TO FINISH THE SCRIPT WHEN WE'RE NOT SURE WHAT WE'RE DOING!
IT COULD BE ABOUT JUGHEAD. I MEAN, HE COULD USE SOME HELP--
ETHEL, THERE ARE SOME THINGS EVEN COMMUNITY SERVICE CAN'T FIX.
HEY, GIRLS! WHAT'S UP?
OUR TIME... ALMOST. WE'RE--
WORKING ON A BLOCKBUSTER HIT!
A BLOCKBUSTER?
OKAY, OKAY. THE NEXT GREAT BBS DOCUDRAMA!
HOW CAN YOU SAY THAT, RAJ? I HAVEN'T FINISHED THE--
WE HAVE AN OUTLINE, SORT OF. AND I'VE WORKED OUT A GREAT OPENING SCENE!
2

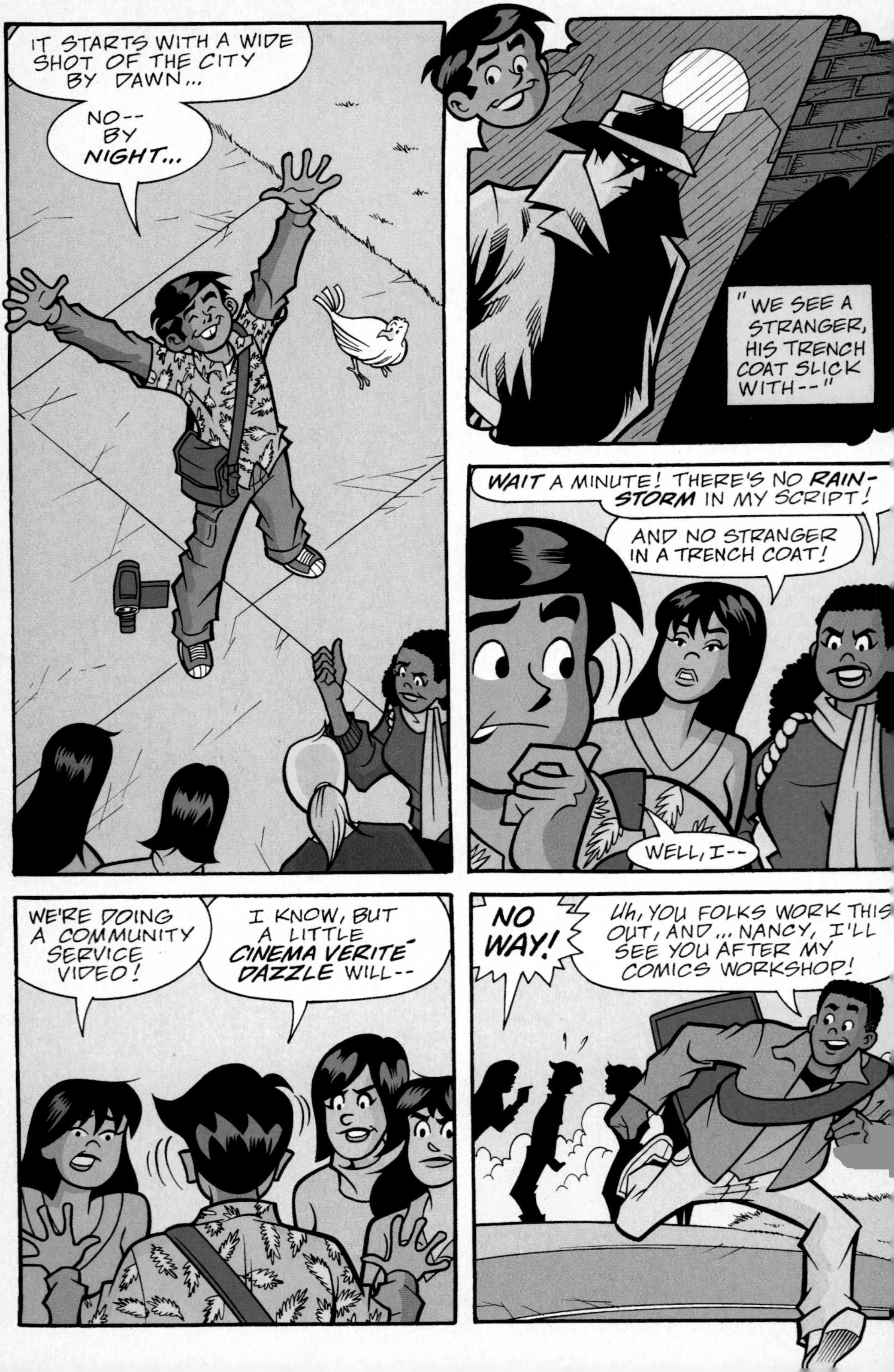
IT STARTS WITH A WIDE SHOT OF THE CITY BY DAWN...
NO-- BY NIGHT...
"WE SEE A STRANGER, HIS TRENCH COAT SLICK WITH--"
WAIT A MINUTE! THERE'S NO RAINSTORM IN MY SCRIPT!
AND NO STRANGER IN A TRENCH COAT!
WELL, I--
WE'RE DOING A COMMUNITY SERVICE VIDEO!
I KNOW, BUT A LITTLE CINEMA VERITÉ DAZZLE WILL--
NO WAY!
Uh, YOU FOLKS WORK THIS OUT, AND... NANCY, I'LL SEE YOU AFTER MY COMICS WORKSHOP!

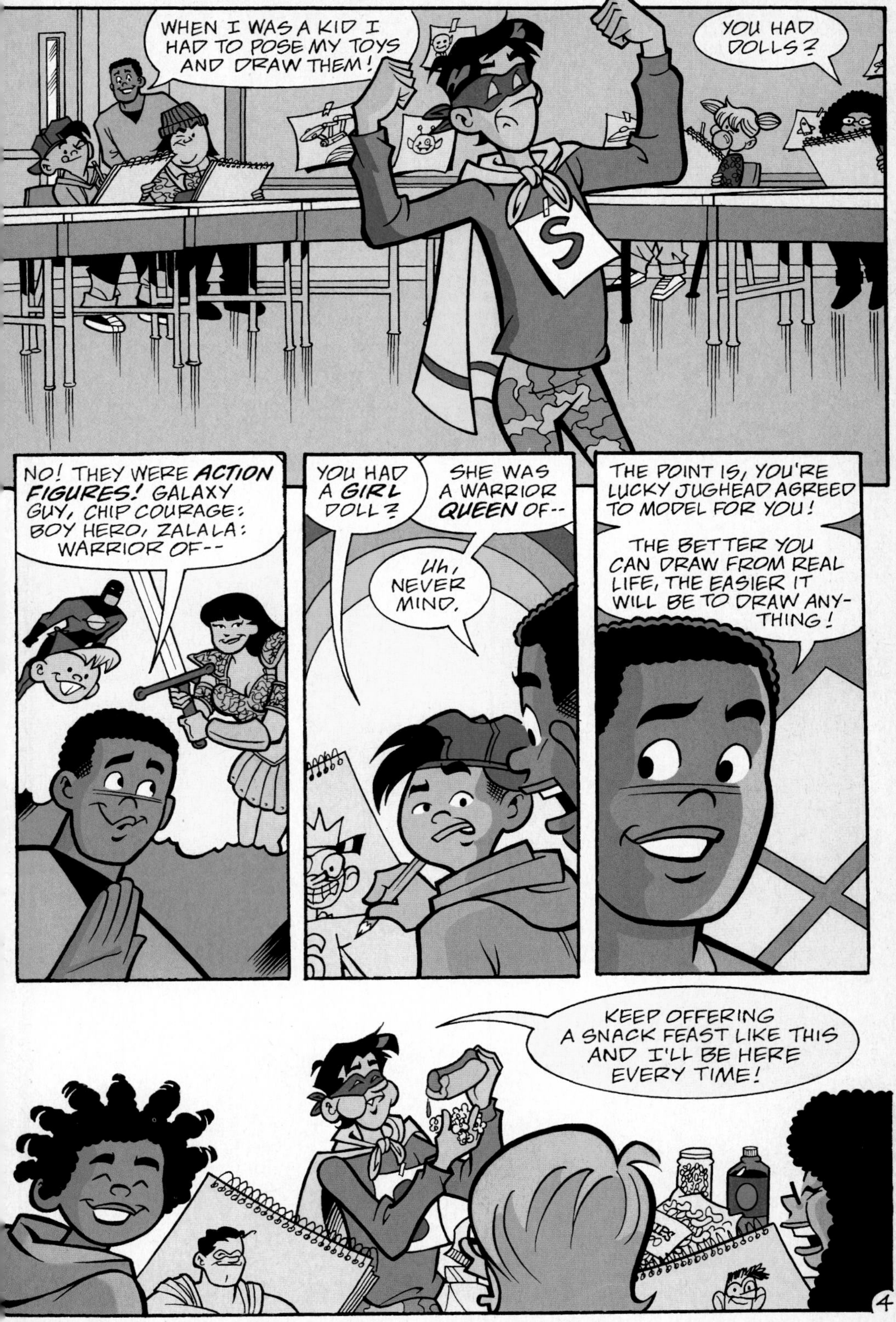
WHEN I WAS A KID I HAD TO POSE MY TOYS AND DRAW THEM!
YOU HAD DOLLS?
NO! THEY WERE **ACTION FIGURES!** GALAXY GUY, CHIP COURAGE: BOY HERO, ZALALA: WARRIOR OF--
YOU HAD A **GIRL** DOLL?
SHE WAS A WARRIOR **QUEEN** OF--
UH, NEVER MIND.
THE POINT IS, YOU'RE LUCKY JUGHEAD AGREED TO MODEL FOR YOU!
THE BETTER YOU CAN DRAW FROM REAL LIFE, THE EASIER IT WILL BE TO DRAW ANYTHING!
KEEP OFFERING A SNACK FEAST LIKE THIS AND I'LL BE HERE EVERY TIME!
4

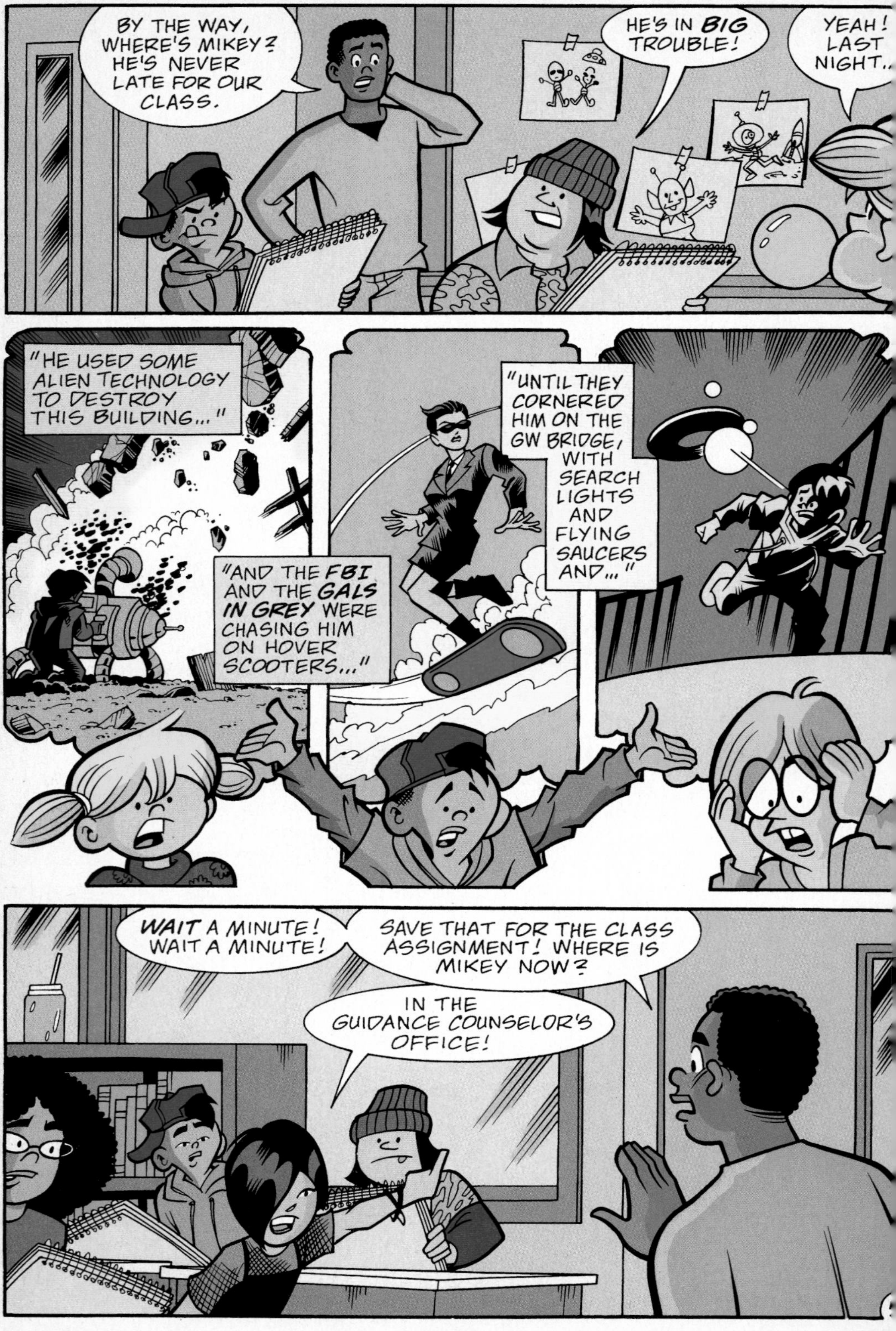
BY THE WAY, WHERE'S MIKEY? HE'S NEVER LATE FOR OUR CLASS.
HE'S IN BIG TROUBLE!
YEAH! LAST NIGHT...
"HE USED SOME ALIEN TECHNOLOGY TO DESTROY THIS BUILDING..."
"AND THE FBI AND THE GALS IN GREY WERE CHASING HIM ON HOVER SCOOTERS..."
"UNTIL THEY CORNERED HIM ON THE GW BRIDGE, WITH SEARCH LIGHTS AND FLYING SAUCERS AND..."
WAIT A MINUTE! WAIT A MINUTE!
SAVE THAT FOR THE CLASS ASSIGNMENT! WHERE IS MIKEY NOW?
IN THE GUIDANCE COUNSELOR'S OFFICE!

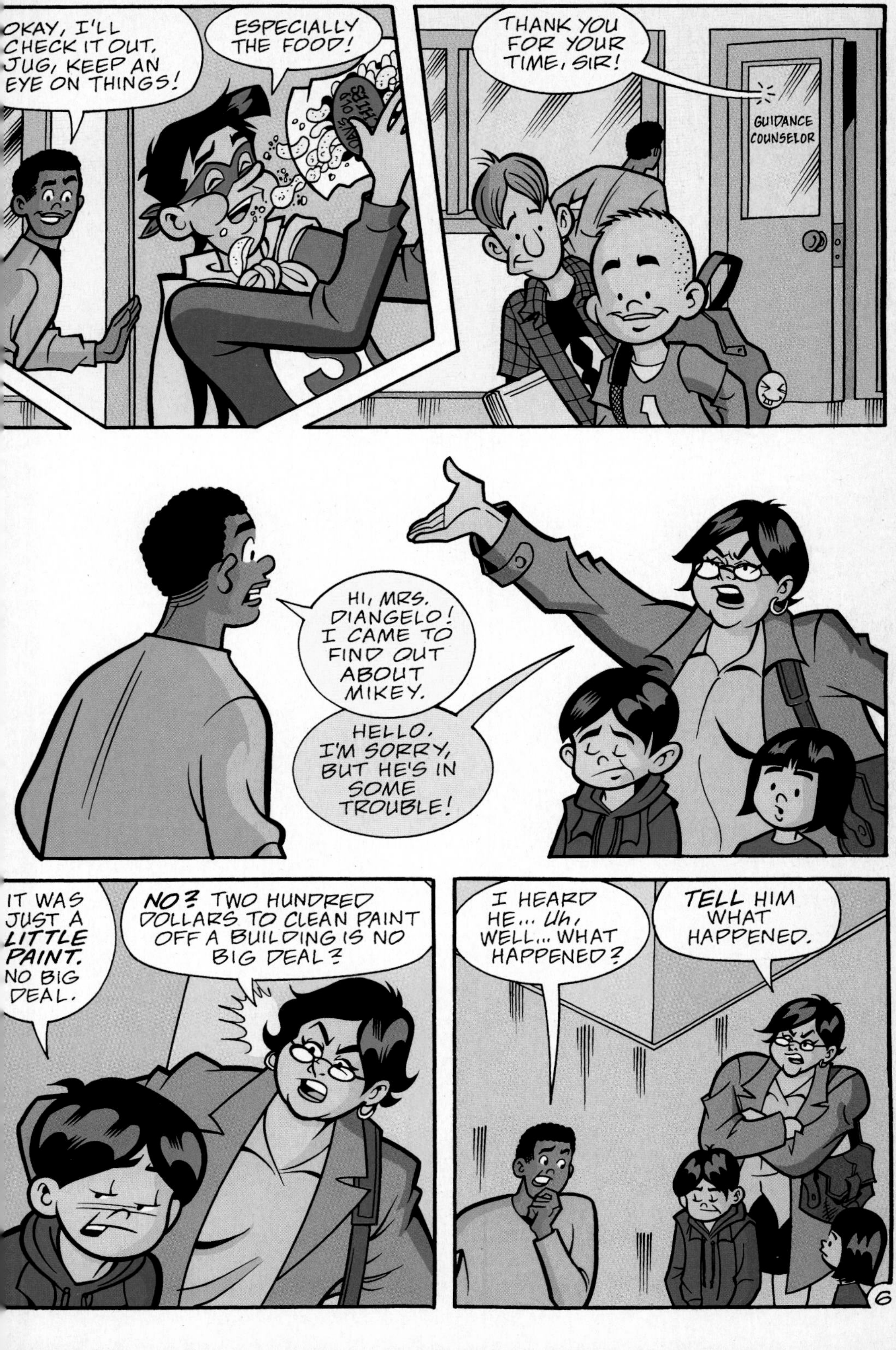
OKAY, I'LL CHECK IT OUT. JUG, KEEP AN EYE ON THINGS!
ESPECIALLY THE FOOD!
THANK YOU FOR YOUR TIME, SIR!
GUIDANCE COUNSELOR
HI, MRS. DIANGELO! I CAME TO FIND OUT ABOUT MIKEY.
HELLO. I'M SORRY, BUT HE'S IN SOME TROUBLE!
IT WAS JUST A LITTLE PAINT. NO BIG DEAL.
NO? TWO HUNDRED DOLLARS TO CLEAN PAINT OFF A BUILDING IS NO BIG DEAL?
I HEARD HE... Uh, WELL... WHAT HAPPENED?
TELL HIM WHAT HAPPENED.
6

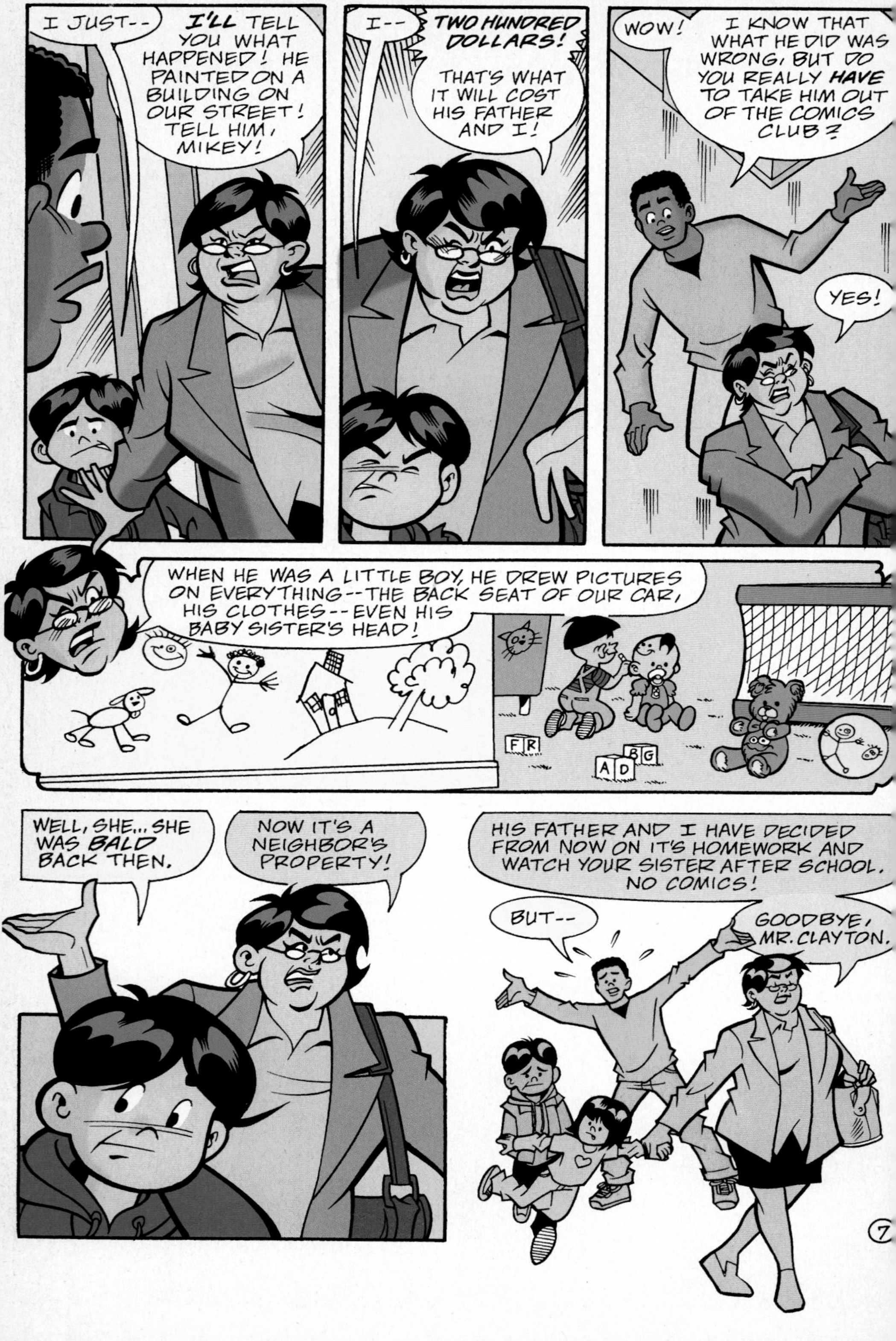
I JUST--
I'LL TELL YOU WHAT HAPPENED! HE PAINTED ON A BUILDING ON OUR STREET! TELL HIM, MIKEY!
I--
TWO HUNDRED DOLLARS!
THAT'S WHAT IT WILL COST HIS FATHER AND I!
WOW!
I KNOW THAT WHAT HE DID WAS WRONG, BUT DO YOU REALLY HAVE TO TAKE HIM OUT OF THE COMICS CLUB?
YES!
WHEN HE WAS A LITTLE BOY, HE DREW PICTURES ON EVERYTHING--THE BACK SEAT OF OUR CAR, HIS CLOTHES--EVEN HIS BABY SISTER'S HEAD!
F R
A D
B G
WELL, SHE...SHE WAS BALD BACK THEN.
NOW IT'S A NEIGHBOR'S PROPERTY!
HIS FATHER AND I HAVE DECIDED FROM NOW ON IT'S HOMEWORK AND WATCH YOUR SISTER AFTER SCHOOL. NO COMICS!
BUT--
GOODBYE, MR. CLAYTON.
7

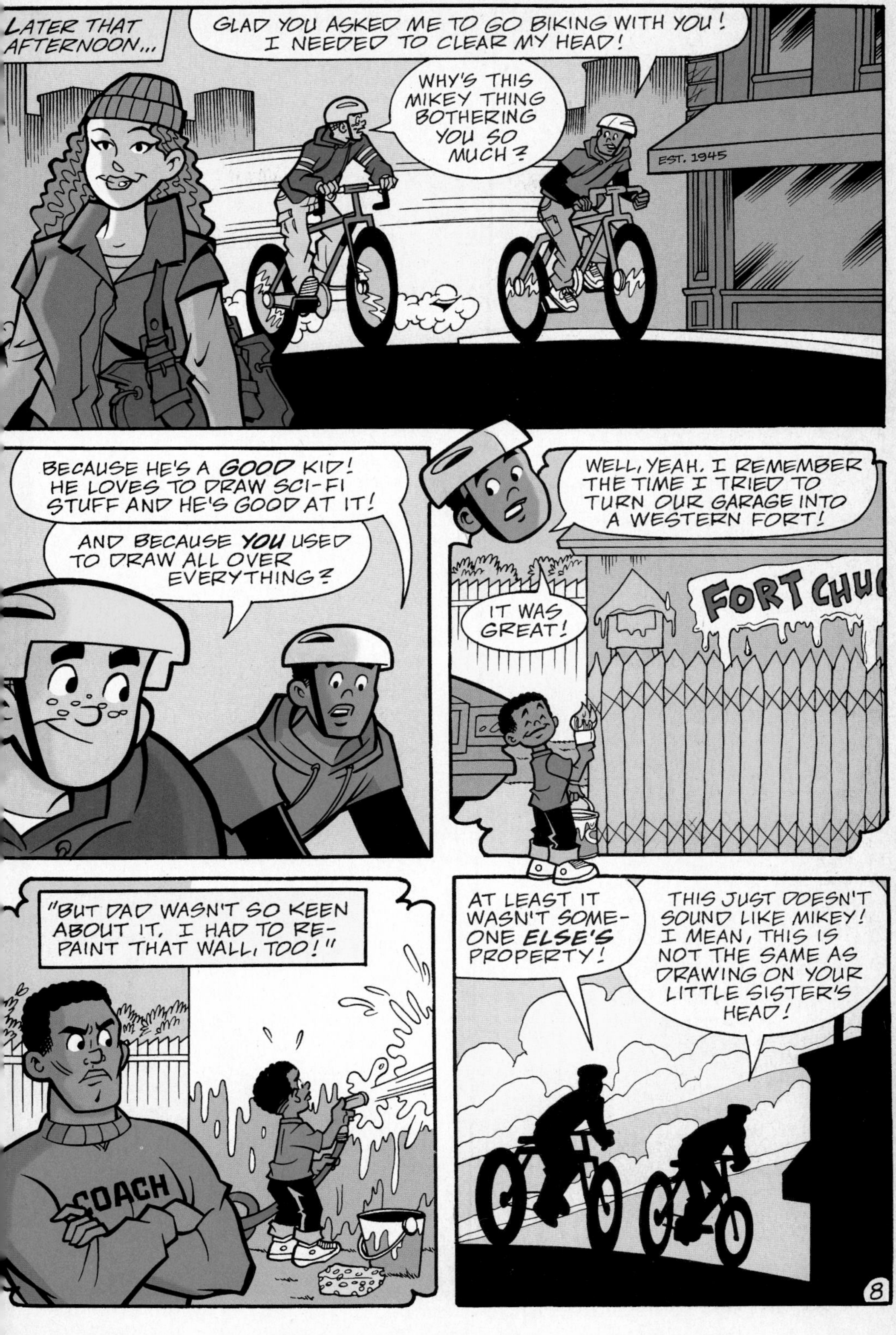
LATER THAT AFTERNOON...
GLAD YOU ASKED ME TO GO BIKING WITH YOU! I NEEDED TO CLEAR MY HEAD!
WHY'S THIS MIKEY THING BOTHERING YOU SO MUCH?
EST. 1945
BECAUSE HE'S A ***GOOD*** KID! HE LOVES TO DRAW SCI-FI STUFF AND HE'S GOOD AT IT!
AND BECAUSE ***YOU*** USED TO DRAW ALL OVER EVERYTHING?
WELL, YEAH. I REMEMBER THE TIME I TRIED TO TURN OUR GARAGE INTO A WESTERN FORT!
IT WAS GREAT!
FORT CHUC
"BUT DAD WASN'T SO KEEN ABOUT IT. I HAD TO RE-PAINT THAT WALL, TOO!"
COACH
AT LEAST IT WASN'T SOME-ONE ***ELSE'S*** PROPERTY!
THIS JUST DOESN'T SOUND LIKE MIKEY! I MEAN, THIS IS NOT THE SAME AS DRAWING ON YOUR LITTLE SISTER'S HEAD!
8

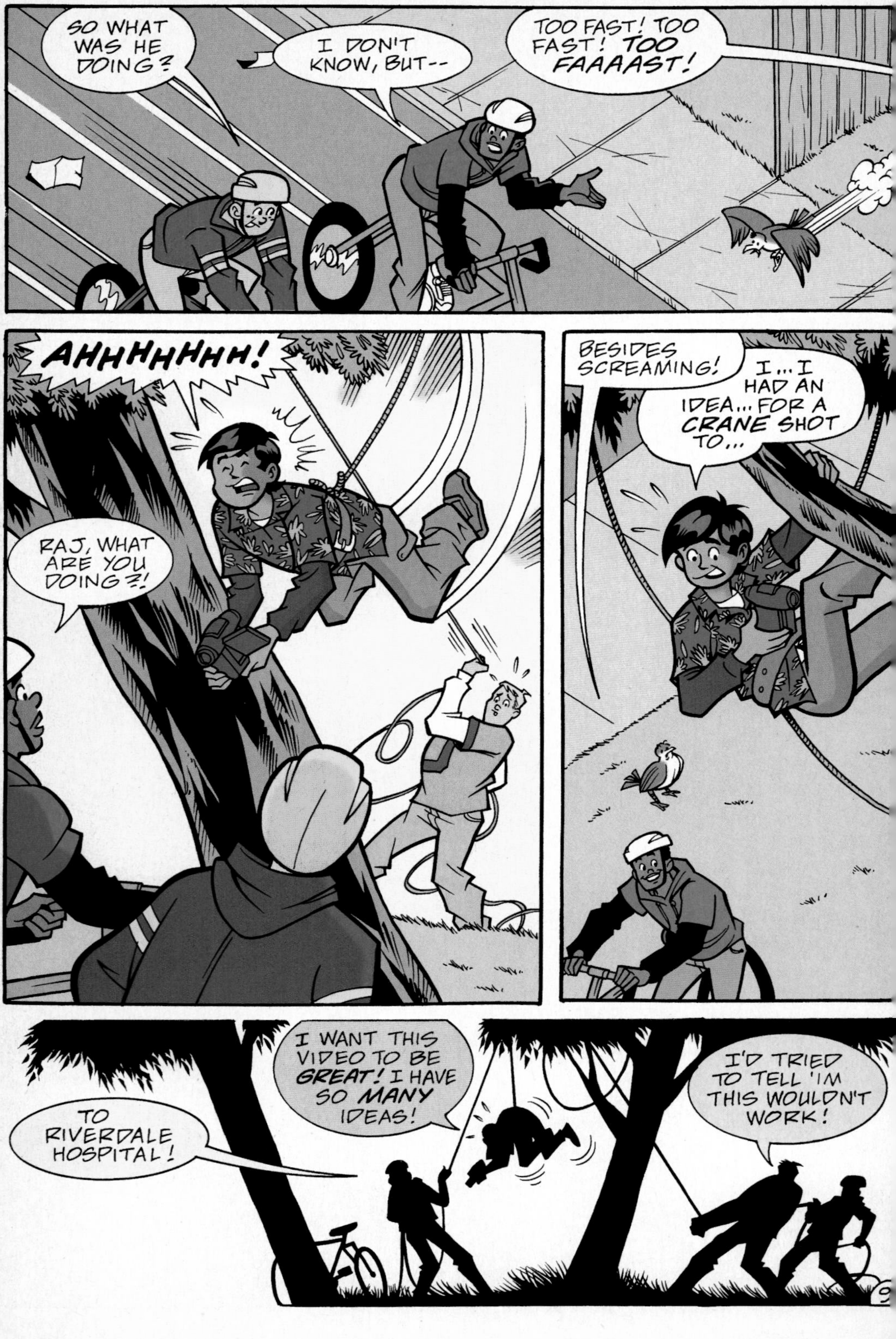
SO WHAT WAS HE DOING?
I DON'T KNOW, BUT--
TOO FAST! TOO FAST! TOO FAAAAST!
AHHHHHHHH!
RAJ, WHAT ARE YOU DOING?!
BESIDES SCREAMING!
I... I HAD AN IDEA... FOR A CRANE SHOT TO...
TO RIVERDALE HOSPITAL!
I WANT THIS VIDEO TO BE GREAT! I HAVE SO MANY IDEAS!
I'D TRIED TO TELL 'IM THIS WOULDN'T WORK!

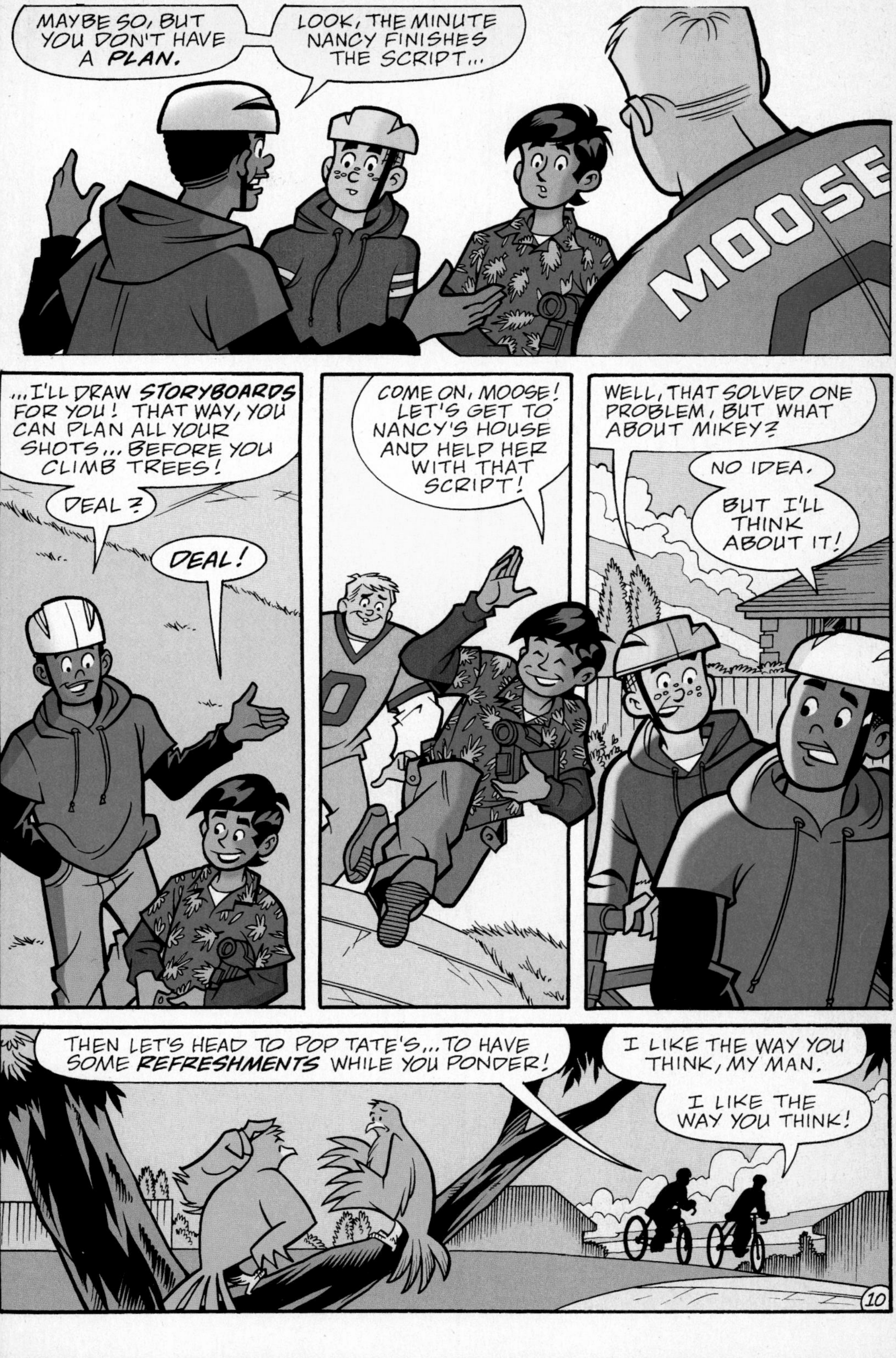
MAYBE SO, BUT YOU DON'T HAVE A PLAN.
LOOK, THE MINUTE NANCY FINISHES THE SCRIPT...
MOOSE
...I'LL DRAW STORYBOARDS FOR YOU! THAT WAY, YOU CAN PLAN ALL YOUR SHOTS... BEFORE YOU CLIMB TREES!
DEAL?
DEAL!
COME ON, MOOSE! LET'S GET TO NANCY'S HOUSE AND HELP HER WITH THAT SCRIPT!
WELL, THAT SOLVED ONE PROBLEM, BUT WHAT ABOUT MIKEY?
NO IDEA.
BUT I'LL THINK ABOUT IT!
THEN LET'S HEAD TO POP TATE'S... TO HAVE SOME REFRESHMENTS WHILE YOU PONDER!
I LIKE THE WAY YOU THINK, MY MAN.
I LIKE THE WAY YOU THINK!
10

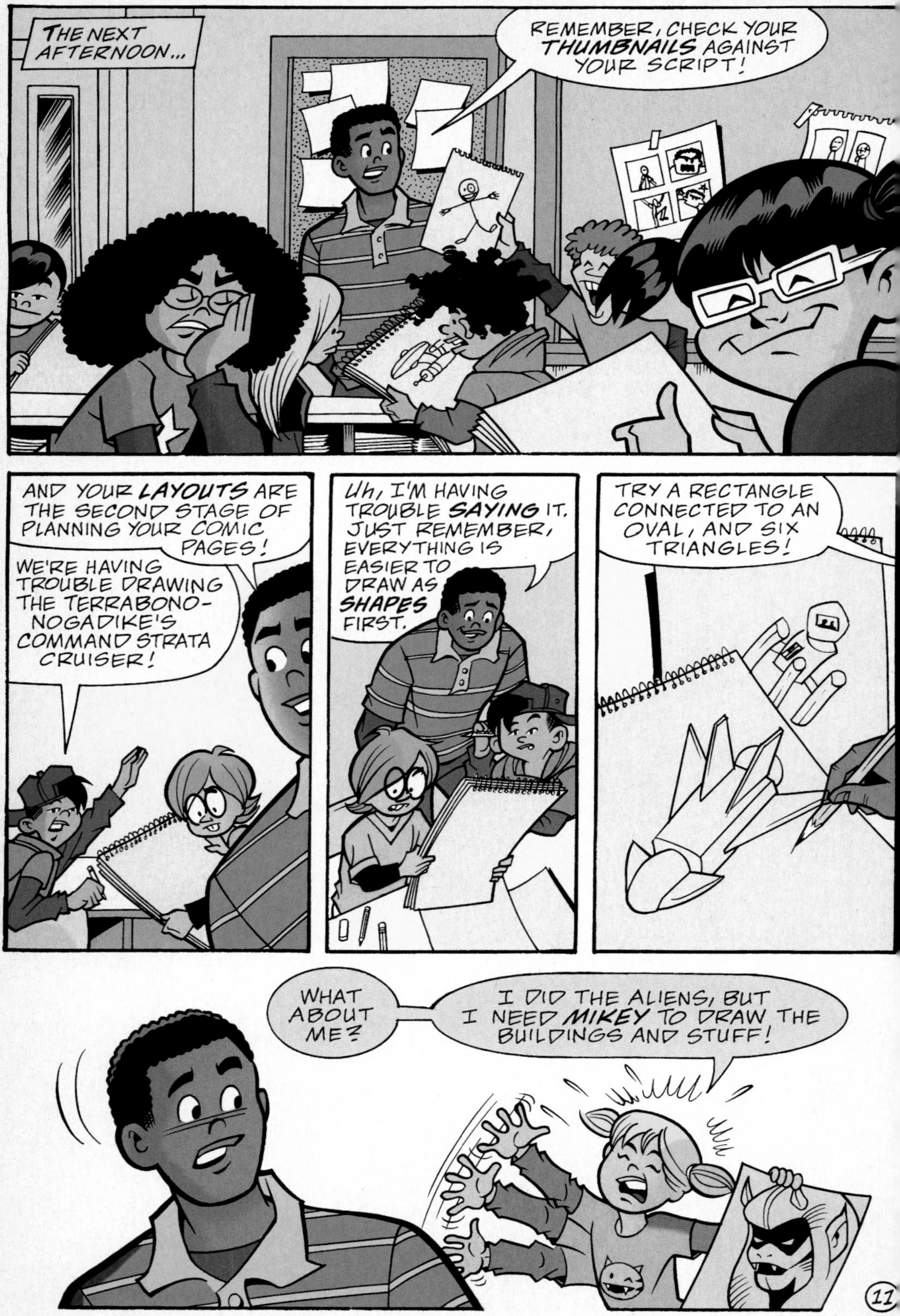
THE NEXT AFTERNOON...
REMEMBER, CHECK YOUR THUMBNAILS AGAINST YOUR SCRIPT!
AND YOUR LAYOUTS ARE THE SECOND STAGE OF PLANNING YOUR COMIC PAGES!
WE'RE HAVING TROUBLE DRAWING THE TERRABONO-NOGADIKE'S COMMAND STRATA CRUISER!
Uh, I'M HAVING TROUBLE SAYING IT. JUST REMEMBER, EVERYTHING IS EASIER TO DRAW AS SHAPES FIRST.
TRY A RECTANGLE CONNECTED TO AN OVAL, AND SIX TRIANGLES!
WHAT ABOUT ME?
I DID THE ALIENS, BUT I NEED MIKEY TO DRAW THE BUILDINGS AND STUFF!
11

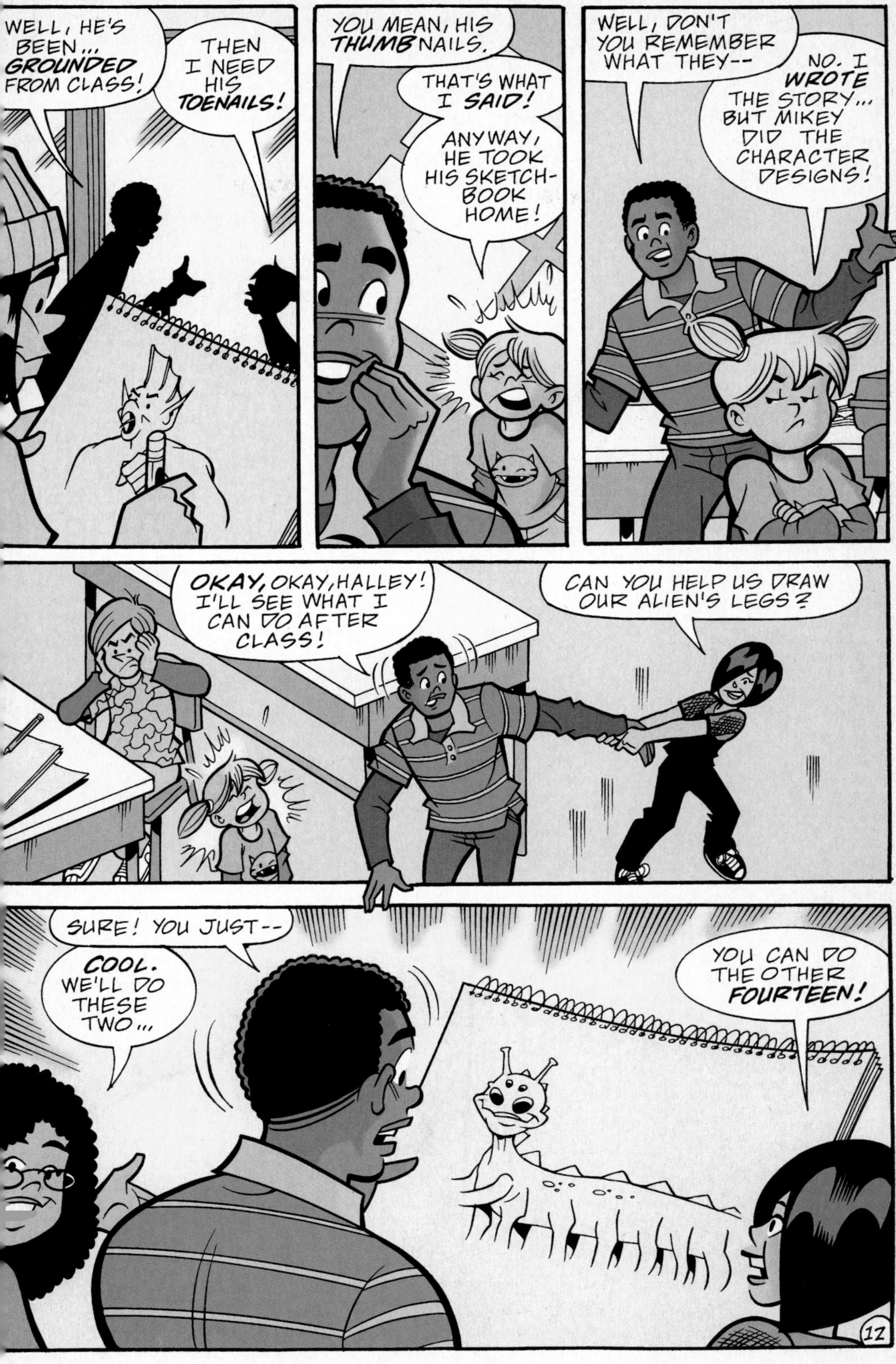
WELL, HE'S BEEN... GROUNDED FROM CLASS!
THEN I NEED HIS TOENAILS!
YOU MEAN, HIS THUMBNAILS.
THAT'S WHAT I SAID!
ANYWAY, HE TOOK HIS SKETCH-BOOK HOME!
WELL, DON'T YOU REMEMBER WHAT THEY--
NO. I WROTE THE STORY... BUT MIKEY DID THE CHARACTER DESIGNS!
OKAY, OKAY, HALLEY! I'LL SEE WHAT I CAN DO AFTER CLASS!
CAN YOU HELP US DRAW OUR ALIEN'S LEGS?
SURE! YOU JUST--
COOL. WE'LL DO THESE TWO...
YOU CAN DO THE OTHER FOURTEEN!
12

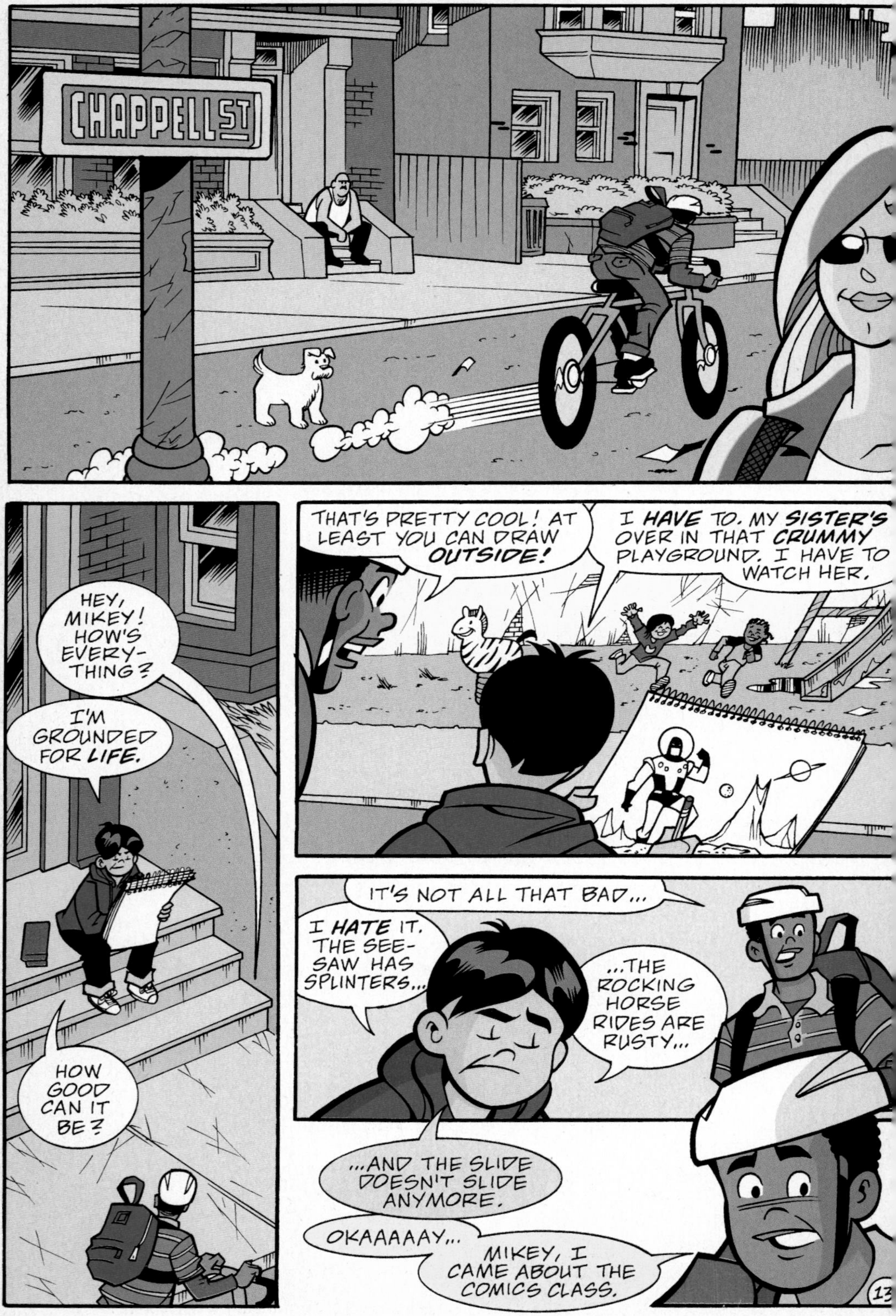
CHAPPELL ST
HEY, MIKEY! HOW'S EVERYTHING?
I'M GROUNDED FOR LIFE.
HOW GOOD CAN IT BE?
THAT'S PRETTY COOL! AT LEAST YOU CAN DRAW OUTSIDE!
I HAVE TO. MY SISTER'S OVER IN THAT CRUMMY PLAYGROUND. I HAVE TO WATCH HER.
IT'S NOT ALL THAT BAD...
I HATE IT. THE SEE-SAW HAS SPLINTERS...
...THE ROCKING HORSE RIDES ARE RUSTY...
...AND THE SLIDE DOESN'T SLIDE ANYMORE.
OKAAAAAY...
MIKEY, I CAME ABOUT THE COMICS CLASS.
13

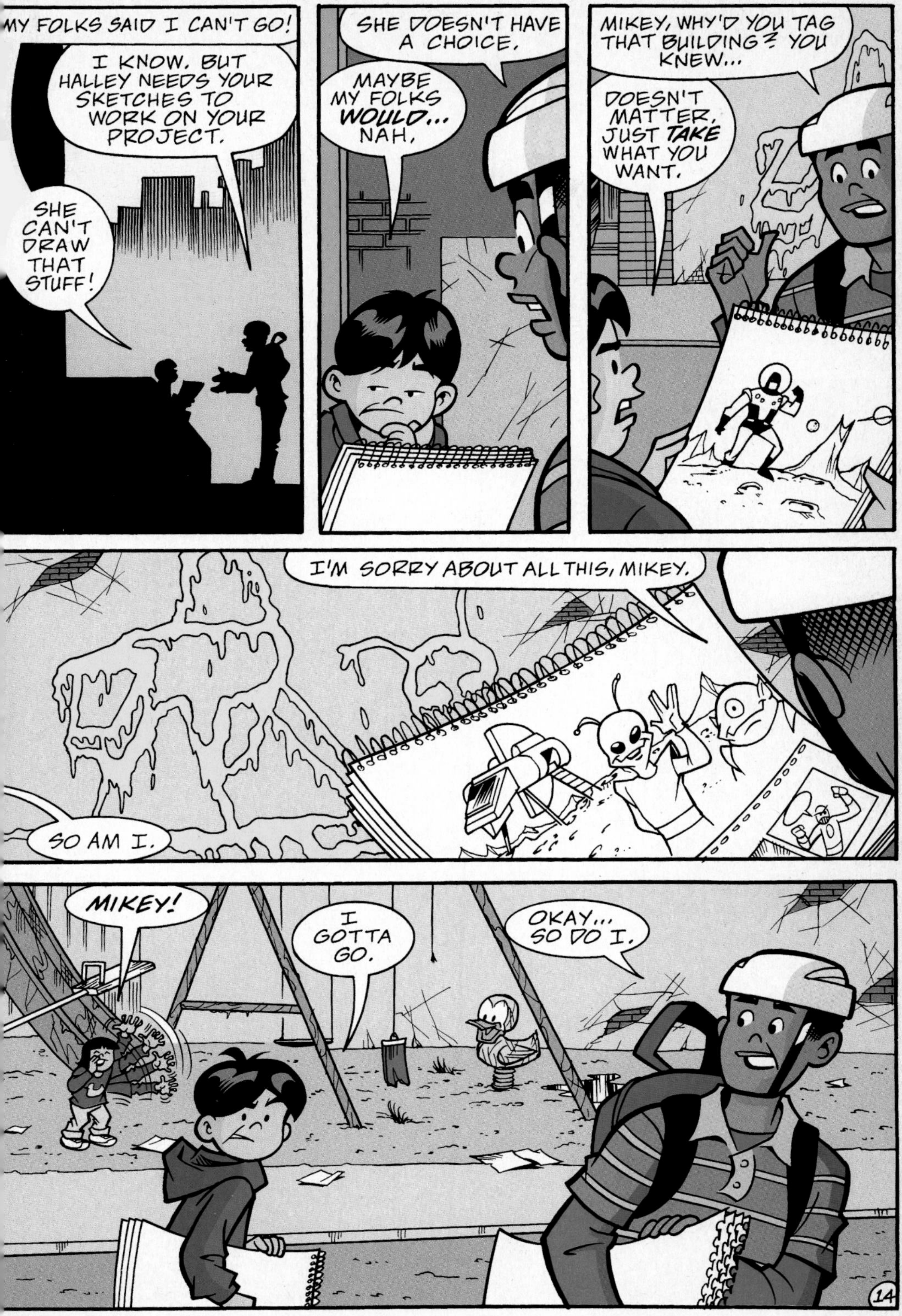
MY FOLKS SAID I CAN'T GO!
I KNOW. BUT HALLEY NEEDS YOUR SKETCHES TO WORK ON YOUR PROJECT.
SHE CAN'T DRAW THAT STUFF!
SHE DOESN'T HAVE A CHOICE.
MAYBE MY FOLKS **WOULD...** NAH.
MIKEY, WHY'D YOU TAG THAT BUILDING? YOU KNEW...
DOESN'T MATTER. JUST **TAKE** WHAT YOU WANT.
I'M SORRY ABOUT ALL THIS, MIKEY.
SO AM I.
MIKEY!
I GOTTA GO.
OKAY... SO DO I.
14

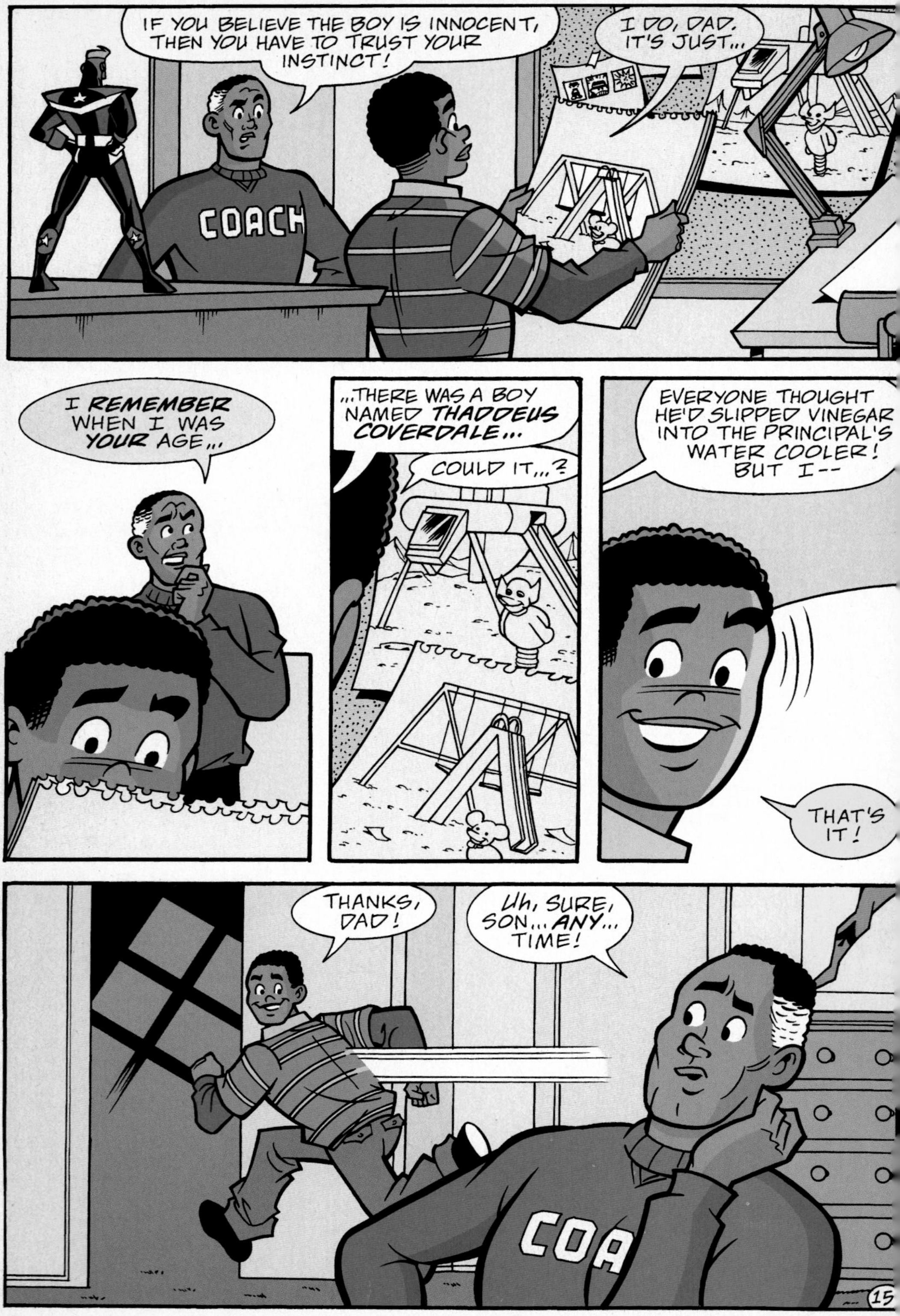
IF YOU BELIEVE THE BOY IS INNOCENT, THEN YOU HAVE TO TRUST YOUR INSTINCT!
I DO, DAD. IT'S JUST...
COACH
I REMEMBER WHEN I WAS YOUR AGE...
...THERE WAS A BOY NAMED THADDEUS COVERDALE...
COULD IT...?
EVERYONE THOUGHT HE'D SLIPPED VINEGAR INTO THE PRINCIPAL'S WATER COOLER! BUT I--
THAT'S IT!
THANKS, DAD!
Uh, SURE, SON... ANY... TIME!
COA
15

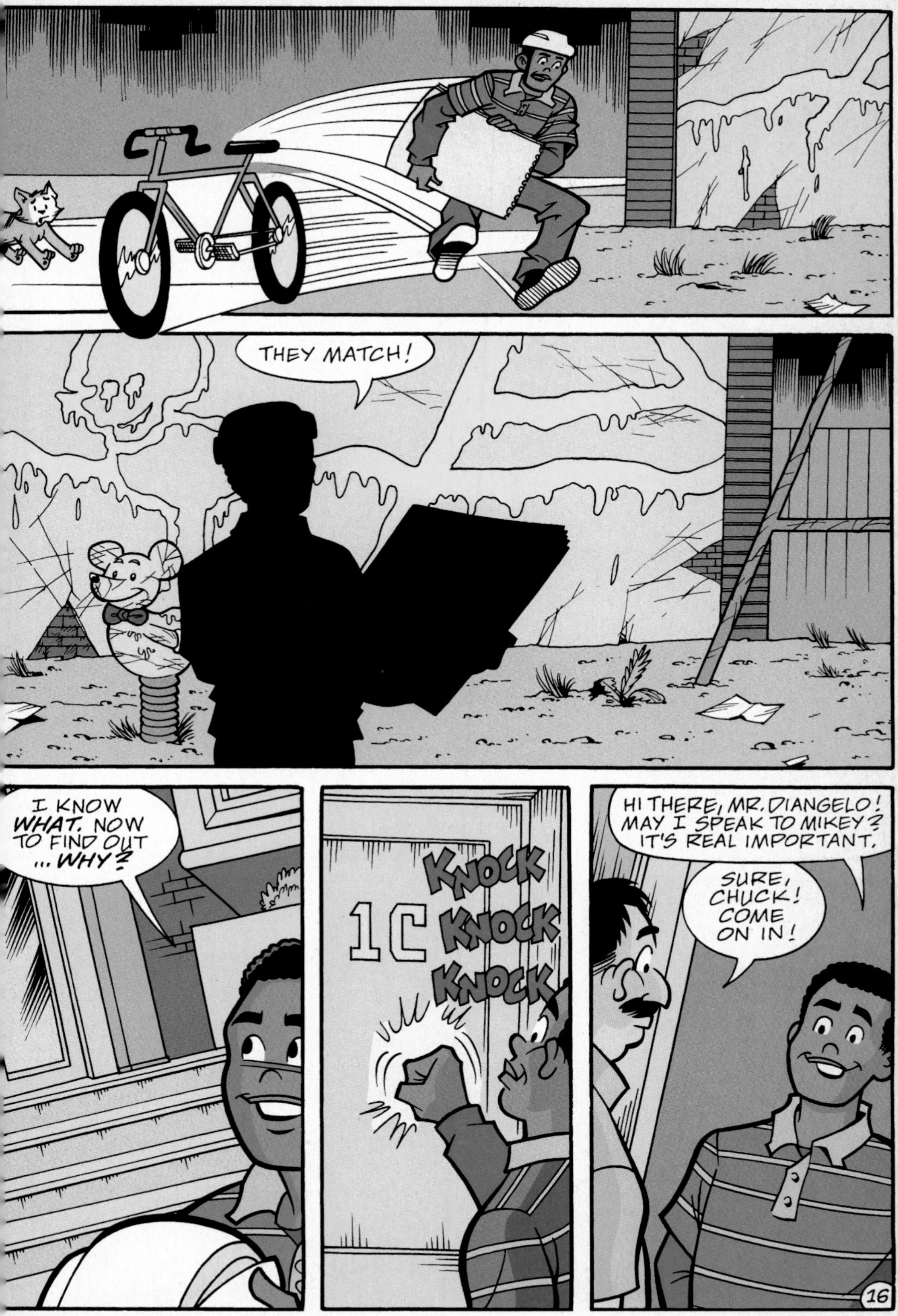
THEY MATCH!
I KNOW WHAT. NOW TO FIND OUT ...WHY?
1C
KNOCK KNOCK KNOCK
HI THERE, MR. DIANGELO! MAY I SPEAK TO MIKEY? IT'S REAL IMPORTANT.
SURE, CHUCK! COME ON IN!
16

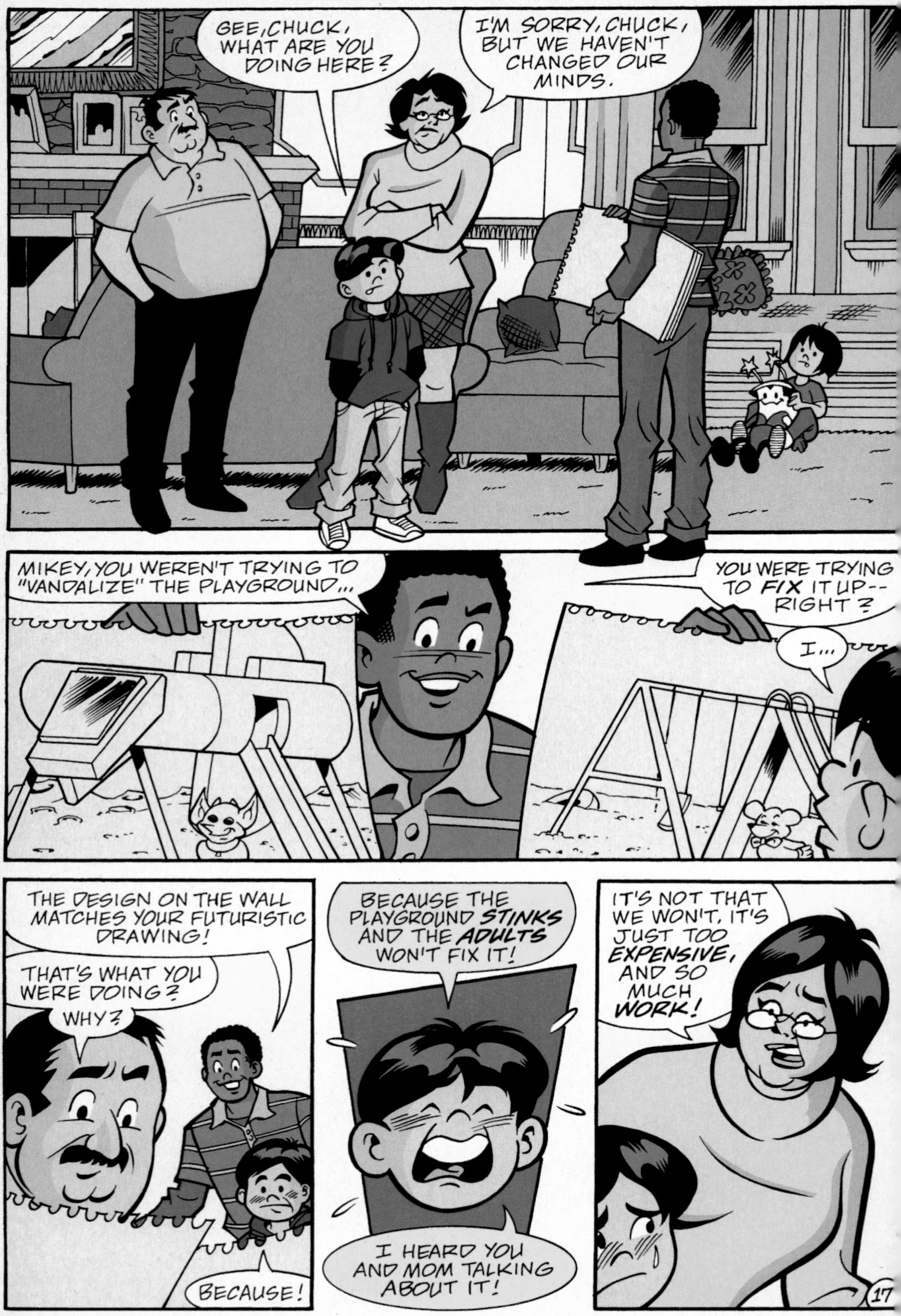
GEE, CHUCK, WHAT ARE YOU DOING HERE?
I'M SORRY, CHUCK, BUT WE HAVEN'T CHANGED OUR MINDS.
MIKEY, YOU WEREN'T TRYING TO "VANDALIZE" THE PLAYGROUND...
YOU WERE TRYING TO FIX IT UP-- RIGHT?
I...
THE DESIGN ON THE WALL MATCHES YOUR FUTURISTIC DRAWING!
THAT'S WHAT YOU WERE DOING?
WHY?
BECAUSE!
BECAUSE THE PLAYGROUND STINKS AND THE ADULTS WON'T FIX IT!
I HEARD YOU AND MOM TALKING ABOUT IT!
IT'S NOT THAT WE WON'T, IT'S JUST TOO EXPENSIVE, AND SO MUCH WORK!
17

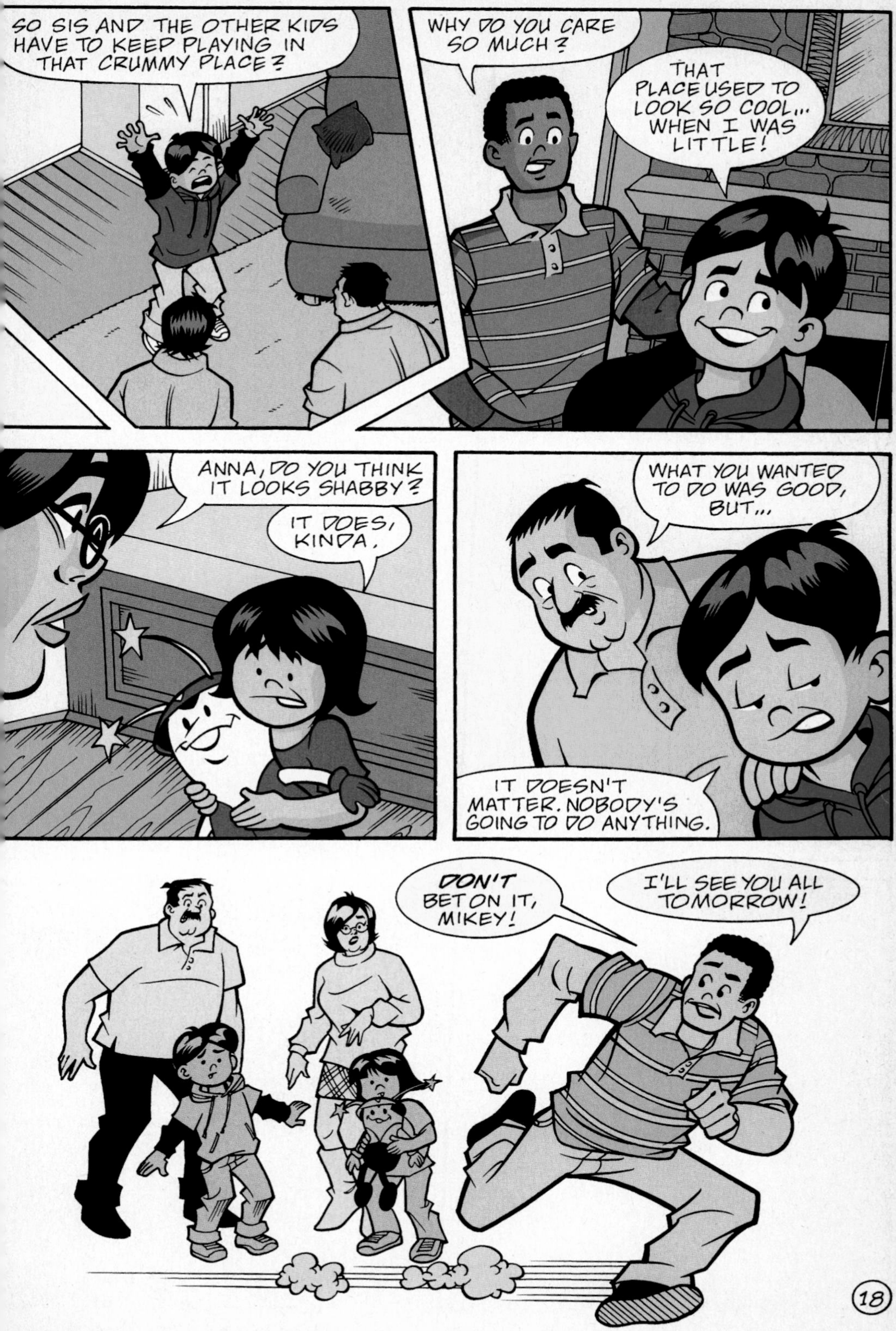
SO SIS AND THE OTHER KIDS HAVE TO KEEP PLAYING IN THAT CRUMMY PLACE?
WHY DO YOU CARE SO MUCH?
THAT PLACE USED TO LOOK SO COOL... WHEN I WAS LITTLE!
ANNA, DO YOU THINK IT LOOKS SHABBY?
IT DOES, KINDA.
WHAT YOU WANTED TO DO WAS GOOD, BUT...
IT DOESN'T MATTER. NOBODY'S GOING TO DO ANYTHING.
DON'T BET ON IT, MIKEY!
I'LL SEE YOU ALL TOMORROW!

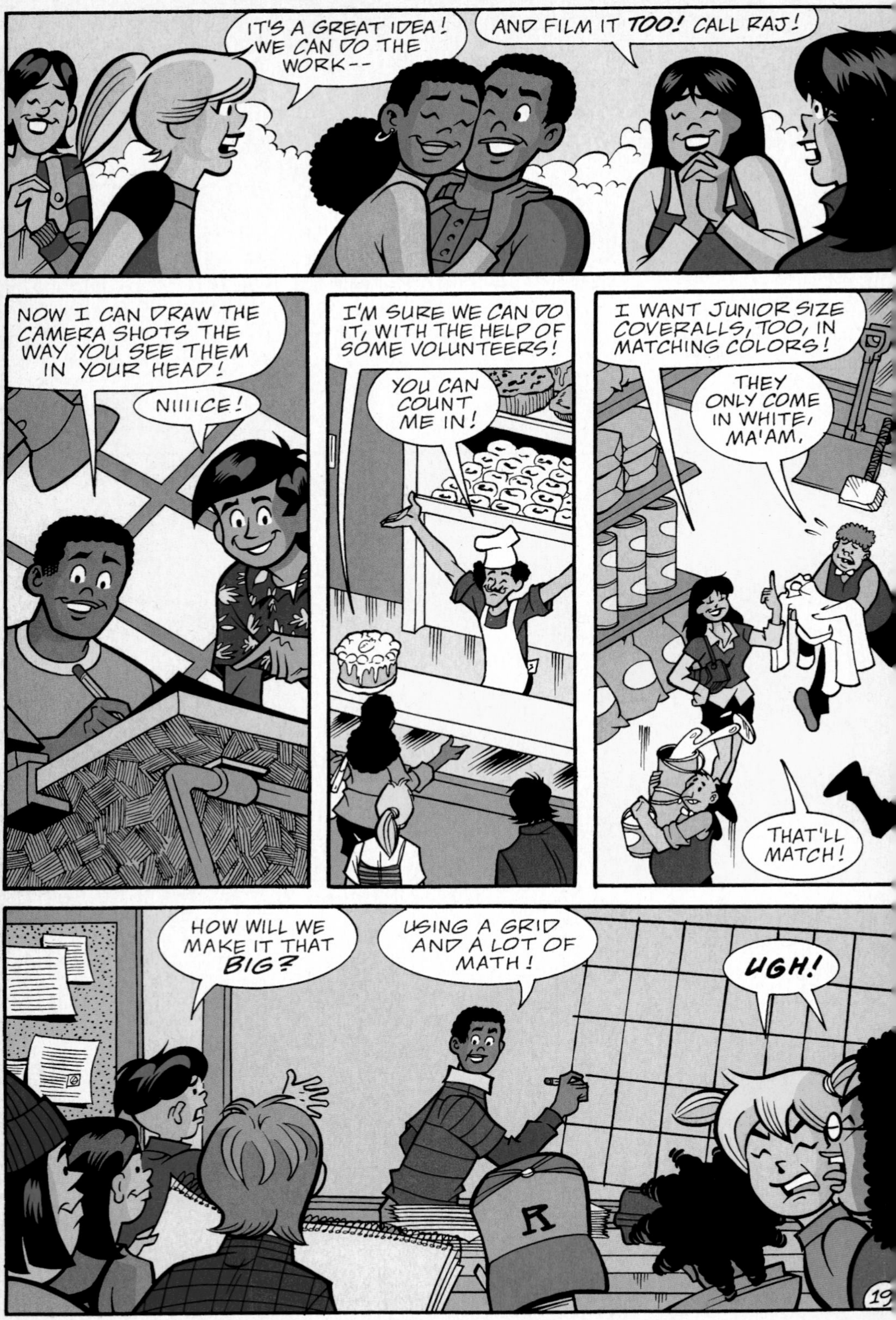
IT'S A GREAT IDEA! WE CAN DO THE WORK--
AND FILM IT TOO! CALL RAJ!
NOW I CAN DRAW THE CAMERA SHOTS THE WAY YOU SEE THEM IN YOUR HEAD!
NIIIICE!
I'M SURE WE CAN DO IT, WITH THE HELP OF SOME VOLUNTEERS!
YOU CAN COUNT ME IN!
I WANT JUNIOR SIZE COVERALLS, TOO, IN MATCHING COLORS!
THEY ONLY COME IN WHITE, MA'AM.
THAT'LL MATCH!
HOW WILL WE MAKE IT THAT BIG?
USING A GRID AND A LOT OF MATH!
UGH!

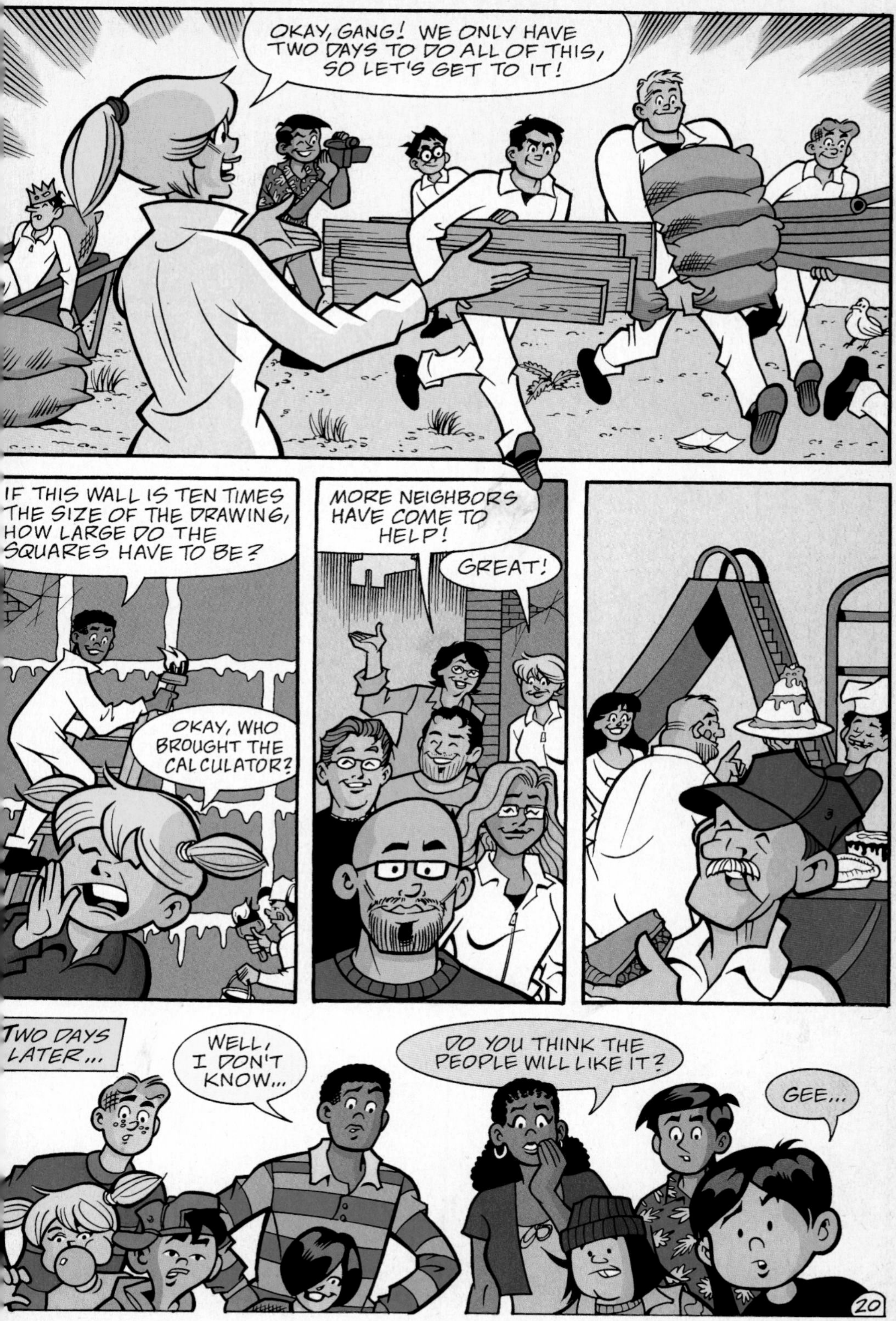
OKAY, GANG! WE ONLY HAVE TWO DAYS TO DO ALL OF THIS, SO LET'S GET TO IT!
IF THIS WALL IS TEN TIMES THE SIZE OF THE DRAWING, HOW LARGE DO THE SQUARES HAVE TO BE?
OKAY, WHO BROUGHT THE CALCULATOR?
MORE NEIGHBORS HAVE COME TO HELP!
GREAT!
TWO DAYS LATER...
WELL, I DON'T KNOW...
DO YOU THINK THE PEOPLE WILL LIKE IT?
GEE...
20

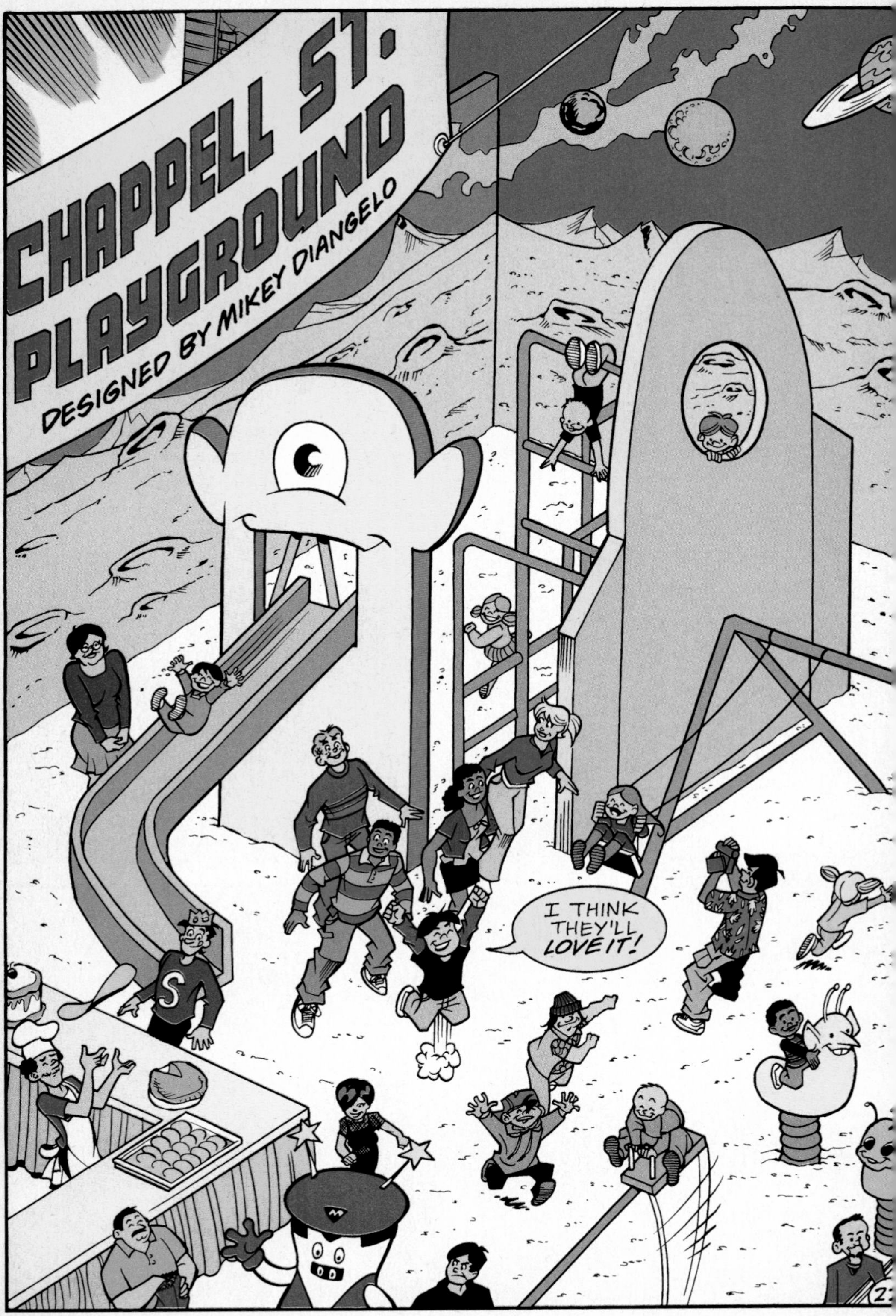
CHAPPELL ST. PLAYGROUND
DESIGNED BY MIKEY DIANGELO
I THINK THEY'LL LOVE IT!

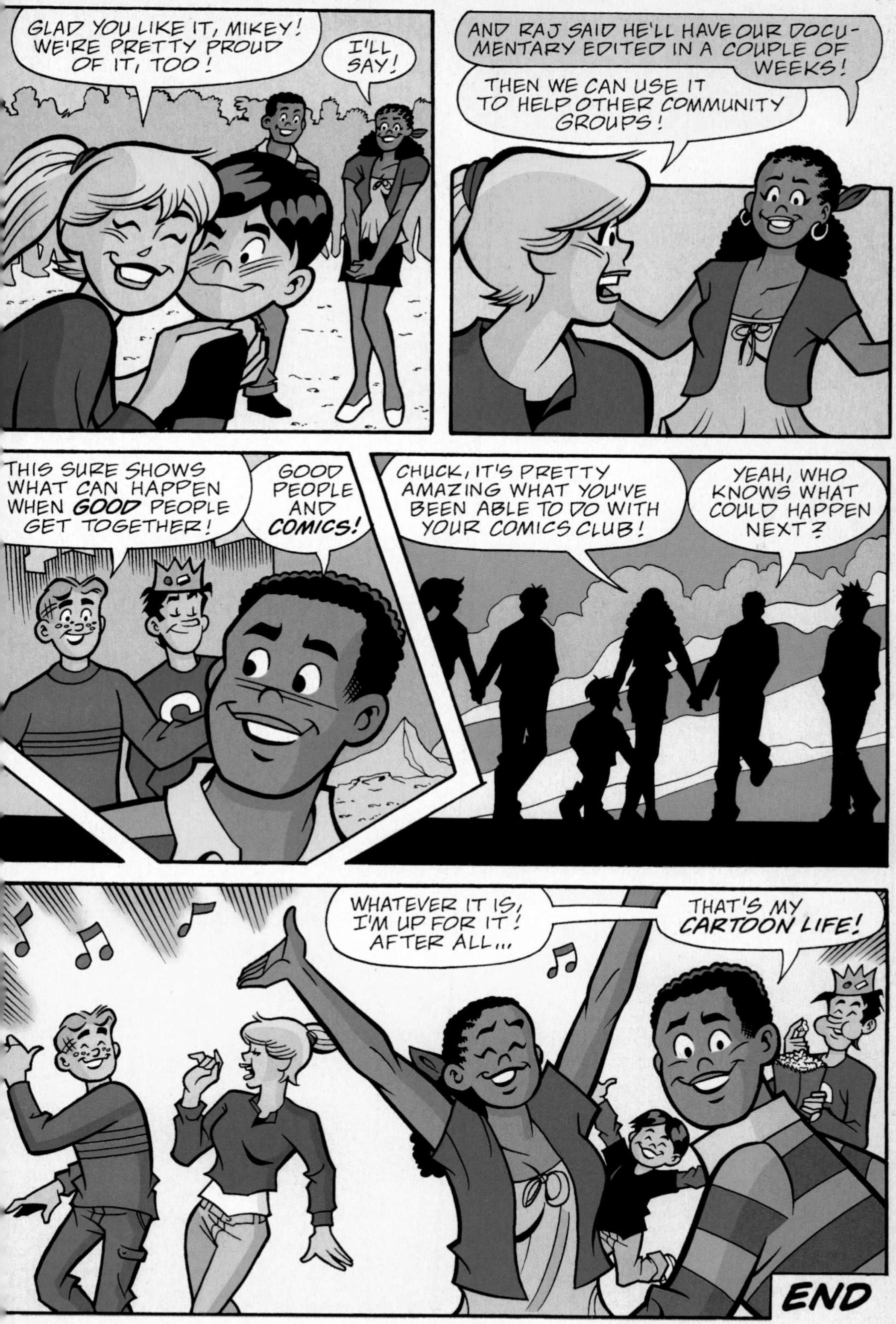
GLAD YOU LIKE IT, MIKEY! WE'RE PRETTY PROUD OF IT, TOO!
I'LL SAY!
AND RAJ SAID HE'LL HAVE OUR DOCU-MENTARY EDITED IN A COUPLE OF WEEKS!
THEN WE CAN USE IT TO HELP OTHER COMMUNITY GROUPS!
THIS SURE SHOWS WHAT CAN HAPPEN WHEN GOOD PEOPLE GET TOGETHER!
GOOD PEOPLE AND COMICS!
CHUCK, IT'S PRETTY AMAZING WHAT YOU'VE BEEN ABLE TO DO WITH YOUR COMICS CLUB!
YEAH, WHO KNOWS WHAT COULD HAPPEN NEXT?
WHATEVER IT IS, I'M UP FOR IT! AFTER ALL...
THAT'S MY CARTOON LIFE!
END

CHUCK CLAYTON'S CREATING COOL COMICS PART 1: TERMS

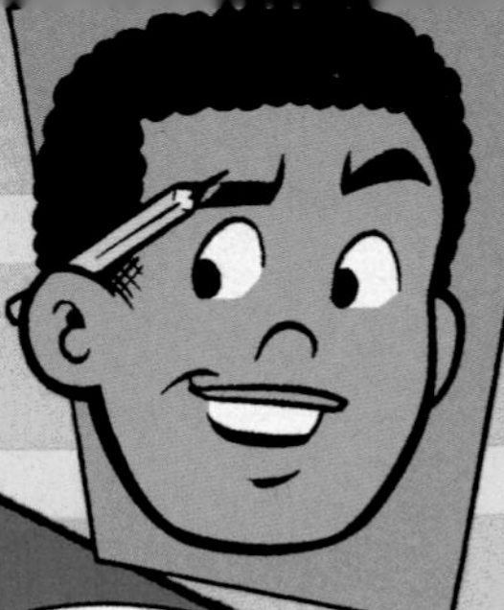

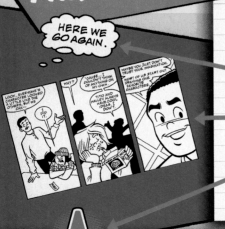

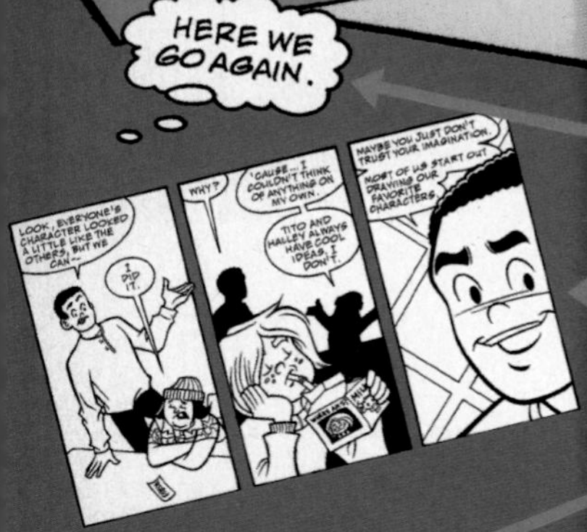
HERE WE GO AGAIN.
LOOK, EVERYONE'S CHARACTER LOOKED A LITTLE LIKE THE OTHERS, BUT WE CAN--
I DID IT.
WHY?
'CAUSE... I COULDN'T THINK OF ANYTHING ON MY OWN.
TITO AND HALLEY ALWAYS HAVE COOL IDEAS. I DON'T.
MAYBE YOU JUST DON'T TRUST YOUR IMAGINATION.
MOST OF US START OUT DRAWING OUR FAVORITE CHARACTERS.

TERMS OF THE TRADE

CAPTION BOXES
THOUGHT BUBBLES
SPEECH BALLOONS
COMIC BOOKS
COMIC STRIPS
PANELS
CHARACTERS
LOGOS
LAYOUTS
THUMBNAILS

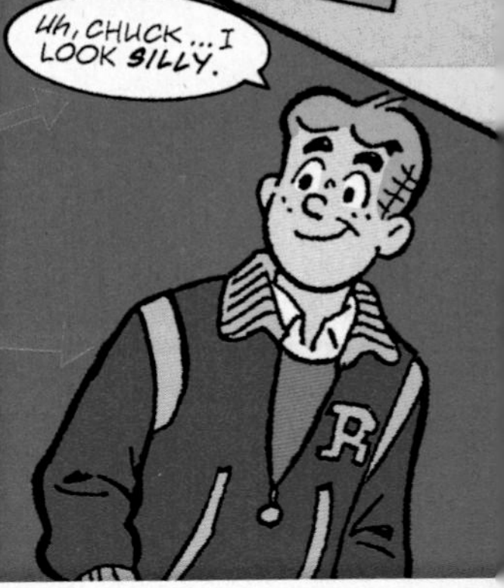
UH, CHUCK... I LOOK SILLY.

ARCHIECOMICS.COM

FIVE IMPORTANT PEOPLE IN COMICS

THE WRITER WRITES THE STORY.
THE PENCILER DRAWS THE WHOLE STORY WITH PENCILS.
THE INKER GOES OVER EVERY LINE THE PENCILER DREW WITH INK.
THE LETTERER PLACES ALL THE WORDS ON THE COMIC BOOK PAGES.
THE COLORIST COLORS THE PAGES.

OTHER IMPORTANT COMIC BOOK JOBS

GRAPHIC DESIGNERS, COVER ARTISTS, PRODUCTION STAFF, AND PRINTERS ALL HELP TO MAKE A COMIC BOOK GREAT!

ALL OF THESE PEOPLE ANSWER TO THE EDITOR, WHO MAKES SURE THAT EVERYTHING IS CORRECT.

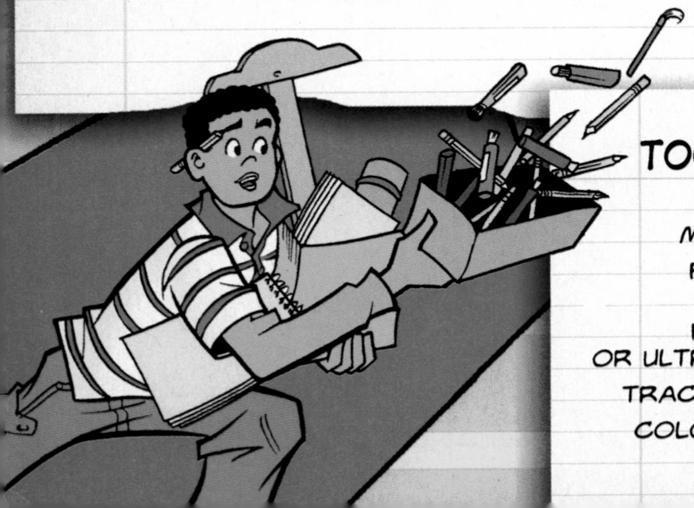

TOOLS OF THE TRADE

PENCILS, ERASERS,
MASKING TAPE, A RULER
PAPER (8 X 11 OR 11 X 17, WHITE, UNLINED)
INKING PENS: MICRONS, OR ULTRA SHARPIES FOR BEGINNERS
TRACING PAPER (GOOD QUALITY)
COLOR PENCILS AND MARKERS

CHUCK CLAYTON'S CREATING COOL COMICS PART 2: SCRIPT

1. LET'S MAKE A COMIC STRIP. A COMIC STRIP HAS 3-4 PANELS.

IMAGINE YOUR STORY AS IF IT WERE A MOVIE. WRITE DOWN:

WHERE DOES IT TAKE PLACE?
WHAT IS THE FIRST THING WE SEE?
WHAT STORY DO YOU TELL?
HOW MANY CHARACTERS ARE IN IT?
WHAT TIME OF DAY IS IT?

2. ONCE YOU HAVE THE STORY OR JOKE, WRITE IT DOWN PANEL BY PANEL LIKE THIS:

PANEL ONE
ACTION:

PANEL TWO
ACTION:

PANEL THREE
ACTION:

NEXT TO THE WORD "ACTION" WRITE DOWN WHAT HAPPENS IN EACH PANEL, LIKE THIS:

PANEL ONE
ACTION: *ARCHIE AND CHUCK ARE RIDING THEIR BIKES DOWN A MAIN STREET.*

3. THEN WRITE WHAT YOUR CHARACTERS ARE SAYING, LIKE THIS:

PANEL ONE
ACTION: *ARCHIE AND CHUCK ARE RIDING THEIR BIKES DOWN A MAIN STREET.*

ARCHIE: SO HOW IS THE COMIC BOOK CLASS GOING?
CHUCK: JUST GREAT, IF YOU DON'T COUNT THE FOOD FIGHT WE HAD AT SNACK TIME.

DO THIS FOR ALL OF YOUR PANELS.

4. WHAT DO YOUR FIRST AND LAST PANEL LOOK LIKE?

LIGHTLY SKETCH THESE TWO PANELS, OR WRITE A DESCRIPTION OF HOW YOU WOULD LIKE THEM TO LOOK.

THEN DO THE SAME THING FOR THE PANEL OR PANELS IN BETWEEN..

YOUR SCRIPT IS DONE!

THE TRICK IS TO USE A SMALL NUMBER OF WORDS AND ACTIONS TO SAY A LOT!

HAVE SOMEONE YOU REALLY TRUST READ YOUR SCRIPT. MAKE SURE THEY GET IT!

CHUCK CLAYTON'S CREATING COOL COMICS PART 3: THUMBNAILS

NOT EVEN CLOSE TO FUNNY.
JUST TELL MR. WEATHERBEE YOU CAN'T DO IT.
TELL THE BEE THAT HE WON'T BE ABLE
UNLESS...
PRIMATES
UNLESS WHAT?
WHAT?

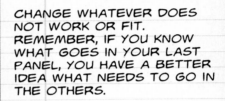

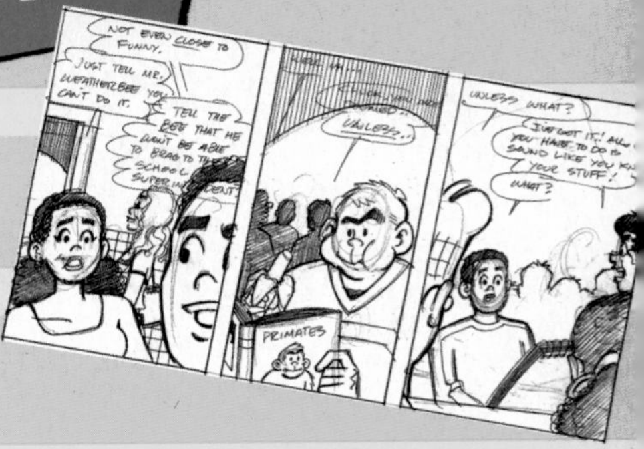

SOMETIMES IT IS EASIER FOR AN ARTIST TO MAKE THEIR STORY BY DRAWING IT A FEW TIMES BEFORE FINISHING IT. THERE ARE ALWAYS THINGS TO CHANGE OR IMPROVE WHEN YOU ARE WORKING OUT A STORY OR A JOKE. THAT'S WHY YOU SHOULD WRITE YOUR SCRIPT AND DO YOUR THUMBNAILS FIRST.

SO, CHECK YOUR SCRIPT AND THEN START SKETCHING OUT YOUR THUMBNAILS, ROUGHLY. IT DOESN'T HAVE TO BE PERFECT; IT IS ALMOST LIKE DOODLING. JUST LOOSELY DRAW THE PANEL LINES. THEN SKETCH IN THE CHARACTERS THE WAY YOU WANT THEM. MANY ARTISTS WILL DRAW CIRCLES OR STICK FIGURES. ONCE YOU HAVE LOOSELY SKETCHED OUT YOUR IDEA, WRITE DOWN THE DIALOGUE LOOSELY TOO.

CHANGE WHATEVER DOES NOT WORK OR FIT. REMEMBER, IF YOU KNOW WHAT GOES IN YOUR LAST PANEL, YOU HAVE A BETTER IDEA WHAT NEEDS TO GO IN THE OTHERS.

ONCE YOU ARE SATISFIED WITH YOUR THUMBNAIL SKETCHES, YOU ARE READY TO DRAW YOUR ACTUAL COMIC STRIP. YOU'LL NEED PENCILS, ERASERS, AND A RULER. OH YEAH, YOU'LL NEED FRESH PAPER TOO!

DRAW A RECTANGLE 2 X 9 INCHES, OR 5 X 18 INCHES. DIVIDE THE RECTANGLE INTO 3 OR 4 PANELS. USING A RULER AND A #2 PENCIL, DRAW IN YOUR PANELS.

NOW START PENCILING YOUR STORY. REMEMBER TO LEAVE ROOM FOR YOUR LETTERING!

BAM

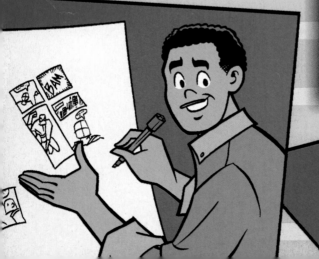

DAILY STRIPS **RUN MONDAY THROUGH SATURDAY.**

SUNDAY STRIPS **ONLY COME OUT ON SUNDAY. THEY ARE USUALLY IN COLOR AND HAVE PANELS.**

CHUCK CLAYTON'S CREATING COOL COMICS PART 4: INKING & LETTERING

WE'RE ALMOST FINISHED NOW, TEAM!

LETTERING

AFTER YOU HAVE FINISHED PENCILING YOUR COMIC STRIP ART, TAKE A PENCIL AND A RULER AND DRAW LIGHT GUIDE LINES WHERE YOU PLAN TO PLACE YOUR LETTERING. IT'S FINE IF YOUR NEW LETTERING GOES OUTSIDE OF THE ROUGH SPEECH BALLOONS.

NEXT, DO YOUR FINISHED LETTERING IN PENCIL ON THE GUIDELINES. ONCE YOU HAVE FINISHED AND YOU ARE SURE IT ALL FITS, DRAW THE BALLOON AROUND THE TEXT. FINALLY, DRAW YOUR POINTER FROM THE BALLOON TO THE CHARACTER SPEAKING.

CHECK YOUR WORK. MAKE SURE EVERYTHING IS SPACED NEATLY. YOUR COMIC STORY WILL ONLY BE GOOD IF YOUR AUDIENCE UNDER-STANDS IT. FIX, CHANGE, OR CUT WHATEVER DOES NOT WORK.

INKING
YOU HAVE TO BE VERY CAREFUL AND PATIENT FOR THIS PART!

TAPE A SHEET OF TRACING PAPER OVER YOUR COMIC STRIP. IF YOU MAKE A MISTAKE, JUST REPLACE THE TRACING PAPER AND TRY AGAIN. INK YOUR LETTERS FIRST, YOUR SPEECH BALLOONS SECOND, AND YOUR ARTWORK LAST. TRY NOT TO LET YOUR SPEECH BALLOONS OR CAPTION BOXES OVERLAP YOUR CHARACTERS.

TAKE AN ULTRA FINE SHARPIE AND GO OVER YOUR PENCIL LINES. IF YOU ARE RIGHT HANDED, WORK FROM LEFT TO RIGHT. IF YOU ARE LEFT HANDED, WORK FROM RIGHT TO LEFT. THIS WILL CUT DOWN ON SMEARS!

WHEN ALL YOUR INKS ARE DRY, CAREFULLY REMOVE THE TRACING PAPER. MAKE PHOTOCOPIES. NOW YOU CAN COLOR IT!

GET TO IT!

CREATE YOUR OWN COOL COMICS AND SEND THEM IN BY EMAIL TO: COMICS@ARCHIECOMICS.COM OR BY SNAIL MAIL TO: CHUCK'S COOL COMICS CLUB ARCHIE COMIC PUBLICATIONS, INC. PO BOX 419, MAMARONECK, NY 10543-0419

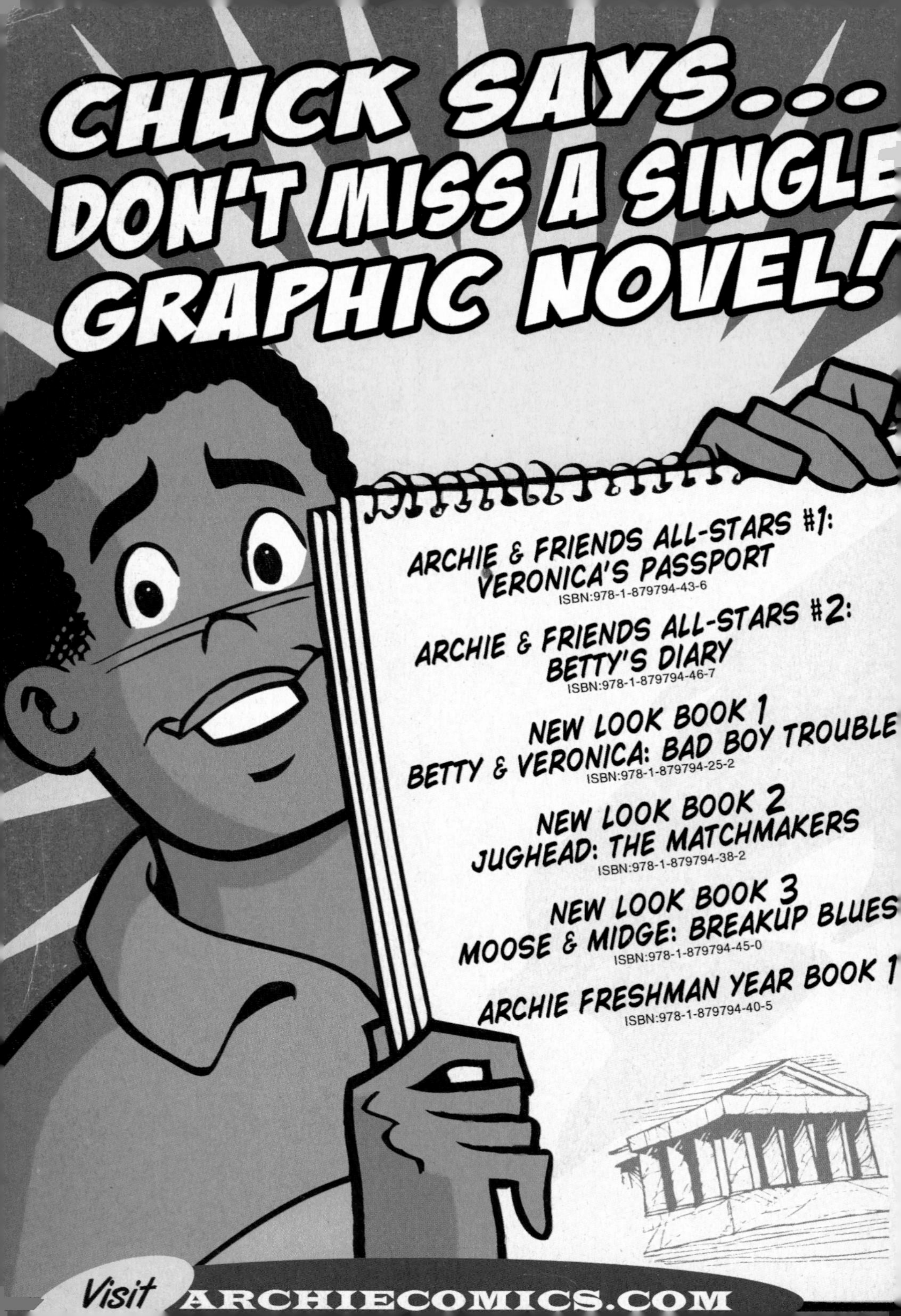

CHUCK SAYS...
DON'T MISS A SINGLE
GRAPHIC NOVEL!
ARCHIE & FRIENDS ALL-STARS #1:
VERONICA'S PASSPORT
ISBN:978-1-879794-43-6
ARCHIE & FRIENDS ALL-STARS #2:
BETTY'S DIARY
ISBN:978-1-879794-46-7
NEW LOOK BOOK 1
BETTY & VERONICA: BAD BOY TROUBLE
ISBN:978-1-879794-25-2
NEW LOOK BOOK 2
JUGHEAD: THE MATCHMAKERS
ISBN:978-1-879794-38-2
NEW LOOK BOOK 3
MOOSE & MIDGE: BREAKUP BLUES
ISBN:978-1-879794-45-0
ARCHIE FRESHMAN YEAR BOOK 1
ISBN:978-1-879794-40-5
Visit ARCHIECOMICS.COM